LOVE LESSONS

LOVE LESSONS

LOVE LESSONS

SARINA BOWEN

Tuxbury Publishing LLC

Dedication

To all our critical inner voices — please take the day off. Actually, take the whole damn year.

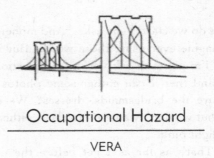

ONE

Occupational Hazard

VERA

July

"THE DRESS HAS to be exactly right," my client says. Even though we're on a Zoom call, I can see that she's wringing her hands.

"What's the occasion?" I ask, my pen poised above my notebook.

"My stepdaughter's wedding. And, well, it's complicated. Even after five years, her mother's family is openly hostile to me."

"Oh, ouch." I set down my pen. "So your dress has to walk a fine line. Beautiful but understated."

"Yes!" Her eyes light up. "It has to be classy but not dull. I need to look stunning but not flashy. And it can't be too young or too sexy, because the bride's mother makes me out to be some kind of slutty Cruella de Vil."

"So I shouldn't show you anything in a Dalmatian print, then?"

"Thanks, but no." She laughs. "My friend told me you would make this fun. I dread this wedding, if you want the truth. The only part of it I'm looking forward to is a new dress."

"We got this," I tell her. "I realize an outfit won't make years of trouble go away. But if the dress is just right, it can change your whole outlook. It can bring you a few hours of much-needed magic."

"So where do we start?" she asks. "And money is no object."

I can't imagine ever using those words. But it doesn't hurt her choices. "I'm going to ask you a few questions about your preferences, and then I can gather some photos to show you. What color are the bridesmaids' dresses? We don't want to match them, but we don't want you to clash, either."

"They're light pink."

"And—" That's as far as I get before the noise starts up outside. *Nrrr-nrrr! Ngggn-ngggn.* It's a deafening buzz—the sound of metal teeth tearing through a piece of lumber.

Oh no. Not again.

My head gives a throb, and I feel like crying. I've been subjected to this all day, on and off—the buzz saw of death—and it's right outside my Brooklyn window.

On the computer screen in front of me, my client flinches on Zoom. She can't hear my apology, so I mime *one moment* and mute my microphone. At least one of us doesn't have to listen to the sound of her own head splitting open.

Oh God. Our meeting was going so well. Not only is this loud and inconvenient, but it's stressful. My personal-stylist business is still in the fledgling stages, and every client counts. If I can't make this work, I'll burn through my savings. Then I'll end up begging for my old job back at the Midtown department store.

Who could build a tiny but stylish empire under these conditions?

The moment the awful sound stops, I unmute myself and smile tightly. "Sorry about that. We were talking about sleeve length. You said this wedding is in September?"

"That's right. It's indoors, so I could really go either—"

Nrrr-nrrr!

2

God, she can't even get the sentence out of her mouth before the sound starts up again. Panicking, I hit mute again. I'm so frustrated I could throw my computer across the room.

I smile instead. This is a new client—a referral. And I desperately need her to think of me as a professional.

"You know," she says when it's finally quiet. "Maybe we should do this another time?"

"Anything you need," I say quickly. "Are you free tomorrow?"

"Yes! You could meet me in my office," she suggests. "Ten thirty?"

My heart drops. "Absolutely," I agree sweetly, even though her office is on the Upper East Side and a forty-five-minute commute away. I don't really have the time for that meeting. But I also don't have the time to drive her away before my first sale to her. "Tell me your address."

AFTER WE SIGN OFF, I pop out of my chair, throw my keys in my pocket, and stomp out of my first-floor unit. I already know who is causing me all this trouble—my new neighbor. I'm going to give him a piece of my mind.

And I'm *not* going to get distracted by his biceps, either. Or his broad shoulders.

I fly out the front door and jog down all seven steps to the sidewalk. I live in a brownstone building on Hudson Avenue, and I used to consider this the perfect apartment on the perfect block. My cozy one-bedroom has an original prewar fireplace in the living room, and a bow window that faces the street. I've lived here for four years, and I never want to leave.

Now that I'm starting my own business, I spend a lot of time at home. That fireplace in my living room makes a great backdrop for the photos I often send to clients. It's classic and stylish —all the things my new business is trying so hard to be.

And yet one muscular hockey player in ripped jeans and safety goggles is ruining the whole neighborhood.

He doesn't even look up as I park my seething self on the sidewalk in front of his godawful saw. Instead, he runs a rugged hand over the beam he's just cut.

I wait. I fume. And I also mentally restyle him, which is kind of an occupational hazard. But nobody needs a glowup quite so badly as Ian Crikey. His brown hair is in need of a trim. He's wearing a threadbare Metallica T-shirt that ought to look like trash. It practically *is* trash—I count three holes along the side seam. Yet it hugs his powerful chest so perfectly I really want to kick something.

This is the other problem with Ian. I'm secretly, uncomfortably, *outrageously* attracted to him. And it makes no sense to me. *He* makes no sense. The man has enough money to buy the building next to mine, which is more money than I'll ever have in my lifetime. The place was listed for over three million dollars.

He's a highly paid famous athlete, and yet I don't think he owns a comb or any clothes without holes in them. It's ridiculous. Bearded men are *not* my type. And don't even get me started on those tattoos peeking out of his T-shirt sleeves. That's not my thing, either. But they work on him somehow. I can't stop staring at them.

It's horrible.

Finally satisfied with his handiwork, he looks up and removes his safety goggles.

Yikes. Now I'm confronted with his cool blue eyes. Their pale, luminous hue is just too pretty for that rugged face. And nobody who's ruining my day should look that good. It's unsettling.

"Something I can help you with, countess?" he asks.

"Are you *kidding* me right now?" My voice is already high and hysterical. "It's the middle of the workday. I'm trying to do calls with clients, but we can't hear each other talk. At all.

You've basically shut down my livelihood. There are probably regulations against making so much noise."

He gives me an irritating smirk. "Regulations, huh? This neighborhood is big on those." He wipes the sweat from his forehead with a muscular arm that I'm absolutely not admiring right now. "Somebody called the cops last night on me and my teammates. Said we were a nuisance."

"Well? Were you?" I demand, trying to keep the guilt off my face. I'd called the precinct last night at midnight, but I probably hadn't been the only one. All I'd wanted was for someone to knock on his door and tell him to turn the music down a little. It had worked—a cop car had pulled up outside, lights flashing. A few minutes later—while I hid in my bathroom, brushing my teeth—everything had gone quiet.

"We weren't that loud." Ian adjusts the Brooklyn Bruisers baseball cap on his head and sighs. Who looks good sweaty and covered with sawdust? It's just not fair. "Would have been better if the neighbors knocked on my door and just asked me to be quiet." He smiles suddenly. "But I guess that's what you're doing right now, yeah? I 'spose the saw is pretty loud."

"Horribly loud," I agree. "You could do this work *inside*, you realize." I point toward the open door of the building he's purchased.

He laughs. "I'm not standing here on the sidewalk for my health, countess. The lumberyard dropped off these posts at a length too long to fit around the corner in there."

"Oh." My face reddens. "Is it going to be like this all summer, though? I'll have to find somewhere else to work."

"Nah, once I demo that awkward entryway, fitting stuff through the door will be easier." He lifts his square chin to indicate what is indeed a narrow doorway with a claustrophobic little hallway beyond. "Live and learn. But after one more cut, I'll be out of your very carefully styled hair."

One of my hands flies up to the chic waterfall braid that keeps my dark hair looking tidy. "What's *that* supposed to mean? If we're comparing hairstyles, I have a few thoughts on your sawdust look."

He shrugs. "Real work is messy. You should thank me. This building was an eyesore. I'm gonna make it look good again. So thank you for welcoming me to the neighborhood with a whole lot of attitude." He pauses to allow those blue eyes to do a slow scan of my body. "Although, the view sure is nice."

And, wow, I am not a fan of the way his hot gaze makes me feel so reckless inside. I let out a squeak of irritation. "Thank *you* for making my workday excruciating and not caring all that much."

He shrugs. "You seem a little wound up, countess. How about I make this up to you? We'll go out for a drink tonight and then work out our *differences*." A smug smile lights his face as he says this, and somehow it comes out sounding dirty.

I give a slow blink, and for half a second, I try to picture it —sitting on a barstool right beside him. He'd prop an elbow on the bar, his big hand cupping a pint glass.

Then I also imagine his devious smile and the swimmy, off-kilter feeling I get when those blue eyes focus on me.

Nope. That's not going to happen. I'm not exactly famous for letting go and having fun. The last guy I tried to date told me in no uncertain terms that I was hopeless.

Besides, it's probably not even a real invitation. He's just trying to throw me off my game. "Even if you were serious," I say swiftly, "I'm sure I'm not your type."

His smile fades. "You're sure, huh? Because I don't use hair gel? Because my shoes aren't shiny?" He takes an exaggerated glance down at the dusty work boots he's wearing. "You don't swipe right on guys like me?"

"I've never swiped right on anyone," I admit, and immediately my face feels hot. That's too much information. If he knew what a prude I was, he'd laugh his muscular butt off.

I've seen the crowd of women hockey players gather—

women who know how to do shots and play darts and flirt like it's a professional sport. That will never be me.

"How many more of those do you have to cut?" I ask, getting down to business. "Is it really only one?"

"Yeah, that one." He points at a board lying between the saw and the building. "You want to do the honors? It's kinda satisfying. Seems like you need to work out your aggressions." He snickers.

"No!" I say quickly. "Not really my thing."

"Suit yourself, countess." He picks up the safety goggles. "Cover your ears."

I do one better. I sprint back to the stoop of my building and leap up the steps, ready to salvage my afternoon. And I swear I feel his eyes on my backside as I go. But it's probably only my imagination.

TWO

A Walk on the Rough Side

IAN

I WATCH Vera walk back up the steps, her ass swaying, her hips in motion, until she disappears into her building. A woman like her—in those designer clothes and shiny high heels—will often enjoy taking a walk on the rough side with me. And Vera feels the urge. Her big brown eyes don't hide much.

But I do not understand that woman. She looks at me like she's starving, and I'm the last bagel at the bakery. But when I try to start something, she shoots me down. That's twice now. I must be losing my touch.

Wouldn't surprise me. These past few months have been a trial.

Still, I could show Vera a good time. We've got nothing in common, but I don't see why that should matter. We could have all kinds of fun together. Doesn't have to mean anything. And I've got a lot of tension to work through, that's for damn sure. Lots of things in my life are suddenly going wrong—even the ones that usually go right.

Last night, for example, I'd thrown a party in the empty space I'm fixing up. It had been an excuse to blow off steam with my teammates. Our season had ended on a rough note for me, and I've been struggling since spring.

A couple months ago, I'd hurt a guy in a fight. Fighting is part of my job. I'm good at it, and I always follow the unwritten code of honor among enforcers. In April, though, something had gone very wrong. The fight hadn't ended with a couple of split lips or a loosened tooth. Somehow, I'd dealt that guy a career-ending injury.

I haven't slept a full night since.

Then came the playoffs. I hadn't been at my best, even as the rest of my team had shone like stars. We'd made it all the way to the third round and had been *this close* to winning the conference. Game seven had gone into overtime, and we could have sealed the deal.

Until I'd fouled one of our opponents. Got mad, tripped him in front of the ref, and took a penalty.

Tampa had won it on the power play, and that had been it for us.

The season ended a month ago, and I'm still not over it. Although renovating the building helps. Construction work is good for the soul. The lower floor of this building I've bought— the commercial space—is empty now. So last night I'd invited my guys into my new space and had fed them pizza and beer. It got a little loud. There was music. There was dancing and smack talk. We are not a quiet bunch.

But then the cops showed up. My temper had flared and I'd argued when they'd said we were a "neighborhood nuisance." That's when a red-faced rookie cop had arrested my ass.

So that was a low point. Never been handcuffed before. I'd felt sick to my stomach when they'd made me stand in front of that mugshot wall and then took my fingerprints.

That's not me. I pride myself on being a good teammate and a good guy.

Until last night.

To make matters worse, I've got a meeting today with the team's management. They want to talk about all my recent "unbecoming behavior."

Christ. Where will my unlucky streak end?

I blow the sawdust off my tools and pick up the scraps of wood off the sidewalk. I'm finished cutting beams, and I have to get ready for my meeting. Working with my hands always calms me down. But even *that* got me into trouble with the neighbors.

Figures.

Summer vacation is supposed to be the most relaxing time of the year. But I'm not relaxed. Not even a little.

I unplug the saw. I'm winding up the cord when I feel eyes on me. Straightening up, I lift my gaze to the front window of Vera's building. There's movement there, damn it. The glare prevents me from getting a clear view inside. But I know what I saw.

She likes watching me. Even if she won't admit it.

I look right at that damn window and smile. Then I lift a hand and give her a wave and a cheesy wink. She'll hate that.

I feel a little better already.

IT'S weird walking into the Bruisers' headquarters on a summer day—like showing up at high school during summer vacation. The practice rink is drained for maintenance, and the locker room is cleared of jerseys.

During June and July, the place runs on a skeleton crew. Management comes in only a couple days a week. The trainers work limited hours, accommodating the athletes who want to use the gym.

There're only two reasons to go to the team HQ in the middle of summer—to lift weights or see management. Since I prefer the former to the latter, I head over early to do a nice heavy workout.

It helps, too. After several sets of squats and lunges in the lonely gym, I'm sweating from every pore and feeling more like myself. In the quiet locker room, I take a quick shower and get dressed.

As I'm leaving the practice facility, I hear voices in the stretching room. Since there's no need to be early for my lashing upstairs, I open the door to see who's here.

Two heads whip in my direction. There's my teammate, Newgate, and the new trainer, Gavin. They both look startled to see me.

"Hey guys," I say into the silence. "Just wondered who was around on a hot July day."

"Hey," Newgate says stiffly. He walks right past me and out the door.

Okay. Whatever. He and I aren't close, but that was kinda rude. "I guess I'm not the only one in a sorry-ass mood today."

Gavin just shakes his head. "Need a spotter?" he asks. "I thought Newgate was going to work out, but it looks like I came in for nothing."

"No, I've got a meeting with the suits."

"Lot of that going around," Gavin says quietly. "Let me know if there's anything I can do to help."

My stomach rolls. "Thanks, man. Appreciate it."

I go upstairs to take my beating.

"IN HERE, Crikey. Thank you for coming in." Hugh Major, our team manager, waves me into his office.

"Of course, sir." I take a seat in the chair opposite his desk. The only other person present is Tommy, one of the co-heads of publicity. I guess that's a good sign—a firing squad of just two.

I can take 'em.

"All right." Hugh slaps a meaty hand on his big, intimidating desk. "Now what the *ever-loving fuck* happened last night?"

Uh-oh.

He fixes me with a stare. "Arrested? Is that really the look you need right now?"

"No, sir," I agree quickly. "But in my defense, it was just a party. I wanted to throw a rager while the place was still in rough shape. But there was no actual raging—just music and dancing."

"Still," Hugh grunts. He seems to be trying some kind of intimidation tactic with his eyes. It's a look that says: *Fly straight, asshole, or I'll have you sent down to the farm team by cocktail hour.* "Have you seen your mugshot? Because every reader of *Puck Raiders* has."

He swivels his laptop around, and I brace myself.

And, yup. It's even worse than I thought. The photo makes me look like a total hooligan. My hair is too long. My eyes are red, because some girl at my party had been smoking. I'm wearing a faded concert T-shirt with a little rip in the neckline.

I look like a deadbeat. "Ouch."

"Yeah, *ouch*." Hugh snorts. "Fans who search your name are going to find this. Hell, your father is probably reading it right now."

I groan and sink down in my chair. He's right, of course, but playing the father card is a low blow. My dad and Hugh had played on the same college team a million years ago. They send each other Christmas cards every year.

God. This is bad. So bad.

"So, let's review," Hugh says darkly. "The record of your arrest is out there in the media. And the last time your name cropped up on the blogs, you'd dealt another player a career-ending injury."

My stomach tenses. That fight still freaks me out. I hit the guy—a rookie from Boston—in the chest. His pads should have protected him. But somehow, they hadn't. His clavicle broke under my bare-knuckled punch. When I close my eyes at night, I can still feel the pop under my fist as I'd hit him.

His helmet had snapped off, and he'd screamed when he went down, bouncing his head off the ice.

Davis Deutsch was the number-three draft pick, and he might never play again. Clavicles are tricky, I hear. He needs multiple surgeries. There were bone fragments...

I suppress a shudder every time I think about it. A couple times a week I wake up in a cold sweat from dreams about the fight.

And yet I don't even know what I would have done differently. I really don't.

"He picked that fight," I remind my manager. "I would'a never thrown down the gloves with that youngster. Clearly didn't know what he was doing. But fighting guys whenever I'm challenged is *literally my job*. There's honor in it."

"Up to a point," Hugh counters. "But there's no honor in a drunken arrest."

I hang my head. And when I do, I notice my khakis have a stain on the cuff, and my Brooklyn Hockey polo shirt is wrinkly. Because of course it is.

"Look," Hugh says. "You have an image problem. Which means your *team* has an image problem. It's also your job to represent this organization in a professional manner. Says so right in your contract."

I swallow hard. "The lawyer you guys found for me said we can get those charges dropped," I point out. "The cop overstepped."

"That's true," Tommy the publicist offers. "In fact, the lawyer got the charges dropped an hour ago. It was only the cop's second night on patrol, apparently."

Thank fuck. My shoulders drop with relief. "Wow. Okay. So now I can move on, right? I swear the party wasn't *that* disorderly."

"Legally, you're in the clear," Tommy says. "But nonetheless, we're going to ask you to work hard on your image this summer. Both the Brooklyn hockey teams are doing well, which is great, but we're more visible than ever. So I'm going to need some buy-in from you."

"Sure," I say quickly. "Whatever you need. And I could, uh, do some extra charity work next season, maybe?"

"Oh, that's just a given. No more loud parties…"

"No parties, *period*," Hugh says.

"I need you looking approachable at all times, in case you're photographed. Nice clothes. Nice haircut. No beer in your hand."

"Ever?" I gasp.

Tommy shrugs. "Don't drink in public. What have you been up to this summer, anyway?"

"Rehabbing the building I bought. Usually, I go golfing somewhere with the guys or hiking in Vermont. But this year…" I hesitate.

"Yeah?" he asks, looking up from the notes he's taking.

"Drake has invited a bunch of us to his villa in Italy. It's a house—" I almost say *party*. "Gathering. On some lake."

"Right. Lake Como," Tommy says. "I've heard that place is amazing. Lots of paparazzi there, though. The place is crawling with the rich and famous."

Oh shit. "They don't even play hockey in Italy. Nobody over there cares about me."

"They care about Neil Drake, though," Tommy points out. "His family attracts attention."

"I'll be a good boy," I say. *Please don't take away my vacation.* "We're going in a few days. Picking up the itinerary tonight."

"No photos with drinks," Tommy says, as if I might have already forgotten. "Are you bringing a girlfriend on this trip? Pictures of you in resort-wear holding hands with a fiancée… That wouldn't be so bad."

"No girlfriend and no fiancée," I mumble. "And what the hell is resort-wear?"

Tommy shakes his head, as if my ignorance disgusts him. "Look, just pay closer attention to the way you present yourself. You and I are going to stay in touch for the rest of the summer. And I'm going to hook you up with a stylist." He pulls a card out of his pocket and slides it across the desk. "He's expecting your call. I gave him some guidelines, told him we want to soften your image."

Soften my image. Like that's going to help anything. I hate posturing. And anyone who circulates that mugshot is just a gossip looking for cheap thrills. They don't know me. I shouldn't have to pander to that kind of attention.

My only real regret is breaking that kid's collarbone. If I could undo that mistake, I would do it in a heartbeat.

I pocket the stylist's card. I have to. These men hold my future in their hands, and there's nothing I can do about that. "Okay, I'll call your guy. And I'll watch my nose."

Hugh is still giving me his eagle-eyed stare, which is uncomfortable. "And get a damn haircut," he says as I rise from my chair.

"Yessir," I say, as if my entire career is riding on it.

It might be, which is stupid. But I'm not in a position to point that out.

A FEW HOURS LATER, I'm sitting across from my teammate Neil Drake, drinking my first beer of the evening. "Here's to Tommy in PR," I say, raising the bottle in the air. Not that the publicist can hear me. I'm seated in Drake's fancy kitchen, bitching about my day. "I feel like sending Tommy a photo of me with this beer and my middle finger raised."

"I bet you do," Drake says, grabbing the kind of wooden pepper grinder you see only in steakhouses. With the flair of a five-star chef, he seasons the meat on the platter in front of him.

Up on the roof, a few more of my teammates are prepping the grill for our dinner. A night with friends is just what I need.

"It was the cop's second night on patrol, and he puts *me* in the paddy wagon," I grumble after another gulp of beer.

"Was there an actual paddy wagon?" Drake asks, salting a

dozen impressive-looking steaks.

"It was more like a van. Smelled like piss."

"Gross," his wife Charli says from the opposite counter where she's tossing a salad.

"Are you sure there isn't something I can do to help you kids?" I ask.

"Nope," Charli insists. "Just sit there and tell us your tale of woe. You're still coming to Italy, right?"

"You bet," I say heavily. "If you'll take an ex-con like me on your fancy jet."

Drake chuckles. "Pretty sure you're not an ex-con if those charges were dropped, buddy."

"Yeah, yeah." I clear my throat. "But I've got to ask you guys not to take any photos of me with a drink in my hand. The publicity team is gonna stalk me all summer. They even made me call a *stylist*." I shudder. "I hated him immediately. I bailed on the call after only a couple of minutes."

"Oh, the horror," Drake says. "You know our friend Vera is your neighbor, right? She's a stylist. She could take care of your wardrobe problem, and you wouldn't even have to leave the block."

"Who says I have a wardrobe problem?" I argue. "Besides, Vera is not a big fan of mine."

"How do you know?" Drake asks with a grin. "Did you hit on her and strike out?"

Bingo. But I'm not admitting that. "Apparently, I'm a noisy neighbor. She threatened to report my construction noise to the city! Like I need more legal trouble."

Both Drake and Charli crack up. "Nothing would smooth that over quicker than paying her styling fee," Drake points out.

The doorbell rings, and Charli drops the salad tongs to zip out of the room. "I think that's Vera now."

Oh Christ. "Why is she here?" I ask Drake. "I thought we were planning our Italy trip tonight?"

Drake removes the empty beer bottle from my hand and

swaps it for another one. "She's invited on the trip. She and Charli are tight."

"Wait, what?"

Drake doesn't even have time to answer before I hear the *tap, tap, tap* of high heels on the wood floors. Vera sweeps into the room, and I almost swallow my tongue. She's wearing a little black dress. Strapless. It shows off smooth shoulders and a kissable neck. She's the finest thing in this very chic room, and it's hard to look away.

"*Oh*," she says softly as her big, dark eyes land on me. "Hi."

"Hi, neighbor." I grin.

That's when Vera blushes. Like, *really* blushes. A deep flush creeps up her face, and I see her swallow hard. "I, um, brought..." She looks down at the bag in her hand, like she'd forgotten it was there. "Prosecco," she manages to say.

"Excellent," Drake says, taking it from her. "We'll have a toast."

"What's prosecco?" I demand, wanting her eyes back on me.

And *boom*. Her brown-eyed stare is back. She takes in my tattoos before jerking her eyes guiltily up to my face. "Prosecco is, uh, sparkling wine from Italy."

"Like...champagne?" My knowledge of wine is nonexistent.

"Right," she says, nodding quickly. "Except you can't call it champagne unless it's from a certain region of France."

"Yeah?" I laugh. "What happens if I do? Will the champagne cops show up and arrest me? Just what I need for my rap sheet."

Her color deepens, and she doesn't say anything. The girl is flustered. She's attracted to me, but she doesn't want to be.

That's fun in its own way, I suppose. And it's just dawning on me that we're going to have to get along on this trip to Italy.

New plan—forget the stylist. I'll spend the entire trip shirtless and working on my sixpack in the Italian sunshine.

She'll hate it.

Suddenly, I'm in a vacation kind of mood.

THREE

Fashion Slut

VERA

HOW MANY RUN-INS can one girl have with Ian Crikey? This guy is everywhere.

Suddenly I feel a little too bare in the dress I'm wearing, but it's probably just my hormone rush talking.

No, you're definitely overdressed, announces my critical inner voice. *You look like you're trying too hard.*

That little voice has a lot to say lately. And she's kind of a bitch.

"I'm going to set the table," Charli says.

"And I'll help you," I announce, grateful for the excuse to leave the kitchen.

I feel Ian's eyes on me again as I go. The purpose of tonight's gathering is to plan our trip to Italy. So what is he doing here?

Uh-oh.

I follow Charli into the dining room, trying to think of a subtle way to ask about Ian. There's a stack of linen napkins at the ready, so I pick up one of them and fold it into a swan shape.

"That's cute!" Charli says. "Show me how you did that."

I give her a quick tutorial. After clearing my throat, I say, "I noticed that my neighbor is here."

Charli laughs. "Kind of hard to miss Ian, right? He makes his presence known."

"Is he going on the trip?" I ask carefully.

"Sure is. Why? Is that a problem?"

I shake my head. "No, of course not." I don't want to admit that he unsettles me. I don't even have a good reason.

"He is a little rough around the edges," Charli says. "But he doesn't set off my jerk-meter, and that sucker is finely tuned."

"Oh, I'm sure," I say quickly. Charli is an excellent judge of character. She's one of my newest friends. We only met in February, but I liked her so much that a few months later she became my first and only employee. "I'm sure he's a solid guy if Neil likes him. Have I met everyone else who's coming?"

"Think so," Charli says, folding another swan. "Heidi Jo and Jason Castro. Anton and Sylvie. My teammate Fiona might join us at the last minute if she can make it work."

"Nice," I say. "You know I really can't wait."

That's not an exaggeration, either. Like Charli, I've never been to Europe. I've barely been anywhere, really. A free trip to Italy on a private jet? I was beside myself when Charli invited me to come along. Nobody ever ran to the passport desk at the post office faster than this girl.

The fact that Ian Crikey will be there too shouldn't make any difference. I'll be too busy touring Italian villas and planning day trips to Milan, the fashion capital of Europe.

I won't even notice he's there.

Much.

"So tell me about this guy," Charli says as we fold the last two swans.

"Guy?" Visions of Crikey's strong forearms swim into my brain.

"The ex. The one who's been texting you."

"Oh! Danforth." I give myself a shake. "I forgot we spoke about him."

"Really?" She gives me a sidelong glance. "He's all you could talk about on the subway the other day."

I cringe, because it's probably true. Danforth is my ex. He and I met in college, at CUNY. We were both ambitious; I was going to storm the fashion world, and he was going to become a venture capitalist.

We made a perfect couple. I loved him, and we were planning a future together. Or so I thought. But then he'd been accepted to Harvard's business school, and I assumed I'd move to Boston to be with him. He dumped me instead. That had been three years ago.

Then, just last week, he moved back to New York to work at a big Wall Street investment bank. I'd had a hunch it would happen, because I stalk him on LinkedIn. But I didn't expect a text from him, asking how I'd been.

In a major victory, I made myself wait two hours before answering it. Since then, we've continued the conversation.

"Are you two still chatting? Are you going to see him?" she prompts.

"We're texting on and off," I admit. "Still making myself wait before I answer any of his messages. Like I'm too busy to fit him in, you know? It's nearly true."

"You *are* busy," Charli says loyally. "You're launching a dream. And I get to put makeup on it."

"Facts." Charli is the best self-trained makeup artist I've ever met. With her onboard, I've begun incorporating some beauty offerings into my business. There's a nice markup on beauty products, and my growing stable of regulars have been loving their sessions with Charli.

"What do you think he wants?" she presses. "And what do *you* want? Do you want to kiss him or slap him?"

"All good questions." I let out a sigh. "The sad truth is that

I'm still a little hung up on Danforth. It's really tempting to go running back to him."

Not that he's asked you to, my critical voice interjects.

Charli's hands pause on the steak knives. "But maybe he doesn't deserve you?"

"He doesn't." I place a swan in the middle of a plate. "He treated me like used goods at the end. But maybe he's learned some things, you know? Maybe he's matured."

"Maybe," Charli says carefully.

"Hey girls!" We look up to see Heidi Jo Castro bounce into the room. "The steaks have been flipped, and Neil said to tell you both that it's almost time for dinner."

"Yay!" I say, enthusiastic for Neil's cooking. "I'll open the prosecco."

"The glasses are in here," Charli says, crossing to a cabinet full of stemware. "Let's do this."

———

TEN MINUTES later we're sitting around the table. Because everyone else is coupled up, I end up beside Ian. He's seated to my left, exactly how things are situated on our little block on Hudson Avenue, too.

But I'm ignoring him, of course. I'm busy passing out glasses of prosecco.

"Give us a toast," Charli demands.

"To Italy!" I say raising my glass. "The birthplace of DaVinci, prosecco, Prada, and Armani."

Ian lets out a snort. But he raises his glass—with a tattooed arm—along with everyone else. I touch my glass to his without looking at him.

I'm just cutting my first bite of steak when Jason Castro asks, "So how much trouble are you in, Crikey? Heidi says the GM is pissed off at you."

My neighbor grimaces. "The charges were dropped this

morning. The cop overreached. I'm not in any legal trouble, but Hugh is real mad."

"Charges?" I gasp.

"Got arrested last night." He grunts. "The cop who showed up to the party got a little overzealous."

My insides seize up, and I forget to breathe. Oh my *God*. He got *arrested*?

"So what happens now?" Heidi Jo asks. "That mugshot was unfortunate."

A chuckle ripples around the table.

"Go ahead and laugh," Ian says, ignoring his prosecco glass to grab his beer. I watch his thick fingers close around the bottle. He takes a sip, and his throat works as he swallows. "But nobody take my picture in Italy, okay? I'm supposed to avoid attention. They're having me do a bunch of volunteer work when I get back." He shakes his rugged head. "The meeting was torture, but the email they sent me afterwards was worse."

"How so?" Sylvie asks.

He grimaces. "How many times can the word *disappointed* crop up in one email? Hugh and Tommy say that I don't do enough charity work and that I haven't been representing the team in a way that makes it easier to shrug off this mugshot headline. So they want me to spend the summer working on my image. They want weekly calls with me. *Lots* of charity work next year, which is fine. But they want me to work with a stylist and maybe an image consultant. They said to buy some new suits and, like, basically make over my entire life."

There's a collective groan from all the hockey players around the table—men and women. "That's bullshit," Anton says. "There's nothing wrong with you. And everyone knows summer is for rest and recuperation, and for thinking about things that *aren't* related to the hockey season."

"He's just pissed about the end of the season," Neil suggests. "It's basically his job to get us to the final round, so he's processing the loss badly."

"His job? I think that was my job," Ian says darkly. "He's still pissed about the penalty I drew, right?"

Heidi Jo reaches over and pats his hand. "It could have happened to anyone. And Hugh will eventually realize that making it to the *conference final* is not exactly a stain on his legacy."

"Yeah, yeah," he grumbles. "Didn't know I had a visit to the NYPD holding tank on my bingo card, but it is what it is. And you know I'm going to spend the summer kissing management's ass. I'll do the charity work. I'll get a haircut."

"Don't forget the stylist!" Charli chirps. "You're sitting next to one, so…"

My face heats immediately. "Happy to help," I say, hoping I sound like I mean it. The truth is that I could use another famous athlete on my client roster. I could use *all* the famous clients. Even the ones who intimidate me.

"No need for a stylist," he says quickly. "What I need is more of Drake's cheesy cauliflower. Stuff is addictive."

"I know, right?" Charli passes the dish to him. "Leave me some, though."

Dinner table conversation turns to Italy, as it should. But I'm still sitting here in shock. I can't believe Ian got *arrested*. That's terrible.

It's absolutely my fault. I'd dialed the police. I'd brought this problem to his door.

I hope he never finds out.

AFTER DINNER, Neil hands out the itinerary. We're flying out of Teterboro on one of his family's private jets. We're taking limos from Milan to Lake Como. There will be day trips to Milan, Switzerland, and an opera night in Verona.

It's going to be magical.

When I say goodbye to Charli and Neil, something unexpected happens. Ian offers to walk me home. "Makes sense, right? We're headin' to the same place, basically."

I'm flooded with mortification. I got this man arrested, and now he's being neighborly. "Not necessary," I insist. "You probably want to go out."

He shakes his head. "Not partying for a little while. Let's roll."

So that's how I find myself alone with him on the short walk from Water Street to Hudson Avenue.

Not that we're talking. I'm drowning in guilt, and I can't really think of anything to say. Except for one thing. "If you decide you need a stylist, I'd totally help you."

"Nah. Tried calling one this afternoon," he says. "It's not like I don't see the appeal of having someone else do my shopping, you know? But I couldn't answer any of the questions he asked me. He used a lot of words I don't know, like 'spread collar' and 'placket.' So I just felt stupid the whole time. Like I was going to pay top dollar for him to make me feel like an idiot."

"Whoa." I stop right on the sidewalk. "Hey—that guy is a jerkface, obviously."

"A jerkface?" His lips twitch. "Strong language, countess."

"But a stylist shouldn't bury a client under a bunch of jargon. That's not how it's supposed to work. It's his job to ask you a few simple questions and meet you where you are with fashion."

"Maybe it's me, not him." He shrugs. "But I don't like paying people to make me uncomfortable."

"Of course not."

"All I really need is a haircut," he says. "But the little place I like is closed on weekends, and it's Friday night, so I can't even do that for three days."

"I'll cut your hair," I hear myself offer. "Right now, if you want."

He gives me a sideways glance. "What? That's not a thing just anyone can do."

"No kidding. I hadn't done it for years until Neil got really desperate during the playoffs. I gave him a haircut as a favor and remembered that I'm still good at it." And Neil was *very* grateful. I'd been headed to his place anyway to talk to Charli. So I'd brought my clippers and scissors along. Easy peasy. And then I got to watch a billionaire vacuum his kitchen floor.

Ian sniffs. "I assumed Drake went to some salon where everyone has a French accent."

I let out a snort of laughter. "He sure does. But so what? He's confident in his masculinity. And then we have you—the guy who's afraid to let me cut his hair."

"Didn't say I was *afraid*," he argues.

"Uh-huh. If you weren't, you'd let me give you a haircut." I surprise myself by pressing the issue. "We can send your grumpy PR guy a photo afterwards. Maybe he'll leave you alone if he thinks you're quick to take his advice."

Ian is quiet for a few paces. I can tell he's considering the idea, but I can't decide if I actually want him to say yes. Guilt made me offer. But running my hands through his hair? That's a little more contact than I really need from a guy who unsettles me.

"Okay," he says suddenly. "You're hired. Grab your scissors. Let's do this."

Gulp.

"Wait," he stops. "You won't make me look like a fashion slut, right? I mean, the *slut* part would be fine. I'm just not sure about the fashion."

And I have to stop walking for a moment, because I'm doubled over with laughter.

FOUR

Let's Go, Champ

IAN

WHILE VERA RUNS into her place for her clippers, I set up the ground-floor retail space for a haircut. I put a chair in the center of the empty room and turn on the lights. Then I head upstairs to my apartment for two cold beers from the fridge.

I don't really understand Vera's enthusiasm for getting her hands on me unless she's actually *getting her hands on me*. But I try not to judge other people's kinks, you know? And a free haircut is a free haircut.

As long as she doesn't make me look ridiculous. Maybe I shoulda thought this through.

But Vera is back in a flash, so I can't exactly chicken out now. She's got clippers and barber's scissors in a professional-looking case. She's even shaking out one of those capes that drapes over your shoulders to keep the hair off. "Sit, sit!" she says. "Let's do this."

Warily, I drop into the chair and let her snap the cape into place. She grabs the extension cord I use for my saw and plugs her clippers into it. Then she pulls a spray bottle out of her bag and starts misting the back of my head.

I guess we're doing this.

26

"Wow, your hair is so thick." She runs a hand up the back of my neck and into my hair, and suddenly I have goosebumps.

Huh. My usual barber is a nice guy in his fifties, and I barely notice when he touches my head. But now there's a hot chick running her fingers through my hair, and my body is all, *Let's go, champ! Get on that!*

I guess my playoffs dry spell was a few weeks too long. "Don't go too short, okay? I like leaving it a little long."

"That was then, this is now. You're trying to make a state-ment here. I'm not going to shave your head, but I am going to make you look tidy and very law-abiding."

I let out a growl, but it's half argument, half horniness. It doesn't help that Vera smells amazing. She's wearing some kind of expensive perfume—it's citrussy with a whiff of fresh flow-ers. As she turns on the clippers and gently works them up the back of my neck, I find myself inhaling deeply to take in more of her scent. And when she puts a soft hand on my shoulder, the heat of her thumb at my neck makes me feel crazy.

Down, boy.

She works in silence while I fantasize about her putting her lips on my neck instead of those clippers. And when she cups my jaw to work on my sideburns, I have the worst urge to turn my head and lick the sensitive skin at her wrist, like the dirty boy that I am.

But then I realize she's eased her clippers onto my beard. "Hey!" I argue. "What's up with that?"

"Hold still," she orders. "I'm going to give you a Brad Pitt scruff worthy of a magazine spread."

"Never wanted to be in any magazines," I grumble.

"Didn't I just tell you to hold still?"

She's all up in my space, her hand on my face, her dark eyes just inches away. Usually when I'm this close to a woman, we're making out. If Vera happened to look down right now, she'd get an eyeful of how I feel about being so close to her.

Then? She strokes my face and makes a pleasing sound that

makes me even harder.

"This whole thing is silly," I growl through a clenched jaw. "I never do this. I never kiss management's ass." Although I'd like to kiss Vera's...

"It's not silly," she insists. "People are visual creatures who respond to subconscious impulses. They'll treat you differently depending on how you present yourself. That's just a fact." She releases my face and steps back to admire her work.

I'm sweating now, and I'm also reminded of how we don't see eye to eye on basically anything. "What difference does it make?" I ask. "Why should I change myself to play other people's reindeer games? Where I'm from, we call that shallow."

Vera gasps. Then she trades her clippers for her scissors. "Here's a pro tip—it's a bad idea to call someone *shallow* when they're holding a very pointy object."

"Christ, I didn't say *you're* shallow. I just don't subscribe to that way of thinking—like I should change my hair to make other people more comfortable with me."

Vera goes silent. She's crimping sections of my hair between her fingers and scissor-trimming the strands at the crown of my head. It's not exactly a noisy process, but somehow each little snip sounds angry.

After a long moment, I have to ask, "What the fuck did I say? Didn't know being myself was a controversial statement."

"It's not," she says tightly. "For *you*. So long as you shoot the puck into the net, they'll keep paying your salary. Even if you get arrested again. Even if your secret hobby is kicking puppies."

"Hey! No puppies are kicked on my watch. I only *look* like a mugshot hooligan. I'm seriously a nice guy. Ask anyone. Especially the ladies."

My attempt at humor makes her snort. "I bet."

I hold back a sigh. And I also hold back the invitation that pops into my head. *Come upstairs with me, and I'll show you just how nice I can be.*

Like that's happening.

There are a few more minutes of silent trimming before Vera reaches for a giant brush and begins to sweep away the snipped hair from my neck. "This is a haircut that management will be proud of," she announces. "Come outside and I'll take your picture so you can see it."

"I do own a mirror," I grumble, because she probably thinks I don't. But then I get out of the chair like a good boy, grab the beers, and follow her outside.

The light is fading, and the bricks of Brooklyn all have a rosy twilight glow. "Quick, before we lose the light," she says. "Sit on my stoop. It's nicer than yours." She points at her building, which has the wider staircase. "I'll snap a shot, and you can send it to PR."

It's not the worst idea, honestly. As much as it pains me to do anyone's bidding, it will help my case if they think I ran right out to toe the line. So I plunk down and look up at the phone she's aiming in my direction.

"Not like *that*," she says immediately. "Sit up straight. Lift your chin. And do you really want those beers in the photo?"

"Oh, for fuck's sake." I move the bottles and sit back down again so Vera can give me a dozen tiny corrections as she takes a million photos. "Eyes over my shoulder. No—the other shoulder! Turn your nose a couple degrees to the left. Now smile. A *real* smile. You look like you want to punch someone."

"What if I do? Use this one." I lift my middle finger toward the camera, and she scowls.

"Come on. Work it, Crikey. Make love to the camera."

I bust out laughing and that camera shutter goes off with a frenzy. "YES! Now we've got it." Vera finally stops shooting. She's wearing a triumphant smile as she climbs the steps. "What's your number? I'll text you the best one."

"Don't I get to pick?"

"No," she says, plopping down beside me. "You'd send them a photo where you're flipping off the camera."

It's possible she's right.

"Here—look at this. Seriously, I'm a miracle worker."

She hands me her phone, and I brace myself. I hope she didn't give me a freaky haircut, and I hope I can find the patience to sound enthusiastic if she did.

But when I look at the photo, I'm kinda stunned. It's a shorter haircut than I've had in a while. It's tidy, but it's sleek on the sides, and more generous on top. The beard trim is so good that I might keep it that way. And she's caught me with a half-smile, like I'm just about to laugh. I look happier and more relaxed than I've felt in weeks.

In short, it's a killer haircut, and I didn't even have to go to the barber shop. "Christ, you're good at this."

The smile she gives me lights up her pretty face. "That is really nice of you to say. I put myself through college by cutting hair. It's a handy skill." She claps her hands together. "Now all we need is some makeup for you. I'll get Charli to do your eyebrows and some concealer for that cut on your face. And maybe some contouring."

"What?" I yelp. "No fucking way."

Vera hollers with laughter. "Gotcha. Who's a gullible boy? I wouldn't even try, stud. But thanks for the giggle."

"You're welcome," I grumble, texting her photo to my own phone, so I can send it to the damn PR department. "Want a beer?" I stand up and retrieve the bottles, then I dig out my key chain and make use of the opener I've got on there with the team logo on it.

"No, thank you," Vera says primly. "I'm not a fan of beer."

Strike... one million. "Sorry, I'm all out of pinot noir." I pronounce it wrong just to sound like a punter. But like I told her before, I don't have any interest in changing myself to make other people happy.

Except for this haircut. I can live with that. "What do I owe you for your trouble?"

"Nothing at all." She taps her kissable lips and considers me.

"I did that for fun. But you know what would be *really* fun?"

Try me, honey. "I can think of *several* things. But let's hear yours."

She hesitates. "Well, I want to style you. I only have one other male client—Neil Drake. But my portfolio needs more bragging rights, so I would do it at cost." She gives me hopeful eyes. "Please say yes. And I wouldn't ask you a million questions. I'd just bring you some choices, and you'd say yes or no. It would be so easy. I promise."

Oh man. "Sorry, that's never happening."

"But why?" She visibly deflates. "Everyone has to wear clothes, Ian. I'm just offering to do the donkey work of dragging them next door to your man cave."

She doesn't see the problem—that she'll be measuring my inseam for a suit, and I'll be thinking dirty thoughts about tying her up with her tape measure and whipping out my dick. "You don't get it. The things I want from you aren't sold in stores. It's *not* true that everyone has to wear clothes, you know. Your goal is to put clothes on me, but I just want to take yours off."

Her mouth falls open in surprise.

"Yeah. Only a dick would hire someone for a job and then hit on them the whole time. So we obviously can't work together."

Her cheeks turn pink as she says, "You're making fun of me now."

"What? No fucking way." I study her for a moment, especially her uncertain brown eyes. "Countess, I'm not joking. Why is that so hard to understand? Run your hands all over my face again, and I'll give you a demonstration of all the big ideas it gave me."

Her eyes go soft and dreamy, and I think I've finally made my point.

But then we're interrupted by a wolf whistle, and it's aimed at me. "Who the hell is that hottie in the new haircut? Can I have that stud's autograph?"

FIVE

Night, Countess

IAN

WHEN I TURN MY HEAD, I see Patrick O'Doul—my team captain—parking his ass on the railing of Vera's staircase. "Doulie, don't tease. I had a rough day. Vera here did the haircut, though. You can thank her for making that mugshot look like old news."

O'Doul chuckles. "Vera, you're a miracle worker. This guy usually looks like an overgrown shrubbery. Anyone drinking that extra beer?"

"Come and get it," I offer. "Vera's not a fan."

"Doesn't make me a bad person," she says stiffly.

"Did I say it did?"

I open the beer for Patrick, and he takes a seat on a stair just below us. It's a beautiful night, which means that front stoops all over Brooklyn have beckoned people into doing exactly this. I drink my beer, while O'Doul makes some small talk with Vera. She seems charmed by him. Hell, I think she likes everyone better than she likes me.

A taxi glides up to the curb, and someone exits the backseat. It's nobody I know, though. Just some guy in a tailored suit and very shiny shoes.

Vera glances his way and does a major double take. "Oh

God," she whispers. Her eyes go very round. *"Shit."* She jumps to her feet like the stairs are on fire, and I see her take a critical glance down at herself before hastily brushing off her dress.

Maybe there's a bit of my hair on her, but it can't be much. She looks as sexy as she did a few hours ago when she first walked into Drake's kitchen. Maybe she has plans with this guy?

The man spots her and smiles. *"Vera!* There you are. You haven't answered my texts tonight."

"Danforth. Wow," she says. "Sorry. I've been occupied." She's smiling, but it looks oddly nervous.

Hmm. Who is this guy?

And why do I care?

Mr. Suit strides toward the steps. He eyes me and O'Doul with a dismissive glance and climbs toward Vera without a word to us. "Let's catch up," he says to her. "Tell me everything."

"One moment," she says a little stiffly. "Ian?"

"Yo!" I look up at her nervous face.

"Can I leave my things with you for now?"

It takes me a second, but then I realize she means her clippers and scissors. "Sure, honey. Thanks for everything. Who's your friend?"

"This is, um, Danforth. And Danforth, these are my neighbors — Ian and Patrick."

"Pleasure," the dude says stiffly. He doesn't offer a hand, he just moves to stand beside Vera's front door, waiting with obvious impatience for Vera to open it.

"'Night, countess," I say.

"Goodnight," she says softly. Then she unlocks the door, and the two of them disappear inside.

O'Doul takes a sip of his beer. "Something going on between you two? Did I interrupt?"

"Nah." I sigh. "I'm down for it. But she'd rather pick out ties for me. And not for bondage, either."

My captain laughs. "I heard management is all over you to clean up your image. Maybe you could do both at the same time."

"She shot me down more than once already. And only an asshole hits on someone who's hired to do a job."

"Maybe you should just hire her anyway, though? Nice girl. And you hate shoppin'."

"True," I concede. "But I hate pretense more. I'm a simple man. You of all people should understand."

He nods. Swigs his beer.

O'Doul and I have a lot in common. We both skipped college to play junior hockey and never looked back. He's also a team enforcer—a fighter when necessary. He's basically my mentor. When I said I wanted to take some fights, he put protective gear on both of us and got me into the ring to learn how to do it right.

We still spar once a week. It's my favorite thing in the world.

"Look, I know it sucks when the suits come down on you," he says quietly. "I've been there."

He has. More often than me, actually.

"But I think you should take 'em seriously this time. Give them a little of what they want. It won't hurt as much as you think."

Uh-oh. "Et tu, Doulie? What do you know that I don't? Are they looking to *trade* me?"

Oh hell. Maybe they are. And now I'm panicking.

"No, man. Calm down." He shakes his head. "I didn't hear anything like that. But management cares about their reputation, which means they care about your reputation. And nobody wants to see your name in the media over some bullshit."

I make an unhappy grunt.

"Plus, you got a tendency to undervalue yourself, and I don't want to see you do that. So I think you could play their games for a minute here and just let 'em all know that you still care. That they should never count you out."

I suppose he's talking sense. But I still feel some dread. "That mugshot didn't help me at all."

"No," O'Doul agrees. "It's not helpin'. That's why you need to walk the walk. Optics matter. Do you think I'd've been captain of this team for so long if I didn't listen when they got up in my face about optics?"

"Guess not. No." I hate this, but if O'Doul is telling me to listen to the suits, then I guess I'm going to have to.

"I got news, and I don't think you're going to like it. But I wanted you to hear it from me first."

My stomach rolls. "That's ominous. What is it?"

"I'm done, man. I told management yesterday that I'm retiring."

"No shit?" I whisper as another wave of dread rolls over me. "I thought you were going to give it another year." And honestly, I thought he'd probably push it even another year further. He's thirty-six. Most guys don't last that long. But he's special.

"Yeah, I thought so, too. But I need a knee surgery. So that would bite into my last season. And Ari wants to have a baby, so I gotta get on that, too."

I snort. "TMI, man."

"No, I'm dead serious. Before Ari, I never made time in my life for anything but hockey. Retiring used to terrify me. But not anymore. I want to quit while I'm ahead. Before they're saying, 'Look at that poor bastard still trying to compete with the youngsters.' And I want to do a lot of things I've missed over the years."

"Fuck." I swallow hard. And now I'm just depressed. But I won't rain on his parade. "Congrats, man. You know I'm gonna miss you."

"Yeah, you will. For a minute, maybe. Until I'm armchair quarterbacking you after every game. We're neighbors now, so

I think it's my right." He pokes me in the ribs. "And you can help me name a new captain."

"That falls on you, huh?"

"Some of it," he says. "I'll be talking to some of the guys this summer, collecting some input. Maybe while you're on your big Italy trip, you can call and give me your thoughts."

"Okay, yeah. Happy to help. I'm sure you'll pick somebody good."

"It's a hard job, but it's a great job, you know? I think I was a shitty captain those first couple years."

"No, you weren't."

"Yeah, I was, because I really didn't understand the job. I thought it was all about modeling behavior. Like all I had to do was show up early and leave last. Keep my head down and show the youngsters how to have a career."

"Well, that doesn't hurt."

"But anyone can do that. The real job is modeling the struggle. Everyone has bad days. Everyone makes a stupid play. It's what you do next that's most important. When I'm looking back on my time in the game, I'm going to remember sitting with the guys who were struggling. Not some goal I made in a big game."

"Shit, Doulie. You're going from legend to guru right now."

He cracks a smile that only cutting-edge, modern dentistry could provide for a guy who's played pro hockey for eighteen years. "Today I took Newgate out to lunch. He's struggling."

"With our third-round loss?" I ask. Because that's what I'm still battling. "I saw him for a second today, and he was in a foul mood."

He shakes his head. "He thinks he's getting traded."

What? "Why does he think so? It's probably not true. Management keeps that shit locked up tight."

O'Doul shrugs. "His family has a lot of hockey connections, so he heard whispers. I told him I had no idea if it was true. But I bought him a burger and let him rant."

"You're a good captain, Doulie. What are we going to do without you?"

And Christ—no wonder Newgate didn't feel like a workout today. The poor guy thinks he's getting FedExed to a new team.

God, don't let that happen to me. I suddenly feel very paranoid. Because it could happen. Easily.

"You won't even miss me, so long as I choose the right guy," he says. "You can help me."

"Yeah, okay. Sure." I don't think it's that complicated, though. There are two or three guys who'd be the obvious choices.

"When do you take off to Italy?" O'Doul asks, pulling me from my thoughts.

"Thursday. We'll be gone a couple weeks. Drake's using one of his family's jets. All I gotta do is show up with a suitcase and a passport."

"Nice."

"Isn't it? Vacations are awesome already, but not having to buy a plane ticket is a whole new level of awesome."

"Hope you have a great time."

"I'm sure I will." But I'll probably spend part of it worrying about my future in hockey. O'Doul's departure is a bummer. No two ways about it.

"You gonna go visit that kid when you come back?"

I don't even have to ask who he means, because I already know. And I dread that, too. O'Doul wants me to go up to Boston to sit down with the guy who got hurt in that fight in April. "Don't know, man. Don't really think he'd want to see my face again."

"Not true. I asked Trevi's college buddy if the guy would be open to meeting you. The kid said yes."

Well, fuck. "Why'd you volunteer me for that without asking?"

"I didn't. I just opened up the conversation. Besides, I think it would help you to apologize," he says quietly.

"But I already did." I wrote a card to him right after the fight and said I was sorry he'd gotten hurt. Actually, the PR guy did the actual handwriting, because mine is so bad nobody can read it. But we'd sent that sucker off just as soon as we'd heard that the kid needed multiple surgeries. I'd felt terrible.

Still do.

"You should go in person," he says patiently. "Might do both of you some good."

Ugh. "Look, I know what you're trying to do. And of course, I feel bad..."

"You still dreaming about it?"

Christ, I should have never told him that. "Not very often. And, yeah, I feel like shit that it happened. But I can't go set eyes on him just to make *myself* feel better. And he doesn't want that either, right? If some guy ended my career, I'd make a dartboard with his face on it and invite whatever friends I had left to come over and play."

O'Doul chuckles. "If it ever comes to that, I'll bring the beer, man. But I have been in your shoes. Fighting is as hard on the mind as it is on the body. And you have to find a way to make your peace with everything that happens in this game."

I know he's right. I'm not okay with what happened. Not even a little. But I just don't see how visiting that kid will ever change that.

My phone rings, and I pull it out of my pocket. "Aw, fuck. My dad wants to chew me out for that mugshot. Here, answer this and tell him I'm trapped under something heavy." I hand O'Doul the phone.

"Hello?" he answers it. "Hey, Mr. Crikey. Yeah, this is Patrick O'Doul. How you been?" They chat for a second, and I start to relax. And then I hear my captain say, "Yeah, he's right here. And he said he was looking forward to talking to you."

Christ. I give O'Doul a glare, but he just smiles. Then he hands me the phone, picks up our empty beer bottles, and leaves me alone with my father's anger.

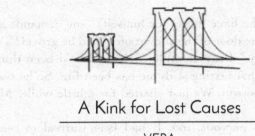

SIX

A Kink for Lost Causes

VERA

"I WANT TO HEAR EVERYTHING, and we've got the time, right?" Charli asks.

We do have the time. We're standing on the sidewalk on Wooster Street in SoHo, inching forward every few minutes in a long line of eager shoppers.

Charli is accompanying me to a huge sample sale. It seems like several hundred other people had the same idea. "Start at the beginning," she says. "When did you break up with this guy?"

"About three years ago. Right after we both graduated." I got an associate's degree, but Danforth had gotten a bachelor's. "Then he got into Harvard Business School, and I expected to move up there to be with him. I thought we had big plans together, but it turns out he only had big plans for himself."

Charli flashes me a pensive look. "Hmm. Well, there's a strike against him." It's a restrained comment coming from her. I love Charli's take-no-prisoners attitude. She's a scrapper like me. We understood each other from the first moment we met.

Hiring her was a great idea. And yet it puts extra pressure on me. These days when I'm fretting about my business, I'm worried about two people's futures instead of just my own.

But it's great having a confidante. "Danforth was my first love," I tell her. "I still have feelings for him, even if they're complicated. Seeing him last night was nerve-wracking. I wasn't ready."

"What did he have to say for himself?" she demands as we inch closer to the door of the showroom. "Did he grovel?"

"Not exactly," I say carefully. "He said he'd been thinking about me and that texting with me has been fun. So he wanted to visit me in person. We just chatted for a little while. Mostly career stuff."

I'd been so nervous, too. It had been surreal to see him sitting on my sofa again after all this time. I'd been jumping out of my skin, wondering what it all meant. "Then, when he was about to leave, he invited me to a big benefit he's attending at the Met. The charity has something to do with solar research."

"Oh boy," Charli says. "I have so many questions. In the first place, *please* don't tell me you're thinking of blowing off our trip to Italy just to be his date for a work party?"

"No way," I say quickly. "I told him about our trip to Italy. But this gala is the first week of August. It's after we get back."

"Okay," Charli says slowly. "Is this a date, though? Like he's hoping to get back together?"

I shake my head. "No, it's not really like that. He asked me as friends—that's the vibe I got. He said he thought I might enjoy it because the dresses will be amazing."

"Are you going to go?" Charli demands. "Did you say yes? Or are you making him sweat it?"

Of course you said yes, my critical voice pipes up. *You'd shine his shoes with your tongue if he asked.*

"I told him it sounded like fun," I admit. "And think of the eye candy. You know I can't resist a man in a tux."

Charli laughs. "Okay, fair. Neither can I, as it turns out."

"See? What was I supposed to do? I told him I'd look at dresses in Italy. I may have bragged a little about Neil's villa. I hope Neil's ears weren't burning." Danforth's reaction, though, wasn't as impressed as I'd hoped. He'd said, *"Oh, I love Italy,"* before telling me about a trip to Rome he'd taken the summer before.

Apparently, he's traveled quite a bit since we broke up. I felt stung just hearing about it, which is silly. His whole visit left me feeling off-kilter. It's just like Danforth to turn up before I was ready to see him. And even as he stood there in my living room —a place I'd often fantasized that he would be—there was a good dose of resentment mixed in with my surprise and satisfaction.

"When did you say this gala was?" Charli pulls out her phone. "The solar-power thing sounds familiar. Neil might be going to that."

"Really?" I perk up. "Does that mean you're going? That would be fun."

She scrolls through her calendar for a minute. "He's scheduled the Urban Solar Initiative Gala in August." She looks up. "Is that the one?"

"I think so! Well, now I *have* to go. What are we wearing?"

"Haven't thought about it," Charli says. "I'm not sure I'm going."

"Why wouldn't you?" I demand as the line moves forward. "We'll try on dresses in Milan. Mine has to be perfect. I'm going to show Danforth what he's been missing. Besides, picture the crowd at this gala—all those socialites who need our services!"

"Good point, sister." Charli cracks a smile. "All right, I'll ask Neil about it later. If we ever get to the front of this line."

We inch forward another three feet. But my head is still back in my Brooklyn apartment last night, where I'd been trying to sort out my feelings about Danforth and his sudden appearance. "Isn't it odd that the one time I played it cool with my ex was the time he got in a taxi to find me?"

"It's educational," Charli agrees. "Maybe you can renegotiate the power in this relationship. You're different now. He's different now. You said you still have feelings for him, but that doesn't mean you have to go right back to the way things were."

"True." Although I'm not convinced. Danforth has a strong personality.

"How did he look? Did you get all the sex tingles?"

"He looked great," I say, answering the first question, but dodging the second.

Danforth is a very attractive man. He's tall, with smooth, coppery skin, gleaming dark hair and eyes, and straight white teeth. We had an accounting class together my first term at CUNY, and I couldn't keep my eyes off him. Even in a Gap T-shirt, he'd looked more suave than any other guy I'd ever met.

And his big brain was at least as attractive to me as his intelligent eyes and perfectly styled hair. I was drawn to his confidence like a fly to honey. He wasn't afraid to set his sights on the best things in life.

He's still that guy, too. Bright eyes. Animated hands as he spoke to me about his new job at Chase Bank where he's on a team who hopes to revolutionize the way public transportation is financed.

I had listened very attentively. It was weird, though. I'd forgotten how it is between us—that a portion of my attention is always performance art. I'd forgotten how long he could talk about his own interests without asking after mine. He freely used vocabulary that I couldn't be expected to understand. "My team will be trying to save spread over LIBOR by leveraging underutilized assets," he'd said, while I'd stood smiling at him in my apartment, wondering whether my makeup was still intact.

And it was hard work finding an opening so I could tell him about my own fledgling business. I wanted so badly to impress him. And maybe I did because he said, "That's boss, babe," when I told him about my growing circle of clients. "The scions of New York won't know what hit them."

Then he invited me to that party. And I was eager to say yes, because I still crave his approval.

The truth is that I want another chance with him. I want him to see what he gave up when he cast me aside.

"So how do you want to play this," Charli asks as we finally approach the doors of the sample sale. "Do we divide and conquer? Or we could stick together."

"I think I'll head straight for the handbags because those get picked over the quickest. Do you want to do a lap and see what else looks hot?"

"Totally!" Charli smiles like a kid on Christmas morning. "Let's turn up the volume on our phones so we can communicate."

I do that, and then I check the group text one more time—the one Neil Drake set up for the Italy trip. This morning I'd let everyone know of our mission.

Vera: Charli and I are hitting a big fashion event in Manhattan. Any requests? Don't forget that we're all getting fancy for the opera in Verona.

I'm so excited—we're seeing Verdi's *La Traviata* in an ancient outdoor arena where spectators have watched live entertainment since Roman times. I couldn't believe it when Neil had shown me the tickets the other night. My nonna used to hum Verdi while she stirred her sauce in her little kitchen.

There are already a couple replies to my text.

Neil: If you see something I need, grab it.

Sylvie: I have my dress all picked out but I'm kind of on the hunt for a clutch purse with a wrist strap. Black or some other dark color. Sparkles optional but welcome.

Ian: Wait. We have to bring a suit on vacation???

He follows that up with a gif from *Home Alone*, all shock and horror.

I don't know whether to laugh or roll my eyes. He and I couldn't be more different. I *love* a good reason to put on a dress. I'm good at my job and if he'd let me, I could make that beast of a man look amazing in a suit. Not only could I solve his problems, but I'd enjoy the smug satisfaction of forcing him to admit that I'm a freaking genius.

But it's not in the cards. He was really clear about not wanting my help. And since I'm still a little intimidated by him, I'm not going to bring it up again.

Probably.

Maybe I have a kink for lost causes. It would honestly explain a lot.

FORTY-FIVE SWEATY MINUTES LATER, we've shopped every corner of the sale. My best finds are two Kate Spade bags—one for Sylvie and one for a client—plus several pairs of Gucci slides in limited edition colors. My Upper East Side clients will snatch them up.

I'm also stocking some Dior lipsticks for Charli's clients and a few other items I couldn't leave behind.

Honestly, I had no idea how valuable Charli was as an employee until this morning. There is nobody fiercer at a sample sale. All that hockey training had come in really useful as she'd fended off the woman who'd tried to literally grab a bag out of my hands. Charli had hip-checked her into a wall and practically bared her teeth. And I'd heard her growl at a woman who was reaching for a shoebox we'd already placed in our shopping basket.

I love hockey players. They're amazing people.

Our last stop is menswear, which always attracts the least attention. You don't see many men at sample sales. "I'll guard the loot while you look," Charli says.

"Good plan."

I set my basket at her feet and take in the lay of the land.

"Those shirts are fun," Charli says, pointing at a rack of men's shirts in colorful patterns.

"Ooh, I love Zegna!" I agree, flipping through the offerings.

"Wouldn't Neil look great in this?" I hold out a shirt with a subtle vine pattern, green on green.

"Yes! That totally shrieks *summer vacation*. Do they have his size?"

I find it and toss it into her waiting hands. "Five more minutes," I say. "Then we'll go and celebrate with lunch."

"Works for me." Charli leans against a display of men's belts and gives an aggressive stare to another woman who's eyeing our finds.

I'm just about finished browsing when I spot a beautiful shirt. It's white and steel blue, with a houndstooth pattern woven into the fabric. It would look *amazing* on a certain hockey player who's been asked to upgrade his image.

And it's only forty dollars, marked down from two hundred.

Forty dollars I can't really spare. But it's so beautiful. Egyptian cotton is in a league of its own. And that woven pattern makes it look expensive.

Crikey had asked me not to think of him as a client, but this shirt would make his eyes pop, and I can tell it would fit him. I can size up anybody at a glance. Professional hazard.

The shirt finds its way into my hands. "Okay, Charli—I'm ready to settle up." I pick up my basket, and we start for the registers.

"Who's that shirt for?" she demands.

"Don't ask. Someone I'm trying to win as a client, but he's not buying what I have to sell."

"Crikey, huh?" She grins. "None of this stuff is returnable, though."

It's true, and Charli is the more practical of us. "That's okay," I insist. "If he doesn't like it, he can use it as a dishrag."

"Please. You'd rather die."

"Let's hope it won't come to that."

THAT EVENING I screw up the courage to walk over to Ian's place with the shirt. There's nobody inside the downstairs retail space, so I ring the buzzer for the apartment on the floor above. I'm pretty sure that one is his.

"Hello?" his rough voice calls a moment later.

"It's Vera. Your neighbor," I add, just in case he knows a few different Veras. Then I cringe.

Awkward much? my inner voice asks.

"Hi, neighbor," he says. "Come on in."

The lock clicks, and I pull the door open. The narrow hallway is dingy, but painter's tape has been applied along the moldings, so I guess Ian is working on that. With a little love and attention, this building could be super cute. The lighting is hideous, though. No paint job in the world will look appealing without better lighting.

I'll probably have to tape my mouth shut to avoid pointing that out.

As I trot up the first flight of stairs, the apartment door swings open to reveal Crikey's big frame in the doorway. He's wearing sweatpants and another tattered T-shirt, this one with paint splotches on it. "Hello, countess."

Yowza. I take in his chilly blue eyes, and I feel… butterflies.

Okay. That's weird. Maybe I have a thing for guys who don't like me all that much. *Nice job, girl. Excellent strategy.*

"Hi," I finally say, and it comes out sounding breathy.

His mouth twitches with an almost-smile. "To what do I owe this honor?"

"Well, you've got my barber's kit. And, um…" The bag in my hand suddenly seems like a terrible idea. "I found a nice shirt at a sale, and maybe it's something you'd like. It's, uh, really simple, but it compliments your coloring."

"My *coloring*," he echoes, like he's never heard the word before. "Usually, I just wear white shirts. Keeps things simple. But I guess I could branch out." He turns around and strides back into his apartment. As if I should follow.

So I do. But two steps into the room, I halt again, because I can't believe the difference between the dingy hallway and the apartment. "Wow. This is *gorgeous*. I guess you started your renovations in here?" There's a generous living space with big windows facing the street. There's an antique fireplace that's even grander than mine. And an open-plan kitchen with a cozy-looking table against the window.

The walls are a perfect snowy white, and the air has that new-apartment smell. "It's going to look nice in here when you get some furniture."

"Thanks," he says easily. "My furniture shows up tomorrow. And I like painting. It's the only kind of work that provides instant gratification."

"*Instant?* Not hardly. There's taping and cutting in and sometimes sanding. And ladders." I make a face, and he rewards me with a smile that emboldens me. "But giving a hot guy a haircut, on the other hand, that's instant gratification."

He laughs, and I feel it inside my chest. "Careful, neighbor. I might start to think you like me." He plucks my barber's kit from beneath a wooden chair and hands it to me. "Here's your stuff."

"Thanks. Sorry I didn't pick it up sooner." *I was too chicken to knock on your door before now.*

"It's no problem. I appreciate the haircut. Management liked it, too. The GM sent back a nicely patronizing reply telling me how well I was representing the organization." He rolls his stormy eyes.

"Okay. Well. Good?" I stammer. I still feel awful for calling the cops to his party. He can probably read it off my face.

"So, let's see this shirt." He crosses his arms across his broad chest. "What does a stylist think I should be wearing, anyway?"

This was probably a bad idea. Nonetheless, I hand over the shopping bag. I hold my breath while he reaches in and pulls the shirt from the tissue paper where I've nestled it.

"Nice color," he says gruffly. "Thanks."

"Try it on," I hear myself demand. I know he doesn't care much about clothes. But I'm dying to know if I've found something that works.

I don't know why I need that shirt to please him. I just do. I'm stubborn like that.

"Later," he says.

"Please?" I hear myself beg. "Guessing people's sizes is my only party trick."

He gives me a dubious look. "That is not a party trick. Tying a cherry stem in a knot in your mouth is a party trick. Balancing a spoon on your nose. Shotgunning a beer…"

"Stop!" I protest. "We've already established that I am not as much fun as most people. Just try the damn shirt on. Just once. That's all I ask. It would make my shallow, ass-kisser heart happy."

He grins. "All right. Stripping for you sounds like fun, anyway." He tugs off his T-shirt in a single, smooth motion.

Suddenly, I'm confronted with acres of muscular glory. And I finally get a full look at that tattoo on his upper chest. It depicts a set of wings, and it stretches the full distance to his shoulders and his upper arms. "*Holy Mary, mother of Jesus,*" I stammer.

"This was your idea, babe." He unbuttons the new shirt with thick fingers. "Already told you my preferences for how we'd spend time together."

Oh god. He probably thinks I have some kind of sexual agenda—making him rip off his shirt in front of me.

What did you think would happen, dummy? my inner voice chides.

I can barely focus until he puts on the shirt and then buttons himself into it. It fits perfectly, which means I haven't lost my touch. "See? I *knew* that would be a good color on you."

He looks nonplussed. He shrugs his shoulders awkwardly. "It fits, right? Does it work with my *coloring*?"

"Um, yup. It'll do," I say, even though he's raised that shirt to an art form with the way it hugs his body in all the right ways.

He gives another awkward shrug and begins hastily unbuttoning it again. But halfway through, he has to stop and sneeze forcefully into his hand.

When he lifts his face again, his eyes are red.

"Whoa! Allergy attack?"

"Something like that," he grumbles, unbuttoning the shirt quickly. "But I'm fine."

He isn't, though. As the shirt comes off, he sneezes again. And even worse, his skin is getting pink where the shirt's shoulder seams had been a second ago.

"Whoa! What the..."

He sighs. Then he bends to snatch his T-shirt off the floor.

But I'm faster and grab it before he can retrieve it.

"Hey! Hand that over." He holds out one broad hand for his tee.

"No way." I hold it behind my back. "Not until you tell me the truth. Did I bring you a shirt that caused an allergic reaction?"

"No big deal," he rumbles. "Happens all the time." He reaches for the tee.

I dodge.

"Vera, jeez. It's just a weird thing with me." He brushes one palm over the reddened skin on his bare shoulder. "It'll go away in an hour or so."

"But... That's *terrible!* Are you sensitive to the sizing they use on new fabrics? Or is it a certain kind of thread?" I've heard men say they're allergic to shopping before. But I never knew it was actually possible.

He shrugs. "I honestly have no idea. But I stay out of stores, and shopping is a damn drag, so I avoid it. The end."

Since I'm still holding his threadbare T-shirt, I quickly turn it inside out. When I run my finger over one of the shoulder seams, it's as soft as a baby's blanket. "No wonder you wear your clothes until they fall apart. Do you have to use a particular laundry soap?"

He looks annoyed at me now. "I buy the kind that's fragrance free. Don't think too much about it, honestly." He reaches over and finally reclaims his shirt. He flips it around and puts it on again.

I grab the new shirt off the chair where he's draped it and squint at it. "I can't believe I made you try on a shirt that caused you to practically *break out in hives*. So much for being a good neighbor."

He smirks at me. "Get over it. I told you not to bother."

"Yeah, you did. And I didn't listen." I pick up my barber's kit, embarrassed. "Sorry, Ian. I'll let you get on with your day."

"Vera, hey," he says. "Don't feel bad about this."

But I'm already gone.

SEVEN

Don't Throw Shade on a woman's Luggage

IAN

I'M CUTTING *boards on the sidewalk. A mountain of boards.*

The PR guy is standing beside me watching me work. "These need to be more even," he says.

"Yessir."

I cut another board, and the saw is loud. It sounds like the jeering of an angry crowd.

But the moment I flip the saw off, somebody gives me a shove from behind. "Hey, asshole. You can't do that here. It's too loud."

"Fuck you. Get off me." Anger zips through my veins like fire, and I try to shake him loose. "I'm not fighting you."

"Pussy. Limp dick."

I turn around, and he's right there on the sidewalk—Davis Deutsch, the rookie from Boston. He's smirking at me. "Come on," he says. "Swing."

Dread pools in my gut, and the crowd is jeering already. Fight! Fight!

He grabs my sweater. And I haven't got a choice, have I? I swing, but don't connect. He swings, and I dodge.

The kid isn't good at this. I know I'm going to win, and it won't take long.

But the dread doesn't ease—not as I take a mediocre punch so I can set up my own.

Every time it unfolds the same way—I hit him once with a glancing blow. But my second punch lands on his body... and sails right through. His body pops with the force of a broken bottle. It shatters. My fist is covered in blood.

When I look down at him, all that's left is his head. It's staring up at me in shock. "What did you do?"

GASPING, I sit up in bed. Or at least I try to. The sheets are tangled around my bare legs, and I'm sweaty despite the AC running full blast.

Goddamn dream. Almost every fucking night it's there. For what—three months now?

I flop down onto my pillow and try to slow my heart rate. The dream doesn't make any sense. It never has. It's like my brain is so full of bullshit that it's taunting me.

After a few minutes of self-recrimination, I notice that the sky is pretty bright outside my windows. I grab my phone and find it's already nine o'clock.

Can we call it progress if my recurring dream has let me sleep in a little before waking me up in a cold sweat?

I throw my legs over the side of the bed and walk through my living room. My furniture arrived yesterday. There are still boxes stacked against the walls, and my electronics aren't plugged in yet. But the place is starting to look livable.

My coffee machine was the last thing I unpacked last night, and I have the satisfaction of walking into the kitchen and merely flipping the switch to get it going.

The grinder starts doing its thing, and I feel a little better. There are some messages on my phone, so I wander over to my sofa to read them. There's one from the PR department, checking in on me, but I'm too grumpy to answer it. I flip to the far more interesting messages. There's a series of them from my neighbor, Vera.

This is a surprise.

I tap on the Play button I use for text to speech and listen to what she has to say.

Ian, you will probably think that I am some kind of obsessive freak, but I have done some research on the chemicals they spray on new clothes. I still feel bad about giving you an allergic reaction.

I bought that shirt because I thought the color would make your eyes pop. But I did not mean for that to happen literally.

That cracks me up. This woman is hilarious.

You can learn anything on the internet. Did you know that many new fabrics are treated with formaldehyde to prevent mildew during shipping? I did not. In other words, most clothes are slightly toxic to humans, at least before that first wash.

Also, when a shirt says 100% cotton that might not include the thread it was sewn with. Isn't that weird? Maybe it's because designers can't do math.

Anyway, I learned a lot that I didn't know before. If I ever have a client who is sensitive to fabrics, I'll know more about how to handle it. So thank you.

And please accept my apology for giving you a rash. In general men seem allergic to me so you'd think I'd be used to it by now.

See you in Italy! —V

I dictate a response: *Hey countess, I told you not to worry about it. Just be glad you're not the team's equipment manager. Dude has to wash my new jerseys a couple times before I can wear them. PS: want a ride to the airport? I'm hiring a car.*

Then I spell-check the hell out of the text and hit send.

She answers almost immediately.

Vera: I'd love to share a car. Are you all packed?

Ian: Packed? We don't leave for 48 hrs. If you're a guy, packing takes fifteen minutes.

Vera: What? Men like to SAY they can pack in fifteen minutes. But then they forget things. They borrow your toothpaste and your shampoo, and they buy a bathing suit at the airport.

Ian: I don't know what guys you travel with, but hockey players are excellent at packing. You can keep your girly shampoo. Ten bucks says you're the one who brings a suitcase the size of a coffin but also forgets something crucial.

Vera: Don't throw shade on a woman's luggage! I need <u>all</u> these shoes. I don't wear bikinis, but I packed five bathing suits and two cover ups. Plus, I heard something about yoga, so I need workout clothes. And the opera means an evening dress and a wrap.

Ian: A wrap?

Ian: Wait, never mind. If you explain it, I'll just forget. Feel free to bring your tiniest bathing suits, though. Have your coffin ready by 7pm.

Vera: If you promise not to mock the size and number of my bags, I will be there. But if you are going to be snarky about it, I will get my own lift.

Ian: I won't make fun of your luggage. Not out loud. And I will carry it for you.

Vera: That won't be necessary. I'm a big girl. And my luggage has wheels.

Ian: Men don't let women lift their own luggage into the cab, countess. That is just the way it is. Meet me outside.

Vera: I will be there. Thank you, Ian.

TWO DAYS LATER, when I actually see Vera dragging her suitcase out the front door of her building, I just start laughing.

"I really don't see what's funny," she says, her voice a little frosty.

I hustle up to the door and grab the thing. "You wouldn't, would you? How long is this trip again?"

"I won't apologize for enjoying myself in Italy."

"Me neither, honey. It's just that my idea of a good time and yours don't have a lot in common."

"Shocker." She crosses her arms across her perky tits. She's wearing a denim skirt and a soft-looking top that hugs her in all the right places.

"It's a good thing I ordered a big vehicle." I point to the black Ford Explorer that's turning the corner to stop at our curb.

The driver emerges to open the rear door. Vera hops off the curb and wrestles her suitcase toward him.

"Come on, now. I told you a woman doesn't wrestle her own luggage on my watch."

"I'd forgotten," she says. "You're willing to make fun of a girl for her luggage, so long as she doesn't have to lift it."

"I didn't make fun of you. I just laughed. I was laughing *with* you." As I say this, she runs back up the steps to her building and disappears inside, only to emerge again with two more bags.

"Oh, for fuck's sake," I say before grabbing them from her.

"Zip it, Crikey."

The driver looks a little nervous, like we might come to blows right there on the sidewalk. He opens the backdoor, and Vera allows him to help her inside, although she'd probably bite my head off if I did the same.

But it doesn't matter. A few minutes later we are on our way to the Drake air terminal at Teterboro.

"You do have your passport, right?" I ask as the car accelerates on the highway. "Be a shame to bring everything you own except the one thing you can't get to Italy without."

"I've got it right here," she says, yanking it out of her bag. "No need to wonder. I'll bet you forgot three things. At least."

I shrug because it really doesn't matter to me.

But Vera must be pretty annoyed at me, because the ride is very quiet. Traffic behaves, and we reach the little airport—

home base for all the private jets of the rich and famous—in no time.

"Wow," whispers Vera after our security screening and check-in take exactly three minutes. Combined.

"Yeah, right? Sometimes I make fun of the things fancy people buy. But you will never hear me make fun of the way fancy people travel. Nobody made me throw out my water bottle or patted down my groin."

"The way you talk, I think you'd enjoy that last thing," she mutters.

"Only from you, countess."

She flushes. God, I love that blush. Wish I could see more of it.

Instead, I steer all her bulky luggage—plus my own—to the unlucky porters whose problem it is now. "Thanks boys," I say, tipping them with a twenty.

We are led outside to the tarmac by yet another uniformed airport employee. "Right up those steps, sir. Enjoy your flight."

"Oh, we will," Vera assures him. But she looks jittery.

Our friends are waiting for us onboard. There is a round of high fives and hugging before everyone returns to their seats. That's when I realize that Vera and I are the only two single people on this trip. Everyone is coupled up. Even Charli's teammate, Fiona—a late addition to the trip—has brought her girlfriend, Aly.

There are only two empty seats left on the ten-seater jet, and they are right beside each other, of course. In the back row, too. I hesitate before claiming one. "Aisle or window, countess?"

While I wait, she chews her lip, as if this is a major life decision.

"I'm about to qualify for the senior discount, here. Which will it be?"

"Aisle," she snaps.

Wordlessly, I move past her and take my seat. Can't imagine

why anyone would give up the window seat, but I'm not going to ask twice.

The seats are leather and generously apportioned. I'm used to flying in style, because the team jet is nothing to sneeze at. But this setup is over the top. Everything is wood or leather, with a big touch screen on the back of the seat in front of me and a pull-out footrest that flattens the whole seat into a bed.

"Nice ride, Drakey," I call out. "Who wants to join the mile-high club with me? Any takers?"

"Tempting," Castro teases. "But I'm already a member of the club."

"No shit?" I laugh. "Heidi Jo, were you in on this?"

"She was!" Castro hoots.

"Oh God, shut your trap," his wife complains. "That's not meant to be general knowledge."

"Too late!" Anton calls.

There's a lot of good-natured teasing after that, but I notice Vera is oddly quiet. I glance at her, and she looks pale.

Oh boy. "Are you a nervous flyer? Really? I didn't peg you for the type."

She pulls a fashion magazine out of her carryon and begins to fan herself with it. "We all have our quirks, Ian."

The jet pushes back and taxis to the runway. The flight attendant introduces herself and does a basic safety announcement. The color comes back into Vera's face, which ought to be a good thing. But when the pilot says, "Prepare for takeoff," over the intercom, Vera is suddenly bright red and breathing a little too fast. As we accelerate down the runway, she grips the armrests with two hands, like a wet cat trying to climb out of the bathtub.

The plane lifts off, and I look out the window. It's a pretty summer day, with only a few puffy clouds. The Hudson River glimmers like a serpent on the ground beneath us. "Lookin' good now, countess. You can unclench."

Except the pilot chooses that moment to bank us into a turn, and a whimper escapes the woman seated next to me.

I check her face, and it's a mask of terror. She's *really* afraid. "Breathe," I order. "Right now."

She gasps, and it sounds ragged.

"Okay, slow-like." I take her hand off the armrest and give it a squeeze. Her grip is like a vise. "Count 'em out. In for four, out for six. Ready?" I inhale slowly, tapping a thumb onto her hand for four measured counts. Then I exhale for six taps.

She screws her eyes shut and grips my hand. But at least she's breathing with me.

Lordy. It's going to be a long flight.

EIGHT

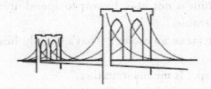

A Ride on the Crikey Express

VERA

YOU ARE A HOT MESS, my inner voice says. *Way to embarrass yourself in front of Ian.*

My shame is complete. But my heart is racing, the engine is loud, and everything is chaos. At least the plane is leveling out again. "Oh God. That's better. Okay. I was sure we were all going to die. I mean, we still could," I babble.

The big man next to me lets out a snort of laughter. "We are all going to die, countess, but not today."

On some level, I'm aware that it makes no sense to worry about my impending death *and* my humiliation at once, because only one of those things can matter at any given time.

But logic is not the boss of me right now. For example, I'm holding Ian Crikey's hand. I'm probably squeezing the life out of it. But he hasn't complained. Not yet, anyway. He hasn't called attention to my freak-out, either.

I never asked to be the girl who's afraid to fly. And it's been a while since I got onto a plane, so I thought maybe it wouldn't be so bad this time.

Now I regret all my life choices.

"All of 'em?" Ian asks, so I must have said that out loud. "Mile-high club offer is still open in case you have a few last

59

wishes. Be a shame to die without experiencing all that life has to offer—like the ride of a lifetime on the Crikey express."

"Oh my God, that ego." I feel a flash of anger, because arguing with him is not how I want to spend my last moments. "You're insufferable."

"Does that mean awesome? That's usually how people refer to me."

"No!" I gasp. "It means irritating."

"Are you sure? If I'm *insufferable* it sounds like you'd suffer without me. We can't have that."

"Jesus, read a dictionary. It means…" I glance up at his face. He's smirking. "Wait, you're joking right now."

He laughs. "You sweet, little, gullible thing. Even this big, dumb jock knows that word. Every teacher I ever had used it on me, so…" He shrugs, and his smile turns smug.

"Figures," I mutter.

"Come on, I'm still awesome, right? You're not putting claw marks into my wrist anymore."

I look down at our joined hands, and I yank mine away. Although, he's right—for a minute there, I forgot to picture my own death. "Maybe I should take a Xanax now."

He grabs his knees and laughs. "You've got Xanax? And you didn't take one yet? Why the hell not?"

"It makes me sleepy."

He roars.

"I know, I know." Gingerly, I lean forward and retrieve my bag from the floor. I'm overly aware of the engine noise and any subtle shifts of the plane. I uncap the bottle of low-dose pills and try to decide between one or two. I've never taken two at once, but my prescription says, *One or two tablets*.

"Do you always need those?" my seatmate asks.

"I just don't know," I murmur. "This is only my second time flying."

"To Italy?"

"No, ever." I tap two little tablets into my palm.

"Ever?" he demands. "Are you really that afraid of flying?"

"I guess." I toss the first tablet into my mouth and dry-swallow it with some difficulty. The real reason I never flew as a child is that I grew up poor. There was no money for trips. Ian wouldn't understand.

He gets up—just rises out of his seat, as if that's not horribly dangerous—and steps past me. In the aisle, he ducks into what must be the galley at the back of the plane and returns with a bottle of water, which he thrusts into my hand.

"Thank you," I gasp. I twist off the cap and drink a third of it in as many gulps. Then I take the second pill.

"So tell me," he says as I finish the water. "What are you going to do first in Italy? And keep in mind that I'm still an option."

I roll my eyes. "I'm going shopping."

"Shopping?" he gasps. "Are any of your suitcases empty? Because how are you going to bring anything home?"

"I might have to buy another suitcase," I admit. He laughs. "But Milan is the fashion capital of Europe, and the lake house is a short train ride from Milan.

"What does that even mean? The fashion capital? Sounds boring as fuck if you ask me."

Later, I'll realize he was just baiting me so I'd stop thinking about death long enough for the Xanax to kick in.

But I'm in no mood to pick up on subtleties. "The name *Milan* comes from the word for milliner, which refers to the creation of fabric and hats. Luxury goods have been made in Milan since the Middle Ages. Armani, Canali, Missoni, Valentino, Versace... so many modern houses of design are headquartered in Milan."

And on and on, I just keep talking. My head starts to feel heavy, and at some point I lose my train of thought and lapse into silence. The seat begins to recline as if by magic, the footrest rising up to cradle my knees.

After that, I spend some quality time staring at the curved

wooden ceiling of the jet, wondering how they were able to shape the panels so perfectly. "Wow, the craftsmanship," I say slowly.

Somebody snickers. But I don't care. I feel floaty and calm.

Later, I smell food, and a female voice offers champagne. I raise one finger off the arm rest in an attempt to get some, because champagne sounds nice.

"Oh no, you don't," says a male voice. "She's cut off. But I would love a beer."

I consider arguing but can't summon the energy.

Eventually the cabin grows dark and quiet. Someone is snoring nearby, but I don't mind the sound. It's soothing. Everything is soothing and sleepy. As it should be.

NOISES. Lights.

"Wakey, wakey, sleeping beauty," says a hunky voice. "We've arrived in the fashion capital of the universe, according to a very long speech you gave right before you started drooling on yourself."

Oooh. Fashion. That is totally my jam. Too bad I'm too sleepy to care right now.

"On your feet, countess." Someone pokes my arm. "Let's go. Step lively."

Nope. Sorry. Go fish.

"Wow, she's really out of it," Charli's voice says.

"I guess we're gonna have to do this the hard way," Neil agrees.

There's a windy sigh. "You guys get her luggage. That's the hardest job. I'll handle the human cargo."

A moment later I'm scooped up into gentle arms. My head comes to rest against a threadbare cotton T-shirt covering warm, solid muscle. I smell soap and cotton and spicy cologne.

It's nice, so I loop my arms around a strong neck and sigh.

Then we begin to move.

I COME to consciousness on the leather seat of a limousine. When my eyes flutter open, I'm looking at Charli. She's wearing a cute, little, red sundress I found for her at Saks, and a big smile.

"Look who's joined us!" she says with a laugh. "Welcome to Italy. We're an hour north of Milan already."

"What?" I blink rapidly and try to clear my dry throat. "But what about customs? Don't I have to show my passport?"

"Oh, you did," Sylvie says with a giggle. "We helped."

Four women are seated around me—Charli, Sylvie, Fiona, Aly. The others must be in another car. "I don't remember getting into this car."

"It went something like this," Charli says, handing me her phone.

"Holy crap," I yelp as I look at the photo. I'm standing in the airport, eyes half open, slumped against Ian Crikey. He's holding me up while I rest my head against his broad shoulder. "I look like a zombie."

"The whole experience was very *Weekend at Bernie's*," Charli says with a nod. "You were a rag doll."

"You must be very well rested, though," Fiona says cheerfully.

I delete the photo and then check Charli's camera roll for more. There aren't any, thank God. Still, I drop my head into my hand and groan. "Why did it have to be Ian? He already thinks I'm a pain in the ass."

You are *a pain in his ass*, my inner voice whispers. *Nice job. And you owe Ian. Big time.*

He'd been a prince when I'd panicked. He'd held my hand and got me water to drink.

I let out a low moan of embarrassment.

"Ian laughed it off," Charli insists. "You clung to him, but you were very well behaved as he steered you around." Charli pokes me in the knee. "Admit it. You have a thing for Crikey."

"I do not," I argue.

"He's a hottie," Sylvie chirps. "And I hear he's single."

"Seems like the kind of guy who's always single," Fiona says.

"This is true," Charli agrees. "It freaks him out that all his friends are coupled up. He says he's never getting married. But that doesn't mean you can't have vacation sex with him."

"Oh God." I lift my head and take in all their smiling faces. "Do *not* try to set me up with Ian. It won't go well."

"Why not?" Charli presses. "You could have a fling with him before you go back to dating what's-his-name. The banker ex."

"You have a banker ex?" Sylvie asks.

"Yes," I say, grateful for the change of topic. "He just moved back to New York."

"He invited her to a gala at the Met. I still want pics of this guy," Charli says. "You promised."

She's right. I grab my phone out of my carryon, which is tucked at my feet. My friends are awesome, because I don't remember putting it there myself.

I open up my photos app and start scrolling. After Danforth dumped me, I archived all our photos, but there's one that's still tucked into a folder somewhere. I just couldn't make myself delete it. "Ah. Here." I pass the phone to Charli.

"Ooh, okay. Wow. He is attractive in a preppy kind of way. I can see why you still carry the torch." She passes it on to Sylvie, who makes a noise of admiration before passing it around the limo.

"I'm not sure how I feel about him," I admit. "It's embarrassing that I still want his attention after all this time."

"Why?" Fiona asks. "You can like whoever you like. Doesn't have to make sense."

"Because he treated me badly," I point out. "And I'm not a stupid girl."

"Hearts are stupid sometimes," Charli argues. "So are pheromones. That's how I ended up boinking Neil in the back-seat of a limo. So don't blame yourself for wanting him. Just don't take any more crap from him."

"Oh, I won't," I assure her. "But riddle me this—do I really want him back? Or do I just want him to grovel. A *lot*."

"Ah." All four women murmur in understanding. "Good question," Sylvie says. "You want him to realize what he gave up."

"*Exactly*," I agree. "I want him to want me. And maybe if he does, I might be able to figure out if I still want him back."

"I've heard worse plans," Charli says. "So what are you going to do about it? Besides dazzle him at the gala?"

"Well…" There's one more complication. "The thing is, when Danforth left town, he didn't just say that we'd grown apart. He made it worse by implying that I didn't do it for him anymore. That I wasn't sexy enough."

Especially in bed, my inner critic reminds me. *He said you were too vanilla.*

As if I could ever forget.

"That is a rat bastard thing to say," Sylvie protests. "So why are we still talking to this chump?"

"That's the million-dollar question," I agree. "But maybe he's missed me. And he realizes that there's more to a relationship than endless entertainment."

Or maybe he just misses the way you worshipped him. Some guys need their egos stroked more than they need their dicks sucked.

My inner voice has a few good points, I think.

Still. "I want to make him eat his words," I admit. "I'm going to this gala, and the gloves are *off*. I'll find a hot dress and spike heels that could make a grown man cry."

"Work it, girl," Aly chimes in.

"But this is exactly why you need a vacation fling," Sylvie

says. "You need to get your mojo back. Flirt with Ian in the hot tub. Work on your tan. Kiss a hot guy under an Italian sunset. I hear this villa has amazing views of the sunset." She gets a dreamy look in her eye.

"I'm looking forward to some sunset lovin'," Charli admits. "Oh Vera—this is for you." She passes me a bottle of orange juice and a bag that contains a lovely Italian pastry.

"Wow, thanks." I take a bite, so I don't have to talk about myself anymore.

Although, I wish I was the kind of girl who had vacation flings. But that's never been me.

What are you waiting for, bitch? that little voice in my head asks. *This is as hot as you'll ever be.*

But it's not like I'd even know what to do. I don't know how to seduce a man. I picture Ian Crikey naked in a bed with a hungry gleam in his eye. And, wow, I don't know if I could handle a guy like that. His style is all animal magnetism and raw sexual appeal.

My style is nervous butterflies and panic attacks on planes.

It would never work.

But a girl can dream.

NINE

Vacation Mode Engaged

IAN

THE CURVY, hilly drive to Lake Como is spectacular. I sip a cup of hot Italian espresso and watch the scenery go by. Little old towns with red rooftops. Church steeples. Lush flowers.

I feel jet lagged and sluggish in spite of the beautiful scenery. Still, this is exactly what I need—a couple weeks away from the city. Maybe I'll be too tired tonight for dark dreams about hockey fights.

"What's the rooming situation?" Heidi Jo asks. "Do I need to elbow any of my girlfriends out of the way to get a private room with my honey?" She puts a hand on Castro's knee.

"We've got seven bedrooms, so no violence will be necessary," Drake says. "Charli and I are taking the king suite, but there are queen beds in all the other rooms. Except—Crikey?"

"Yeah?"

"Your room shares a bathroom with Vera's. If that's okay."

"Sure, man. Of course." I'm planning to walk around the villa shirtless, of course, until she admits she wants me.

My phone buzzes with a text and—speak of the devil who wears Prada—it's my hilarious neighbor.

Vera: I just deleted a picture off Charli's phone of you holding me upright in the airport. If I promise to find you some new shirts with hypoallergenic seams, could we never speak of this again?

Ian: Okay. Does that mean I should delete the photos I took of you drooling on my concert tee? I was gonna light up Instagram first

Vera: IAN!!! Delete them!!!

I laugh, because she is a lot of fun to tease.

Ian: There aren't any photos, countess. Just for the record, you are welcome to take pics of me anytime. You might want some to hang in your apartment.

Vera: My apartment already has very tasteful art on the walls, thanks.

Ian: More tasteful than me in my underwear? No such thing.

She texts back an eye-roll emoji. That's all.

I open Google Translate and look up "countess" in Italian. Then I send one more text.

Ian: Just realized your new nickname is contessa, because when in Rome...

"I see the lake!" Heidi Jo squeals. "There it is!"

I turn to look out the window. "Damn, that's really something." I already knew that Como is a big lake in the shape of a Y, so you can't ever see the whole thing at once. But I was unprepared for the grand villas peeking out at the water's edge, or for the rolling green mountains rising up from the distant shore. I can also see a marina full of sailboats, their masts poking upward toward the deep blue sky. And everywhere else there's the rich green of midsummer dotted with bright flowers in bloom.

Italy is basically heaven. "Vacation mode engaged," I announce. "Who wants first crack at paddle boarding?" I've already arranged for a rental company to drop off a pair of boards for an extended rental.

Every hand in the limo goes up.

This trip is going to be a blast.

TWO HOURS later I'm in my vacation uniform—swim trunks and sunglasses—standing on a private dock, drinking an Italian lager, and watching Heidi Jo race her husband on a paddle board. "You're a beast, Heidi Jo!" I hoot. "Cut 'im off! You got this!"

She goes for it, steering her paddle board toward his like a roller derby queen on attack. But Castro has fifty pounds of muscle on her, so he pulls ahead.

Frustrated, Heidi Jo takes the nuclear option, jumping onto her husband's board and grabbing him around the hips. "It's a tie!" she shrieks as the board tips, and they both pitch toward the lake.

Castro has fast reflexes, which he uses to safely ditch both their paddles as they plunge together into the water.

Laughing, I almost choke on my beer.

They pop back up above the surface a moment later. "Gotcha!" Heidi Jo yells. "I win!"

"You little…" I don't even know how that sentence was supposed to end, because she grabs him and kisses him.

"All right, kids, get a room," I have to yell after a minute. "Your paddles are floating away, guys."

Castro retrieves their gear, and they both climb up onto the dock. "We're going inside. Nap time!"

"Yeah, yeah." I can only imagine what *nap time* means in this context. "So who's next? Anyone?" I turn around and survey the patio above me. It's an elaborate stonework terrace with a hot tub and a dozen wooden lounge chairs wearing cushions in white and orange stripes. Drake has hired some staff for our stay, so a young Italian dude brought me this beer a little while ago.

Like I said, heaven.

Three of my friends are up on that terrace, but Charli and Drake seem to be napping. Only Vera is watching me through a set of classy, mirrored sunglasses that make it difficult to read her expression.

Her little red bathing suit, however, is not hard to read at all. It's skimpy in the best possible way, with a V-neck that shows off her shapely body.

I'm a big fan. "Hey, Vera! Let's go. I haven't seen you on the paddle board yet."

"I don't think so." She shakes her head. "That's not my thing."

Like I'm going to give up that easy? "Why did you risk death to fly here, then? Was it only for the shopping?"

She puts down her book with an angry thump. "I'm not falling for your tricks, Crikey. You're going to push me in the water."

"No way." I set down my beer. "Scout's honor. Come here and try the paddle board. It's as easy as standing up."

She rises from the chair, a wary expression on her face. "If this ends in my humiliation, you'd better not take a photo."

"I don't even have my phone. Now get down here and paddle."

She sniffs. "I'd like to paddle *you*."

"Now, now. I'd prefer if *you* were the submissive. But hold that thought." I kneel down on the dock and steady the larger board in the water. "Sit down on this. Piece of cake, contessa."

She tiptoes toward the edge of the dock and looks down. "Push me in and die."

"Noted."

She crouches down and then gingerly transfers her hot little body to the board, until she's seated with one leg dangling into the water on either side. "There you go." I hand her the paddle and nudge the board away from the dock. "All right. Stand up and paddle. These are nice, sturdy boards."

I watch as she rises to one knee. But then, biting her lip, she shakes her head and sits back down. "I like the view from down here."

Making a *tsk-tsk* noise, I lean out and grab the tail of the board before she's out of reach. "Come back. We'll do this together."

"We will?"

I slide myself down onto the board behind her, and it rocks under my weight.

"Whoa!" Vera grabs my knee with her free hand. "Don't do that!"

"Simmer down, we're fine. And now you can stand up, because I'm providing ballast. The board won't move at all."

She must believe me, because she slowly draws her feet out of the water and onto the board. And—although I've seen ninety-year-olds move faster—she rises to her feet, holding the paddle in two level hands like a tightrope walker. "I'm doing it!"

"You are," I agree, trying to keep the laughter out of my voice. But she's just so fucking cute. "Now try paddling."

Carefully, she dips one end into the lake, and then the other, while I try not to get a face full of water. It's a kindness to say that her stroke is not very efficient. We're about three feet from the dock.

In one smooth motion, I tuck my feet under me and stand up.

"*Oh God,*" she cries. "You made us wobble."

"And yet we're still breathin'," I point out. "Here, girl. Like this." I step forward until my chest is touching the knot in her bathing suit, and I reach around her waist to take hold of the paddle. Then I take a couple of nice, clean strokes to move us away from the dock and out into the lake.

"Okay, wow. We're moving now." She grabs the paddle from me and takes over. All I've got to do is stand here in the sunshine, breathing in the coconut scent of her sunscreen and admiring the smooth, kissable skin of her shoulders.

The wind picks up, and Vera struggles as the rowing gets a little rougher. She has to exert more effort, and she does this by bracing her feet carefully on the board and leaning back against my chest ever so slightly. "This is fun," she puffs. "I get it now."

"I bet you do," I murmur. If it were up to me, she'd be getting a hell of a lot more than paddle board lessons. "So you're ready to race me?"

"No!" she squeals. "Fat chance."

I laugh and turn my face toward the sun. The only thing that would make this vacation more perfect is if she would sneak into my bed later.

As if.

"How far can we go on this thing?" she asks, suddenly an expert. "Could we check that out?" She points at a marble statue peeking out from a niche on the shore.

"Sure. When you want to turn, you take extra strokes on one side. Like this." I grasp the paddle, and we stroke together. Soon enough, we're pointing toward the statue.

"Ooh, yes. We got it now," she says cheerfully. "Okay that's... Which goddess has a helmet and a snake? Athena?"

"No idea, contessa. That's your department. I'm just here for the swimsuit competition." I run one finger over the thin little strap that's tasked with holding her bathing suit up. "This is a particularly nice specimen."

She shivers. "Stop. If you do that, I won't be able to concentrate. We'll fall in the lake."

Because I'm me, I do it again, running a finger up along her sun-warmed skin. "You hate that, huh?"

"No," she says with a wiggle. "Didn't say I did. But you'd better knock it off all the same."

So I do. And we have a nice little paddle down the lake shore. Then I help her turn us around, and we paddle back toward the dock.

Everything is great until the speed boat comes by.

"Oh no!" Vera clenches up immediately. "Is he going to hit us?"

"Nah. He sees us." Sure enough, he steers his boat well out of our path, and Vera relaxes.

"But brace yourself," I warn.

"Why? What are you doing?" she yelps.

"Not me. The wake."

"The what?"

There's no time to explain. I commandeer the paddle, reaching around her body to try to point the nose of the board into the oncoming ripple.

"Omigod, we're doomed!" she grabs my forearms as the waves roll in.

"You can grab me all you want," I say. "But sit down if you're worried about falling in."

She drops onto her seat with the speed of someone bracing for a crash landing.

Still chuckling, I steer us through the wake, while Vera holds onto the board with a white-knuckled grip. "You're hilarious. It's like you've never seen water before."

"I grew up in the Bronx. Not a lot of open water up there."

"Really? The Bronx?" I stop paddling because I'm so surprised. "I took you for an Upper East Sider. Or maybe Greenwich, Connecticut."

"Then you'd be wrong." She shrugs, and her mirrored shades flash in the sunlight.

Huh. One thing I can say for Vera is that she keeps me guessing. Just when I think I've got her figured out, I'm wrong again.

TEN

I Need Tutoring

VERA

MY ROOM in the villa is spectacular. I have a sliver of a lake view, but my window mostly faces up into the green hills. And there's a queen-sized, four-poster bed—the kind you might see in a movie about royalty.

Even better, there's an antique dressing table with a tufted seat and an ornate, antique mirror. I think I'm in love. Sitting there makes me feel like an actual countess. And I can do my hair and makeup there, so I won't always be hogging the jack-and-jill bathroom that I share with Ian.

Ian. Even if our rooms weren't basically connected, I would still be thinking dreamy thoughts about him. Paddle boarding in the sunshine with that dangerous-looking hunk of a man was a nice way to start my vacation.

He and I don't see eye to eye on much, but I'm starting to understand his charms. Or at least his charming physique. I basically have a hormone rush anytime he gets near me.

The shirt I bought for him at the sample sale is stretched out on the bedspread. I don't like to give up, so I've done a lot of work on the darn thing. There's still a half hour until dinner, so I could knock on his door right now and hand it over.

Still, I hesitate, taking another moment to check my reflection. I've put on a simple, clingy dress and a pair of strappy Valentino sandals that I found on Poshmark for a song. I've swept my hair into an updo. My makeup skills aren't as fantastic as Charli's, but I've done a nice enough job. Sultry eyes and red lips look back at me in the mirror.

I look *good*. Fashion is my jam, and I like to dress up. I do it all the time.

But there's no denying that I picked out this outfit with Ian in mind. I want him to notice, even if he rolls up to dinner in swim trunks and one of his ancient tees. Even if he makes a crack about the dress code. I want to see his eyes widen a little. I want to see his eyes drop to the deep V of this dress.

I don't know why. I just do.

Gathering my courage, I pluck the shirt off the bed, march into the bathroom, and knock on his door.

"S'open," he says from inside his room.

I open and then peer around the bathroom door, wondering if he's decent, and then wondering if I'll be disappointed to find that he is.

Ian is standing in the middle of the room wearing a pair of nicely pressed khakis and a faded polo shirt in light blue. But he looks hot and dangerous even in that. The V of the polo shows me a glimpse of his chest tattoo, and his eyes look twice as blue.

You're staring, my inner voice snaps. *And he can tell.*

Sure enough, his eyes are twinkling. "Something you need from me?" he asks, and the question is dripping with innuendo.

"Um, not to beat a dead horse, but I brought you something." I step all the way into his room, revealing the houndstooth shirt in my hands. "First, I washed the shirt in hypoallergenic detergent, to clear away the chemical sizing. Then I removed every single interior-facing seam and sewed each one back in with organic cotton thread. I also removed the tags, because who knows what those are made from. Then I washed, dried, and ironed the shirt again." I hold it up for his inspection. "It shouldn't hurt you now. I hope. If it does, you have my permission to light it on fire."

He laughs. "That sounds like a lot of trouble, honey." He steps forward and takes the shirt from me, inspecting it. "Did you really sew it back together? That's crazy. How many hours did it take?"

"It wasn't that much trouble," I insist.

He already knows you're bonkers. My inner voice laughs. *This is just an obsessive little cherry on top.*

I brace myself as Ian removes his polo shirt with one burly arm and tosses it aside. Those wings on his chest ripple as he puts on the new shirt. "Hmm. Okay. The seams feel a lot better now."

"Oh good," I say, practically melting with relief.

He buttons it all the way up and then looks at himself in the mirror over his dresser. "Nice work, contessa. I like it. And you're right—I never buy anything new because half the time it doesn't work out for me. And a man isn't supposed to whine about his itchy shirt. Nobody wants to hear it."

"I do," I say quickly.

He gives me a sidelong glance. "We all have our kinks."

"Ian! You know what I mean. Solving fashion problems is my calling."

He laughs.

"Look, I know you aren't interested in clothes. But now that I know what you need, I could find you some more. I'd like to do that for you."

He looks wary. "I could really use a few things, I guess. Shirts. A suit or two. And eventually maybe a tux. Mine is a rag."

I'm so excited that I actually clap my hands. "Let me grab my measuring tape!" I dart for the bathroom door.

"I said *eventually!*" he thunders at my back.

"Too late!" I call. "You're stuck with me now." I grab the

tape out of my suitcase, then I hurry back into the room before he can object any further.

He gives me a grumpy look. "You can't measure me wearing that slinky dress, contessa, I'm gonna get ideas."

"Oh, please. This will literally take ten seconds," I insist, handing him the loose end of the tape. "Hold this to your inseam, please."

"You mean my balls, right?" he grumbles. "I don't do jargon."

"Call 'em whatever you want, just hold the tape," I say gleefully. I drop down onto the rug and catch the other end. Then I straighten his trouser leg so my measurement will be accurate. "All right! Thank you." I drop the tape and look up at his stormy face. "See how easy that was? Not exactly the porn shoot you were picturing, huh?"

He actually scowls. "Oh, I'm filming it in my mind as we speak. Honestly, the view of you kneeling at my feet in that dress is as convincing as a hand on my cock."

The way he says that last word makes my face heat. I stare up at him from the floor and realize how close I am to his groin. And now we're *both* picturing something much different than a trouser fitting.

Oh boy.

I know I ought to scramble to my feet and break the moment. But for once in my life, I don't. Somehow, I stay right here on the rug, my heart beginning to pound, my tape measure forgotten. And for a split second I feel like a different person. A bolder one. The kind of girl who drops down onto her knees on a dare.

It's a thrilling idea. Scary, but still thrilling.

That's the kind of girl men want, my inner voice reminds me. *Danforth would have stuck around if you weren't such a drag.*

With courage I didn't know I possessed, I hold my ground. Instead of running away, I lift my chin and look Ian straight in the eye. Then I lick my lips.

"Contessa," he growls. "You can tease me if you like. But know this—I'm thinking *all* the dirty thoughts about you right now."

If that's supposed to scare me off, it doesn't. I hold his gaze and give him a little smile.

"Christ." He takes a step back and parks his hands on his hips. "Mixed signals, honey. I thought you wanted to style me. But now I think you want to jump me, too."

"What if it's both?" I whisper.

"Well, is it or not?" he snaps. "Trying to be a good guy, here, but you make it *hard*." He winks after he says that, and I feel my flush deepen.

For once in my life, my impulse is to break all the rules. But the idea of a sexed-up Ian is intimidating. He'd be expecting me to follow through. And then he'd realize I'm the most awkward human *in the world* when it comes to sex.

I let out a sigh, and I get to my feet. "Hold up your shirt, please. I need to measure your waist."

Ian blinks. Disappointment flashes through his eyes. But after a moment, he does exactly as I'd asked. I quickly measure his waist, but it's more intimate than kneeling at his feet. My knuckles brush against his smooth skin.

When I back away, he's still watching me with a heated gaze. Like he's waiting for me to up the ante.

Like you'd even know how to do that.

"Listen," I whisper. "Has there ever been something in your life that other people just *get*, but you don't?"

He blinks again. "Well, sure. School. All thirteen years of it. The only class where I ever got an A was PE."

"Oh." I picture a much younger Ian sitting alone in the back of all his classrooms. "Was it frustrating?"

"Yeah." He shrugs, like it doesn't matter. But I bet it did.

Because I know all about that feeling. "It might not sound plausible to you, but the subject I've been failing my whole life is sex."

"Oh, honey." He grins. "Not to brag, but if they gave out grades for that, I'd've been an A-plus student."

"I imagine," I say drily. "But don't laugh. If I'm sending you mixed signals, it's because I seem to have a learning disability when it comes to, uh…"

"Sex," he says hotly. "Maybe you're just not sexually attracted? It happens. That's what they tell me, anyway."

"Oh, I am," I say quickly. "But I'm not good at the follow-through. I lack confidence. I think I need…" I make myself look him in the eyes again. "…tutoring."

His grin fades away, replaced by a more serious expression. "Tutoring. Seriously?"

"Yes," I clip. "Tutoring. What if you gave me lessons on how to seduce someone?"

His eyebrows disappear into his hairline. "Lessons on how to seduce someone?"

"Are you just going to repeat everything I say?"

"Maybe." He chuckles. "At least until this starts making sense. Because, honey, all you'd have to do to seduce me is take off your dress."

I'm already shaking my head. "I promise you it doesn't always work that way. There's this guy, my ex. He…" I can't do it. I can't finish that sentence. It's too embarrassing.

Ian's brow furrows. "What did he do? Did he hurt you?"

"Nothing like that," I say quickly. "He just…told me that I don't do a good job. That I had no spark."

"Liar," Ian growls. "That sounds like his own damn excuse."

"Maybe," I concede. "But he's just reached out to me for the first time in years. And I have this idea that I want him to give me a second chance. Or teach him a lesson. One or the other." I take a breath. "What if you could teach me? Tell me what turns a guy on. And, uh, show me. Maybe. If that's not too weird."

He stares.

"Oh God, that is weird, right? I'm sorry. Crap! Forget I

ever mentioned it. Never mind! I'm…" I'm going to flee. I whirl around, because the nearest exit is through the bathroom.

But he catches me by the wrist. "Hold on there, contessa. Not so fast. You didn't wait to hear what I think of this idea."

"Never mind," I say quickly. "I'll just go and die of embarrassment now."

He chuckles. "From the sound of things, that dude is not worth your trouble."

"That's my decision," I point out quietly. Even though Charli might agree with him.

"Look, I'm on board for anything that results in you and me blowing off some steam together. Especially if we're naked in your bed."

"Really?" I'm surprised he'd say that, now that he knows for sure I'm super awkward and also bad in bed.

"Well, yeah." He slides his palm down my wrist and presses my hand between both of his. "I know a fun idea when I hear it. But like I said, there's nothing you can actually learn from me that you don't already know."

"Who are you, the Wizard of Oz? Besides, you're wrong," I insist. "You can tell me what guys want, and how to be more fun and adventurous. It's just like fashion tips, Ian. Everyone wears clothes, but not everyone wears them *well*."

He snorts. "It's not the same at all. Because those of us who *don't* wear clothes well don't care all that much."

"But you're still judged," I point out. "Your manager wants you to look sharp, because the world is judging you on its own terms. How is that not the same?"

"Aw, honey. If I get you into that bed—" He nods toward his queen-sized bed covered with a thick white comforter. "— nobody is gonna judge you. Not on my watch."

You say that now. "Then it's a deal," I say in a slightly hysterical voice. "You show me the ropes. I'll make it worth your while." That comes out of my mouth with far more nonchalance than I actually feel.

"Hot damn. This conversation did *not* go where I expected it to."

"I bet," I say under my breath. But then I plan my exit. As a businessperson, I know how to close a deal, and I know how to quit while I'm ahead. I grab my measuring tape off the floor and leave before he comes to his senses.

ELEVEN

A Living Demonstration of my Awkwardness

VERA

REGRET SETS in about two minutes later, as I'm needlessly touching up my makeup befor dinner. Honestly, what was I thinking? I can't believe I asked him for seduction lessons. Only a loser would do that.

Oh wait, that's me. A confident girl would just…wink at him or something and invite him over later. But me? I give a living demonstration of my awkwardness and then beg him for help.

I lean closer to the mirror and tap the mascara brush against my bottom lashes. As if lush eyelashes will make me less of a freak.

The truth is that I *do* need help in the bedroom. I need some straight talk from someone who knows what turns a guy on. I lack experience. I've only ever slept with one guy—the same one who told me that I wasn't enough between the sheets.

My only source of information up to this point has been women's magazines. From articles with names like "Ten Ways to Thrill Your Man." I've scrolled through dozens of these articles, but their advice is always too generic. *Eye contact is key. Make time for sex. Put on some mood music.*

As if any of that could address the real issue — that I don't enjoy sex that much, and faking it never seems to work.

An antique clock chimes somewhere out in the hallway, and a wave of anxiety rises up inside me. Before I can even deal with the awkwardness I've created, I have to survive a friendly meal with nine other people.

Yikes. I toss the mascara onto the dressing table and trot out of the room. Maybe a cocktail will help. My sandals sink into the rich carpet runner on the grand staircase as I descend toward the main dining room.

I'd been told that dinner would be served "family style" in the villa's dining room. And that might be true, if the family in question were Italian royalty. I step into the room and find the table is already set with china and crystal and loaded down by platters of mouth-watering dishes.

"Wow," I say in a hushed tone.

"Gorgeous, isn't it?" Ian's voice says roughly.

I look up and there he is, leaning that muscular body against one of the high-backed armchairs, wearing the shirt I'd tailored for him, the sleeves rolled up onto brawny forearms. He gives me a saucy wink that makes my heart beat faster.

Could I even handle a night with Ian? If he takes off those trousers, I might just faint. That's one way out of this awkwardness, I suppose.

Charli trots into the room, leading her husband by the hand. "Oooh! Have I mentioned how much I like Italy?" she asks with obvious glee, as she pulls out a chair and sits down in it. "Let's eat."

I take the free chair beside hers, leaving Ian safely on the opposite side of the room.

But guess who walks all the way around the table and seats himself on my right? Yup. Ian Crikey. And just as the rest of our friends hurry in and snag all the other chairs.

And now I'm praying he doesn't say anything about our

awkward conversation. *So, Vera here asked me for the craziest favor…* He wouldn't do that, right?

My stomach churns as Charli passes me a bowl of radicchio salad with hearts of palm and grapefruit sections. And after that, a platter of fresh mozzarella, thinly sliced tomatoes and basil, drizzled with balsamic vinegar and olive oil.

Well, I guess if I'm going to die of embarrassment, this will make a great last meal. When one of the caterers Drake hired offers me some rosé, I hand him my glass without hesitation.

"We're going for a run tomorrow, right?" Ian asks the table. "I'm going to need it after all this food." He helps himself to a spoonful of gnocchi in a buttery sauce. "This smells delicious. Would you like some, contessa?"

"Yes, please."

When he leans in to serve some onto my plate, I get a whiff of his spicy cologne. "There you go. Eat up. You never know what games we'll get up to later." He winks.

I practically burst into flames. I pick up my water glass and down it in a few gulps.

"I love games!" says Fiona from the other side of the table. "I brought Pictionary and Taboo. And I think I saw some more games in the den."

"There's a whole collection," Drake says. "And there's a big screen for movies hiding behind the paneling in the den. We're kinda jet lagged. Maybe a movie is the way to go?"

The conversation turns to which movies we should watch together while we're here. "We can vote," Sylvie says. "I'll make a ballot."

"Wait. They can't all be chick flicks," Anton argues.

"Says you."

As I follow the conversation, Ian shifts in his chair, moving his body a little closer to mine. I'm terribly conscious of his nearness and the throaty sound of his laughter when Anton says something funny. I feel it vibrate inside my chest.

Ignoring him, I try to enjoy my meal. The food is spectacular, and the first glass of wine is making its way into my bloodstream. The sun is setting outside the windows, burnishing the lake and setting it on fire.

Much like my face.

A hand lands on my knee. No — not even a hand, just two of Ian's fingertips. He's merely stroking my kneecap with a feather-light touch.

Okay. Wow. Taking a gulp of my wine, I focus my attention on Charli so nobody will notice. But my body has other ideas. As he continues this delicate assault, I feel a flutter between my thighs. It would be so easy for his hand to slide a few inches to the left...

But it doesn't. And when he finally places his palm over my knee, the touch is almost polite. It just rests there, warm and solid.

Nobody notices, except for me. I notice. A lot. My neck is hot, and my nipples harden. All from the touch of his hand.

My wine glass is suddenly empty, and the caterer comes by to refill my glass. Ian removes his hand, and as the pink wine fills my glass, I feel bereft.

The hand does not return. But I expect it to, so I spend the rest of the meal in heightened anticipation. And, fine, arousal.

I have no chill. It's never been more apparent to me in my life. I overthink absolutely everything, even a hand on my knee. And I can't even follow the conversation, because I'm basically quivering in anticipation of what might happen next.

Suddenly, people are pushing back their chairs from the table. But they all pause when the cute Italian caterer speaks. "Signore e signori, I'm leaving a selection of desserts in the refrigerator. We'll be back in the morning with pastries and other breakfast items. Can I pour anyone another drink before I go?"

"Oh. Me," I say breathlessly. Another drink sounds like a fine idea. I carry my glass over to the bar where he's keeping the wine.

"Easy now," says a low voice behind me.

"W-what?" I whisper, holding my glass out for a refill.

"That's your last glass, contessa."

"Why?" I squeak.

He doesn't answer me until we've both moved away from the bar and out of earshot of our friends. He stops me in the corridor leading toward the den. "Don't drink too much, sweetheart. I have lesson plans for you, but you can't follow along if you're drunk." After delivering this ultimatum, he goes on into the den without me.

Lesson plans. I gulp. A quick glance at the time shows me that it's only eight thirty. In the den, my friends are rolling aside a wall panel to reveal a movie screen. Heidi Jo and Castro flip a coin, trying to settle some kind of feud about the movie.

And I'm standing here like a zombie, wondering what Ian will do next.

"Here, Vera. Sit here." Charli pats the cushion beside hers.

I shake myself a little, walk over to where she's seated with her husband on a huge, tufted sofa, and plop down beside them. Others toss giant floor pillows down in front of the sofa and spread out happily.

Someone turns off the lights, and it gets quite dark as the movie comes up on the screen. It's *Roman Holiday*, which tells me that Heidi Jo won that coin flip.

Audrey Hepburn's perfect face lights up the screen. I'd forgotten the plot of this movie—a princess who escapes her official duties to frolic around Italy with Gregory Peck.

And the clothes are *fabulous!*

I begin to sink into the sofa, my head propped up in one hand. Sipping my wine, I toe off my sandals and relax my limbs. It's been a long day, but I'm enjoying the movie.

Everyone else is, too. Charli rests her head on Neil's chest, and I notice that he's nodded off, his arm around her. It's peaceful, and a gentle breeze blows through the room, scented of whichever purple flowers are climbing the villa's walls outside.

Wait, no. That's the scent of Ian's cologne. As the movie reaches its climax, I realize he's placed a chair behind the sofa and seated himself there. A few heartbeats later, soft lips graze the back of my neck.

My breathing hitches, and I have goosebumps, waiting to find out what he'll do next. I can sense the heat of his body behind me. Anticipation builds inside my belly. But I don't turn around. I don't want to draw attention to myself.

My busy thoughts recede as those sultry lips find the back of my neck again. Since I've forgotten to breathe, the contact makes me let out a windy gasp. My eyes dart to the side to see if anyone noticed.

Nope. All eyes are on Audrey Hepburn as she falls in love in black and white.

"*Relax.*" His whisper is so quiet I might have imagined it.

I make my breathing more level, training my eyes on the screen. And I'm rewarded by another kiss—this one slow and searching. My nipples harden inside my bra as he moves his hot mouth another inch and kisses me again. Then his tongue comes out to play, and he sucks gently on my neck.

Oh God. That's so nice. I mean, it's just a kiss, right? Just your ordinary *secretive* kiss in the dark from a super-hot, bad-boy athlete *in an Italian mansion.*

It must be the romantic setting. Or even the movie. That must be why my panties are already soaked. The man has barely touched me, and I'm this close to panting. I shift a bit on the sofa, propping my other arm on the back cushions, exposing a new spot for Ian to torture.

Which he does, on long, languorous pulls with firm lips and a wicked tongue. I try to breathe evenly, but all I want to do is whirl around and climb into his lap like a bonobo monkey. Heat pools in my body. And who knew that my neck was connected by electric wires to my nipples?

My eyes flicker to the screen, where Hepburn and Peck are kissing madly in the front seat of a car. That's how I feel right now, too—wild and loose. I close my eyes as Ian's tongue takes a naughty trip to the underside of my jaw. It goes on and on, wave after wave of delicious torture. Then he discovers a spot so sensitive that I have to bite my tongue to keep from crying out.

But eventually it stops. It's just gone. I open my eyes, and the movie is over.

"That's it?" Charli says, sitting up suddenly. "She just goes back to her own country and leaves him forever? They don't end up together? What a rip!"

"Hey, I didn't choose this movie," Anton says from a floor pillow. "Nobody even got nakey."

Castro gets up and turns on a lamp, lighting the room with a soft glow. He beckons to Heidi Jo. "Come on, honey. Time for bed."

"I'm beat," she says with a yawn.

I'm not. My heart is still beating madly, and I feel hot everywhere.

"Night, guys," Ian says from the other side of the room, where he's already replacing his chair against the wall. "See you in the morning. What time is yoga tomorrow?"

"Ten," Anton says. "Drag me out of bed by my feet if I don't get up."

I count to ten before I get up off the sofa. "Night, all," I murmur.

And then I make a break for upstairs.

TWELVE

Lesson One: Anticipation is a Powerful Thing

IAN

MY HAND IS on the doorknob to my room when I hear footsteps hurrying along behind me. Smiling to myself, I push open the door and begin to step inside. My body is humming from the torture I've spent the evening inflicting on myself. I want more, starting with her clothes on my floor.

Vera draws up short behind me. But she doesn't follow me into the room. I can feel her hesitation before I even turn around.

Interesting.

I turn slowly, and take her in. We've flown halfway around the world today, but Vera somehow looks fresh and pretty. That dress fits her as if it was designed for her body in a laboratory.

I'm sure that if I got her out of it, the tag would reveal some fancy designer I've never heard of. But I'm starting to realize that her worldliness and confidence is as thin as the delicate fabric hugging her tight body.

It's funny—some people become easier to understand the more time you spend with them. Vera is just the opposite. I used to think she was snobby and a little uptight. But I had it all wrong. Her bravado is fierce, but there's more there than I anticipated. More vulnerability. There's yearning in her soulful brown eyes.

And now she's just watching me, waiting for me to decide what happens next.

"You need something?" I ask.

Her eyes drop immediately to the elaborate rug beneath her feet.

"Just kidding, sweetheart," I whisper, already regretting my dickish question. "But tell me this—what did you learn from my first lesson?"

She gives a slow blink. "Mostly I learned that I am capable of outrageous suggestions."

"That's it?" I study her for a moment. Her cheeks are pink, and her pupils are blown. She wants me, but still, her reply was so self-deprecating. "You're offering me an out. That's the wrong play, contessa. You want to seduce a guy—you don't retreat."

"Oh," she says softly. "I told you. I'm terrible at this."

"I think you need some homework," I say.

"Homework?"

"Yeah, you need to reflect on tonight's lesson."

"Reflect?"

I chuckle. "Are you just going to repeat everything I say?"

Her mouth snaps closed, and her eyes blaze. And I just wanna tug her into this room and push her down on the bed. I want to kiss away that tentative look on her face. I want to make her forget all the bullshit her ex put into her head. That guy sounds like a piece of work. I can make her stop thinking about him. I can make her stop thinking, period.

But I won't—not tonight. I've been awake for more than twenty-four hours, which means I'm equal parts horny and exhausted. I'd rush my time with her; I'd make her scream my name inside of ten minutes, and then I'd pass out like a beast.

That isn't what she asked me for, though. And we have two weeks in the sunshine. What kind of asshole would I be if I didn't teach her right? Seduction is all about anticipation. That's why I spent the whole night torturing us both.

And yet she didn't learn the lesson.

"Here's your homework," I tell her. "I want you lie down in your bed." I point toward her room, like either of us could forget where it is, or how close we are to each other. "You're going to lie down on those sheets and reflect on our time together tonight. What I did, and what I didn't do—*yet*."

Her eyes widen, and her perfect lips part as if for a kiss.

Fuck. I really don't want to send her away. But I'm still going to. "Meanwhile, I'll be right here, worked up, picturing all the things I plan to do to you for lesson number two. I sleep naked, by the way. Just so you have that image in your mind."

Her cheeks pink up, and her eyes do a sweep of my body—head to toe and back again.

I chuckle again, because she's not even trying to hide it. "Lesson one is about anticipation, sweetheart. There's no seduction without anticipation. If you're frustrated right now, then I did the job right."

She swallows hard, and I can tell she wants to argue. She and I have a great capacity for arguing with each other. And it's more fun than I'd like to admit.

Still, now is not the time. I raise one finger to her lips and press it there. "Shh. Lesson one is over. Tomorrow is a new day, contessa. And we'll both be ready for lesson two. Okay?" I trace a line around her top lip and hear her breath shudder again. The sound goes straight to my dick.

Vera blinks up at me, wide-eyed. Then she nods.

"All right, then. Goodnight." And now I should close the door between us. But nobody moves. So I lean in slowly, my eyes on her mouth. Her lips part in pure anticipation.

With self-control that I didn't even know I possess, I swerve at the last second and kiss the underside of her jaw.

"Anticipation," I whisper. "It's a powerful thing."

"Y-yes, it is," she breathes.

"Goodnight, contessa. Go ahead and take the first turn in our bathroom. You know you want to."

She gives me a watery smile as I take a step back and gently close my door.

A moment later I hear her door open and shut. And then I hear the sink flip on as Vera brushes her teeth.

Carefully, I unbutton my new shirt. I can't believe she took it apart and put it back together again. The girl has mad skills. I hang it up and admire it for a moment. It's been a long time since anyone did something so caring for me. A *long* time.

I walk over to my bed and faceplant onto it, my cock hard against the comforter, my senses screaming.

I sure am looking forward to tomorrow.

AROUND TEN O'CLOCK, I wake to the sound of someone knocking on the door. "It's yoga time!" Drake's voice calls. "Get up, sleepy."

I let out a monstrous groan, but then I sit up anyway. I slept without bad dreams—one night in a row. This is possibly because it's only four a.m. in New York right now. Maybe I just didn't get around to the nightmare yet.

"You coming?" my teammate calls.

"Yup," I grunt. Physical exercise, even when tired, is something an athlete knows how to appreciate. If I move around right now, my body might forget it's jetlagged.

I dress quickly and head downstairs, where sunlight is streaming through the windows of the villa. I'm wondering where to find my crew. The house is all marble and finery, and there's no obvious place for a yoga class.

Then I spot movement outside the kitchen window—they're all out on the side lawn, unrolling matching blue yoga mats. I count heads as I cross the expanse of grass in bare feet. I'm the ninth to arrive.

"We're all here," Fiona says. "Aly is sleeping in. She says she isn't into yoga."

"Or bendy athletes in spandex?" Heidi Jo asks.

"Not this early," Fiona says. "But I'm down. Let's do this."

I grab a mat from the instructor's basket and unroll it at the back of the group. Vera's glossy ponytail is in the front row. And somehow—it's unintentional, I swear—I have a perfect view of her ass as we start in child's pose on our mats. She's dressed in a closely fitted yoga top in a purplish color and matching leggings with a cloud-like pattern on them. Her hair is smooth and glossy. And if I'm not mistaken, she's even matched her lipstick to her outfit. She looks like an extra in an exercise video—too pristine to actually sweat.

In contrast, I am wearing a pair of joggers with a hole in the knee and a T-shirt so old you can practically see through it.

We are a study in contrasts. But my libido thinks she's exactly my type. That whole opposites-attract thing seems to be working for us.

And now I've got a whole hour to think about how attractive she is to me. I have a perfect view of her proud little form in mountain pose. And when she sweeps low, bending into a forward fold, I get a split-second glance at her perfect ass before I'm staring at my own ankles.

The instructor takes us through a quick rotation of sun salutations, and my eyes keep returning to the front of the pack, where Vera is keeping up with everything in high style. Her lunges are deep, her warrior stance is strong. That lithe body seems capable of anything.

And I have some ideas for it. All I want to do is throw her over my shoulder and carry her back upstairs to my bedroom. The more I think about it, the harder it is to concentrate. My body feels loose and warm and ready for action.

Horizontal action.

The yoga instructor ups the ante, bringing us into a series of eagle poses. And thank God. I have to force myself to concentrate or I'm gonna topple over in the grass. These balance poses are better suited to an indoor studio than a grassy yard, and I see a lot of wobbling around me.

But it's just what I need. I choose a focal point in the distance — a tree, by the way, not Vera's ass — and give it my best shot.

By the time the hour is over, I'm sweaty and tired in a good way. We thank the instructor, and Charli announces that pastries, coffee, and fruit are now being served on the terrace.

"This place is heaven," Castro says. "You might have to kick us out, because I might not leave willingly."

I don't disagree. I set myself up with a breakfast tray and eat on the shaded terrace. Traveling with the super-rich is a real good time.

As I sip my second cup of coffee, the women are making plans. I hear something about dinner tonight in Bellagio and a water taxi. "Doesn't that sound fun?" Sylvie asks Anton.

"Sure, baby," he says, closing his eyes and reclining in his chair. "Just poke me when it's time to go."

I turn my attention to my phone. There are several messages from yesterday. Two are from the publicist whose glower I'm trying to forget, and three of them are from my father.

Those are the troubling ones. They're all variations of: *Call me back, Ian. I need to speak to you. There's a problem with your purchase agreement.*

Just like that, my vacation vibes are shot. I get up, carry my dishes into the kitchen, and hurry upstairs to call him back. Because — shit! What the hell did I do wrong now? Every call from my father gives me a familiar case of agita. He's never satisfied with anything I do.

My brownstone in Brooklyn is the biggest investment I'll ever make. It's part of my Plan B, which is a thing my dad is always hounding me about. *What are you going to do after hockey? What is your plan?*

I've never had a good answer to that question until I realized that I like working with my hands. And real estate is hands-on work. I could be good at it.

Unless I've already committed a major error.

Even though it's only six a.m. in Massachusetts, I phone my dad. He doesn't answer, so I leave the phone on the bed. I tap on the bathroom door I share with Vera and find the room is empty. I'm brushing my teeth when the phone rings, so of course I do a comically fast rinse and rush for it.

I answer the phone, and it's my mother on the line. "Honey! I was just about to get on the Peloton when I heard your father's phone ring. Is everything okay? You never call this early."

"Yeah, I'm in another time zone. Sorry. And Dad has something he wants to chew me out about."

"Oh dear," she says. "Well, I'll let him have you—except I need to remind you of something. Your RSVP to Jaqueline's wedding is late. She stopped me in the wine shop the other day and asked me if you were coming."

Uh-oh. "What did you tell her?"

"Of course, I said you'll be there. And that I'm sure your RSVP is in the mail. It's *rude* not to reply, Ian. I raised you better than that."

What. The. Fuck. "Did you really just commit me to attending my ex's wedding? Why would she even want me there?"

"Because you're both adults, and you were close for years. And it's a family wedding, Ian. You have to show your face."

"Oh, come *on*. He's my second cousin. We don't even send each other Christmas cards. You're the one who wants to go to the wedding, Ma. So go without me. It's not like I can go all the way to Massachusetts the first weekend of August. That's right before training camp."

"The wedding is just thirty miles from New York—on the waterfront in Connecticut. He picked the venue."

I groan. "I don't want to go."

She lets out a frustrated sigh. "We all have to do things we don't wish to do. Now your father wants to speak to you. Send in that RSVP. It's rude to wait so long. She needs to do her seating chart."

Before I can even respond, my dad's voice is booming in my ear. "Son—I called three times yesterday."

"Hey, Dad," I say, gritting my teeth. "Missed your calls because I'm in Italy on vacation."

"How relaxing," he says drily. "But you'd better get back to New York, because you have a big problem to fix on that real estate purchase."

My blood pressure spikes again. "What kind of a problem?" The truth is that I don't really know what I'm doing. I just didn't think I'd fuck up so soon.

"You bought the place under your own name! That's a disaster waiting to happen. The way this stands, you have a shit ton of liability, son. Any idiot who trips on the front steps can sue you for every penny you made playing hockey."

"Well, fuck." My stomach plummets. And then I ask him the kind of question he loves to hear from me. "What should I do? Can I fix it?"

"You need to incorporate, and then rent your apartment from the corporation."

"Oh," I say slowly. That is the dumbest thing I ever heard. Although it doesn't sound impossible. I'd been expecting worse news—like the deed was fake, or the building was condemned. God knows I didn't read every word of the contract the lawyer drew up for me.

But this is just typical Dad stuff. He makes every mistake I make sound like a fatal disease.

I'm twenty-eight years old, and I make two and a half million dollars a year. I play for one of the most successful teams in hockey, and now I'm the proud owner of a hundred-year-old Brooklyn building. And none of it is good enough for him. Nothing ever will be.

And he's still talking. "...you transfer the property into the corporation to limit your liability. Get on this immediately. Don't hire anyone to work in there without shielding your assets. Are you listening to me?"

"Yeah, I heard," I say with a sigh. "I need to incorporate. I'll deal with it when I get back in a couple weeks."

"A couple *weeks?*" The phone basically explodes with another torrent of advice, until he finally exhausts himself on the topic of my financial ineptitude. "You didn't rent any units yet, right?"

"No tenants yet," I assure him.

"You gotta vet them," he says. "Full background check. Criminal as well as financial. One wrong move and you're stuck with an abusive tenant. Eviction law is not on your side."

"I know," I say, just to shut him up. "I need to go, though. Thanks for your help. I'll get right on that..." What did he call it? "Limited liability thing."

"You'd better."

We say goodbye, and I hang up with a sigh. "Is it too early to drink?" I ask the bedspread.

"Definitely," says a sweet voice nearby. "Talking to your parents?"

I sit up and spot Vera in the bathroom, a hairbrush in her hand. "Just, uh, talking to my dad," I grumble. "Always a pleasure."

She's changed into another one of her little dresses. This one is orange, sporty, and stops just above her knees. Maybe there really was a point to all that luggage. "Your dad wants you to form an LLC?" She's wearing those hot mirrored shades again, so I can't see her expression.

"Right. Sorry if that conversation was not exactly vacation worthy."

She shrugs those smooth shoulders. "I had to do an LLC in April for my business. I have a guy. I could email him for you."

97

"Yeah?" She has all my attention now. "Was it complicated?"

"The lawyer does all the work. All I had to do was sign some papers and pay him almost two thousand dollars. That's a lot of money to me. But I listen to a lot of entrepreneurial podcasts, so I knew I needed to do it."

"Business podcasts, huh?" I give her a wink. "Sexy."

She grabs her mirrored shades off her face and stares me down. "Are you shaming my kinks, Ian? Is that lesson number two?"

A bark of laughter flies out of my mouth. "God. Sorry. We all have different hot spots, huh?"

She smiles, and then her eyes flip downward, as if she's a little shy. "I'll find the lawyer's contact information."

"*Yeah, baby.*" I drop my voice low. "Whisper it in my ear. Attorneys make me horny."

Vera giggles.

"Am I interrupting something?" another voice calls out.

Vera whirls around and trots out of my line of sight. "Hey, Charli!"

"Ready to go biking?"

"Sure," Vera answers. "So long as we can sit in the hot tub afterwards. Wait—I need my sunglasses." She reappears in the bathroom and grabs her shades off the counter.

"Have fun, gorgeous," I say. "I'll be looking for you later."

She gives me a bashful smile before departing.

And just like that I'm in a good mood again. Because there are at least one or two things in this life that I do well. And I intend to show one to Vera later.

THIRTEEN

I Hope That Means Something Dirty

VERA

BIKING IS EASY–UNTIL you do it with professional athletes. The scenery is beautiful, but the sun is hot, and my legs are like noodles by the time we head back to the villa.

"So are mine," Heidi Jo pants when I whine about it. "I'm going to need a nap after this."

"Same."

"How's your room?" she asks. "I hear they're all different. Ours has a window seat that overlooks the terrace."

"Mine is so pretty," I admit. "Like a Disney princess's. It has an old-fashioned dressing table. Although I share a bathroom with Ian, so I have to remember to knock on the door before I open it. Otherwise, I might get an eyeful as he steps out of the shower."

As if you don't want all *the eyefuls*, my inner voice snorts. *Both eyes*.

She's not wrong.

"Mr. Macho probably looks pretty good in a towel," Heidi Jo says. "He's such a cinnamon roll, am I right? Spicy on the outside, gooey on the inside. You should think about jumping on that."

"Now, there's a fun idea." I say it lightly, as if the thought would never occur to me. But heck, if I thought about it any more than I already have, I'd probably fall off this bike.

Last night I was ready to throw myself at him. I thought it was happening. But then he said goodnight and sent me on my way. I was confused.

I still am.

The villa comes into view, and I almost cheer. "There it is! We survived."

"Heck yes." Heidi Jo pedals faster. "Uh-oh—we're not the first ones to hit the hot tub. The men have beaten us to it."

She's right. When we park our rented bicycles beside the terrace, I see all four of them in there, sipping sodas and splashing each other.

"Get over here!" Castro calls. "There's room on my lap for you, baby."

"Five minutes!" Heidi Jo replies. "It's bikini time."

We run upstairs, where I choose my skimpiest bathing suit. I saw Ian in that tub, and I want a reaction out of him. Something that tells me our agreement is still in force.

It works, too. I swear his eyes darken when I slip into the hot tub a few minutes later. I choose the seat directly across from Ian, and he gives me a slow, appreciative smile that practically announces the things we're going to do later.

At least I think we are.

If I don't chicken out.

"Wow! This is the life," Heidi Jo says, slipping into the water between me and her husband. "I knew this place would be amazing, but I really had no idea."

"Isn't it nuts?" Charli asks cheerfully. "This hot tub seats ten people, and we're not even crowded. The Drakes don't do anything like normal people."

"Oh, we do a *few* things like normal people," Neil says with a sexy wink. "We just do them better."

"The ego on you," Charli complains. But she's scooting closer to him anyway.

I sink down into the water and try not to notice that everyone in this tub is snuggling up to a partner. Except for me and the hottie whose gray-blue eyes are watching my every move. Right this moment I'm pretty sure his gaze is stapled to my cleavage, and I applaud my choice of bathing suits.

If anyone in this hot tub were paying the least bit of attention to me right now, they could easily read my thoughts off my face. I'm *so* attracted to Ian. He's not the first man I've admired since Danforth. But he's the first one who makes me feel so flustered. Like there's a butterfly war raging behind the polka-dot tummy of this overpriced bathing suit.

I don't really understand it. Ian has a dangerous vibe that doesn't usually call to me. And we don't even like any of the same things. He doesn't respect what I do for a living, and I don't really understand his job, either.

A big sweaty athlete who solves problems with his fists? That's so not my type.

But whenever I accidentally look into his eyes, none of that matters. I just *want* him. I want to sit in his lap and trace his throat with my tongue. I want to run my hands over those tattoos. And I want him to kiss me until I'm breathless.

Also, I'm staring at his hunky body again.

When I drag my eyes off Ian's chest, I find his cool blue gaze watching me. And then he gives me a slow, cat-like smile that says he knows exactly what I've been thinking.

All of a sudden, this tub is too hot. I take a deep breath of chlorinated air and wonder if it would look weird for me to leap out and run away.

Just as I'm planning my exit strategy, the caterer rolls a beverage cart out of the French doors and onto the terrace. There's iced tea and lemonade in shatter-proof glasses and a tray of sandwiches, too. "Lunch is here," he says.

And I am saved.

AT SEVEN P.M., in the golden light of evening, I gather with my friends on the villa's private dock.

My eye is drawn to Ian, of course. I notice he's wearing the shirt I gave him again. I don't know if it's meant as a compliment, or if he didn't bring any other shirts. With him, it could really go either way.

A crisp white boat pulls up to the dock, and we climb aboard one by one. I take a seat in front on a padded bench, and the steward hands me a chilled glass of white wine before the boat rumbles away from the dock.

"The ride is just ten minutes," Neil tells us as we cut through the shimmering water. "If we took a car, it would be forty minutes."

"I like the way you travel," I say, feeling giddy. As much as it scares me to take time away from my business, this really is a trip of a lifetime. "And I promise all of you that boats don't scare me as much as planes. So there will be no need to carry me off."

Everybody laughs except Ian, who gives me a sexy wink instead.

My tummy flutters.

A few minutes later, I get my first view of the town of Bellagio, with its red roofs and cute buildings crowding the waterfront. We arrive on the dock of the Villa du Lac, and I follow my crew off the boat and up a set of stairs to the restaurant, where Drake checks in with the maître d'.

"Posso prendere la sua giacca, signore?" a young woman asks Anton.

"Um," he says, looking flummoxed. "Sorry?"

"She's offered to check your jacket," I offer.

"Oh!" He brightens. "No thanks, I'm good."

"Molte grazie," I say, as she smiles and turns to help another customer.

"You speak Italian?" Ian says, and the incredulity in his voice makes me smile.

"I do," I say with forced modesty. "Although this is the first time I've ever tried it out on an Italian. My nonna doesn't count —she spoke a messy blend of Italian and English. But my high school offered Italian as part of the language requirement, and I chose it because of her."

"Say something else in Italian," he demands.

"Lasagne. Fettuccini."

Everyone laughs, but Ian just shakes his head. "Christ, contessa. Until ten minutes ago, I thought Bellagio was just a hotel in Vegas."

"You know what? So did I, until I started googling Lago di Como," I admit. "I've always wanted to go to Italy, but I could never afford to."

He gives me a glance that's part puzzlement, part warmth.

"Seguitemi, ragazzi," Neil says, beckoning.

"What did Mr. Fancy say?" Ian asks.

"Follow me, kids," I translate.

We're led into a candlelit room that overlooks the lake and to a table set for ten. The setting is outrageously romantic. I watch my beautiful new friends seat themselves around the table and have the sensation that I'm finally living my dreams.

I do that thing where you hold back a little to see if the hot guy saves you a seat. And when Ian Crikey holds out a chair for me as I'd hoped, I feel victorious.

"Grazie, signore," I say in a silky voice.

His eyes flare. "I hope that means something dirty."

The table laughs, as if he was joking. But his eyes say that he wasn't.

I take the menu that I'm handed, and I try to read it. But I'm overly conscious of the man seated next to me. I wait for his hand to find my knee under the table. But it doesn't. Not yet.

The menu is written in Italian but translated into English, too. I consider a pesto dish but change my mind at the last second. Pesto is loaded with fresh garlic, and I don't want to reek if Ian kisses me later.

He'd better. I can't wait to see what he does next. I edge my knee a little closer to his and wait.

AND WAIT.

And wait some more.

Dinner is taking a very long time. When is the man going to make his move? I've chosen a *primi* of buttery risotto and a *secondi* of lightly grilled fish with olives and herbs. Each one proves delicious.

I've sipped my wine slowly, like a good girl. If Ian doesn't want me to get drunk, then I'll behave.

Yet he hasn't touched me or teased me at all. Not once. I spend the whole meal in reach of his appealing bulk, but not even one fingertip has found my hand under the table. He's as cool as the *acqua frizzante* the waiter keeps pouring into my water glass.

But I am not cool. I'm practically melting with expectation. Every time he laughs, I feel it low in my belly. Every time he smiles, I want to lick him like a brand-new flavor of gelato.

He hasn't made a move, though. What did I do wrong?

Maybe he wised up, my inner critic suggests. *You're awfully needy*.

Yeah, yeah.

When the dessert is finally served and the men settle into their grappa, I can't take it anymore. I excuse myself to go to the ladies' room, but it's just a pretense. I head outside to stand on a darkened terrace, where the cool stonework of the half-height wall feels lovely against my overheated palms.

The lake sparkles under a quarter moon, and I can see lit-up towns on the distant shores. It's beautiful here. But I'm so frustrated.

Sexually frustrated.

"Contessa."

I don't turn around, even though the scrape of his voice makes me prickle with awareness.

Ian moves to stand beside me, copying my posture, his hands on the wall beside mine.

Every cell of my body screams, *touch me!* But he doesn't.

"Did you see *Attack of the Clones*?" he asks. "With countess what's-her-name and Anakin?"

"Sure. It sucked," I say sourly. "Worst dialogue ever written for a major motion picture."

He chuckles. "All those scenes of her, though, standing on a terrace and staring out at the lake? They were filmed at a villa near here. The whole secret-love-affair thing. Just like this." He moves his hips to playfully knock into mine.

"We're not having a secret affair," I point out. "You just like to tease me."

"Not true," he says immediately. "But I gave you some homework, and I don't think you got the message. I'm a little disappointed in my student. I had high hopes."

I turn to him, wearing an incredulous expression. "What the hell do you mean? I'm right here waiting for you."

His smile is a little too smug for my liking. "That's the problem, honey. You're waiting, when you could be practicing your technique. I gave you some pointers last night. I showed you the way. But today? Nothing. No footsie in the hot tub. No feeling me up under the table in there." He jerks his head toward the restaurant. "Get off the bench and show me some hustle, rookie."

I stare up at this hot creature beside me and realize he's serious. "You were waiting for me to seduce you?"

"Of course. Isn't that what you wanted to practice? How's Mr. Banker Man going to know you're interested if you just wait for him to make all the moves?"

It's a perfectly good question, but I still don't like it. "Women are cultured not to initiate," I point out. "This is harder for me than it is for you."

"Didn't say it wasn't." He spreads his muscular arms in a show of acceptance. "But you asked me for help, lady. And seduction is all about confidence. It's not how you use your tongue, or the one right way to touch a guy's balls. It's the presumption of success."

"I see." Although I'm still full of questions. Like—*there's one right way to touch a guy's balls?* "Ian, I stink at this. The whole thing! Where do I find some confidence?"

He cocks his hip against the stone wall and gives me a smirk. "It's like anything else in life, contessa. It comes from practice. So, if you want this…" He points at his hot self. "You'd better come and get it. I'll give you ten seconds."

"What? Right now?"

He glances down at the watch on his wrist. "Somebody had better kiss me in the next eight seconds, or I'm gonna go find someone else who wants to practice seducing me."

Why do I feel like smacking him instead?

FOURTEEN

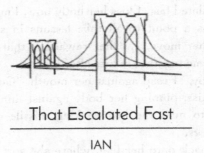

That Escalated Fast

IAN

VERA NARROWS HER EYES. She's looking up at me with a fierce glare that's half annoyance, half yearning. That's good. The woman needs to get out of her head. "I just have one question."

"Yeah?"

"Is there really one right way to touch a man's balls?"

Startled by the question, I laugh. And *then* the little minx makes her move. She leans in and presses her mouth to the underside of my chin, which is probably as high up on me as she can reach.

And it feels so fucking good. Soft lips kiss my stubbled skin. My heart thumps with joy as I act on pure instinct, widening my stance and tipping my chin down so she can reach my mouth.

We slide together in a heated kiss. I let her kick things off for at *least* two seconds. I'm the worst teacher ever, but that's all I can wait. My mouth captures hers, and my whole body shouts *finally!* Hers does, too. She lets out a breathy moan as I deepen the kiss.

Big brown eyes lock on mine as I encircle her waist with my hands. The fabric of her dress slides against her body, the same

107

way I'd like to. I tug her closer and lick my way into her mouth. She tastes like bubbly wine, and she smells like heaven.

Her arms wrap around my neck as my hand finds her ass. Hell, that escalated fast. I kiss her hotly now. I'm vaguely aware that there was a point to all this: lessons in seduction. Vera finally made her move, and her reward is that I'm losing my mind as we come together in kiss after kiss.

"Fuck, baby," I rasp against her mouth. "Gold star." I give her one last kiss, pinning her body against mine so there's no way for her to miss the heat-seeking missile of my erection between her legs.

I set her back onto her feet, where she sort of sways for a moment before righting herself. We're staring at one another, our breathing too fast. As if we've just run a sprint together. Neither one of us wants to stop.

It was brave of her to ask me for help. I can see the courage flickering in her eyes right this second. And the honesty.

I don't know if I'm worthy of it. It's been years since I really laid myself bare for anybody like she does. I haven't tried, and I haven't bothered. Hell, I feel more like a villain than a super-hero right now. More Darth Vader than Anakin, that's for sure.

"Wow," she says softly. "Sign me up for the next lesson."

"I think you're ready. Your room or mine, later?"

"Whichever," she says, her voice dreamy. She lifts a hand, and I wait to see where it lands. Its destination turns out to be the bridge of my nose, where a single fingertip smooths a line between my eyes. "You get a crinkle right there sometimes. Like you're thinking too hard."

My eyes fall closed as she slowly rubs that spot. Up and down. I feel like a kitty cat in the sunshine.

"That's better," she says softly.

Her fingertip travels over my eyebrows, one at a time. It's... nice. It's not what I think of when I imagine seduction. But at the same time, it's unexpected. Points for that.

Her fingertip trails down my cheek and then she cups my chin. "Look at me," she says softly.

My eyes flip open, and I take her in. She's studying me like I'm a puzzle she can't quite solve. "You wore the shirt again tonight," she says. Then she smiles. "I'm flattered."

"It's nicer than all my other ones," I admit. "You'll probably see it tomorrow, too."

"Your collar size is larger than Neil's," she says as her fingertips stray to my neck.

"You know what they say—big neck, big…"

"Shirts," she says, as a playful smile finds its way onto her lips. Her fingertips skate down my throat now, tickling the open V of my shirt collar. "I've been wanting to touch you here, you know. And here." She flattens her hand onto my chest. "Ever since that day when you took off your shirt to try the new one on."

"I already told you that dressing me won't be half as fun as undressing me. Now are you convinced?"

Her thumb teases the top button of my shirt, as if she'd like to unbutton it right this moment. "I hope to be. Although once your boyfriend tells you that you're boring in bed, it's easy to believe that he's right."

Well, fuck. "Baby, I told you already—some guys just want variety. He should have manned up and said so. The problem wasn't you, it was him."

"You say that now, but maybe he was right." She gives me a sad smile. "Better bring your A-game to our coaching session, big guy."

Then she turns and leaves the terrace.

FIFTEEN

Don't Forget Canada

VERA

THE BOAT RIDE home seems to take forever. I'm all keyed up on hot kisses and anticipation.

And *nerves*. I don't expect Ian to laugh at me, but I still have stress about sexy times. He probably has no idea.

After Danforth, I did some sporadic dating. I tried, anyway. But it's hard to meet available men, and I never found anyone who was worthy of a second or third date, let alone sex. Nobody made the cut.

As we cross the lake, the stiff breeze gives me goosebumps. My sleeveless dress isn't really cutting it anymore. All the other women onboard snuggle up to their boyfriends or girlfriends. It's been years since I was half of a couple. I can't even remember what that feels like—to have a person who's ready to hold you when it's cold.

I don't have any delusions about who Ian and I are to each other. So I stay put on the end of the bench, my arms wrapped protectively around myself. It's only a ten-minute trip back to the villa, even if it feels like hours.

Ian looks to be checking his messages on his phone. But I hope he's secretly as distracted as I am right now.

When the boat finally docks, I stand up so fast my knees

pop. Ian shoves his phone in his pocket and gives me a secretive smile.

And then Neil ruins everything. "Okay, fellas. It's poker night! Meet me in the den. I asked the caterer to leave us a card table and a bottle of scotch."

"Wait, is this men only?" Charli yelps. "What the *hell?*"

"No way." Neil puts a hand on his wife's back, steadying her as she climbs onto the dock. "There are plenty of seats and plenty of chips. Let's go, wifey. Ante up."

Charli gives him a sly smile over her shoulder. "I guess I don't actually want to play. I was just checking."

"I'm not going to play, either," I announce. "I'll be up in my room, planning out that shopping trip for tomorrow."

Ian is silent. I feel his eyes on me, and I like it. But as we file into the villa's side entrance, Anton specifically asks him to play cards. "You're in, right? I need a rematch after that bloodbath in Chicago."

"Uh, sure," he says. "Only for a couple of hands, though. I have to call my, uh, parents. See how they're doing."

"Yeah, let's go," Castro says, oblivious to my pain. They march off to the den, and I make my way upstairs to my bedroom.

Once there, I let my hair loose and brush the tangles out of it. On the one hand, this delay isn't so bad. I'll have a few minutes alone to make myself beautiful.

On the other hand, I'll have a few minutes alone to have a fashion crisis. What does a girl wear for sex with a professional athlete? He's the kind of guy that women proposition after every hockey game. He's probably had sex in every US city that has a hockey team.

Don't forget Canada, my inner voice says.

Right.

I open the top drawer of the bureau, where I've deposited all my underwear and night things. I pull out a simple little silk nightgown and give it the side-eye.

Not that, my inner voice complains. *Too demure. You don't even own the kind of lingerie that would turn his head.*

I drop it again. Holy macaroni. What was I thinking? I didn't pack right for this kind of adventure.

Now I'm spiraling. I actually pick up my phone and google: *Ian Crikey girlfriend*. I know he's single at the moment. But self-flagellation is an art form, and I need to know what I'm up against.

My stomach drops as the screen loads a stream of results. There's a whole smorgasbord of photos of Ian at various charity events with a different glamorous date on his arm in each one. There's a leggy redhead in an emerald dress. There's a stunning Black woman with model-worthy cheekbones, wearing a pleated Chloe maxi dress that I could never pull off. Next, we have a curvy woman with impressive corkscrew curls wearing a strapless ball gown. Her intricate shoulder tattoos curl artfully above the neckline.

Every one of those women is exactly the kind of kickass beauty that I would have expected to see on his arm. But then, as I scroll down even further, many of the older photos of Ian feature one particular woman. The captions read: *hockey player Ian Crikey and Miss Jaqueline Everston*. And they go back a few years.

Huh. Ian had a girlfriend before he became a man about town.

I zoom in on Miss Everston, taking measure of her wide, polished smile. It's worthy of a toothpaste commercial. She's *very* well-dressed, even if her taste runs to the conservative — Chanel jackets and silk blouses.

And she's super photogenic. The glossy hair. The perfect smile. The scarves tied just so. She's sleek and well-accessorized, sort of the way I'm trying to be.

Well, almost. I'd never choose those pumps. Or that pencil skirt.

You're too short for those clothes anyway, my inner voice chimes in.

Even so, Ian's ex is not what I pictured. Maybe Ian broke up with her to date carefree, adventurous women. Maybe she was too boring in bed.

Gulp.

I can't stop scrolling, though. And then it occurs to me that I can google her name by itself and find even more photos.

Boom. There she is in dozens of other pictures. She pops up in news stories about Connecticut politics. She works in the government? That explains the pencil skirts. And the confidence. And—wait—there's a new man in a lot of these photos. She's engaged to be married. To... the lieutenant governor of Connecticut?

Okay. Well. That's not intimidating at all.

A muffled shout from the main floor startles me out of my reverie, and I guiltily toss my phone down onto the bed. I don't hear footsteps, though. That was merely the sound of someone winning a high-stakes hand of poker downstairs.

Still, it makes me realize I'm sitting here stalking my hookup's clever ex-girlfriend. Like only a loser would do. I grab my phone and kill all the browser tabs. Then I hurry into the bathroom to brush my teeth.

Maybe I should shave my legs again.

Or take another shower?

Would it take too much time to paint my toenails?

Do men notice toenails?

Wait—are foot fetishes real?

You're getting off topic, my inner voice snaps. *It doesn't matter what you do, because Ian has already forgotten you're up here.*

There's that. But just in case, I'm brushing my hair for the third time when I hear the door to Ian's room open. "Hello? Anybody call for room service?" I hear him call in a teasing voice.

And I say... nothing.

113

Brilliant, my inner voice says. *Keep up the good work*.

"H-hi?" I squeak. Then I make an effort to pull myself together. I straighten my spine and set the brush down on the counter. "In here." I reach for the door that leads to his room and open it.

And there he is, his shirt sleeves rolled up onto those strong forearms. He's holding a scotch glass in each hand. "Hey, lady."

"Hey," I manage.

"You like scotch?"

"Not, um, much?"

My inner critic just rolls her eyes.

"No problem," he says, striding right past me, thorough the bathroom and into my bedroom. "I'm not really in the mood for more scotch either."

"You're not?"

"Nah." He sets both glasses down on the windowsill. Then he turns around, takes me by both shoulders and takes my mouth in a hungry kiss.

I'm startled, but only for a moment. This is good. No, this is *great*. Now I don't even have to make small talk. Instead, I wrap my arms around him and tilt my chin up, like an Italian sunflower reaching toward the light.

And maybe I *do* like scotch, because Ian tastes of dark, peaty liquor and pure man. His broad hand cups the back of my head as he takes control of another kiss.

Okay. Wow. Yup. Kissing Ian Crikey is my new favorite thing. It's intense, like he is. But it's also surprisingly playful, the way he nips my lower lip and then smooths it with his tongue. The way he smiles as he tilts his head the other way and draws me nearer.

I got this. I can do this. My bravado holds steady even as he steers me toward the bed. He pulls us both down, and I land on top of him. It's getting real. Hot kisses on the terrace are one thing, but now we're horizontal. Which means we're inching closer to the moment when he realizes I'm a disaster.

Ian rolls us to the side, and I catch a glimpse of his smile before he kisses me again.

That's what keeps me going—that smile. It's rare on him. So I must be doing something right. My hands fumble for his shirt buttons. My fingers are shaking a little as they brush against the thick fabric.

This *is* a kickass shirt. I do have my talents. The first button is undone, and I scramble onward to the second. His chest is a work of art, so I hurry to reveal it.

"Get it, girl," he says in a low, teasing voice. "Can I take this dress off you? I've been wanting to do that for hours."

"Yes! Good idea."

He chuckles. Then clever fingers work the zipper down my back. The metallic whine it makes is wonderfully sexy. It's the sound of boundaries crossed.

A rush of cool air hits my skin. When he lifts the dress over my head, I suddenly feel very naked in my camisole and panties.

But then Ian says, "Oh fuck yes." His voice is full of admiration. His hands land on my bare skin—one on my shoulder and one at the curve of my hip.

His touch is so much different than Danforth's. As his fingertips slide down my thigh, they're confident, with a side of possessiveness.

I like it. And *somebody* should have some confidence around here.

"Touch me," he whispers. "You know you want to."

He's right. I do. The moment I reach up to run my fingertips through the trimmed hair of his chest, I forget all my fears. Ian's body is *very* distracting. It's like something from a fitness influencer's Instagram photos. The skin is soft, but the bumps of his abs are firm under my fingertips.

Wow. And those pecs. I guess I'm a chest girl. And I have a thing for the stripe of hair running down his belly. So rugged. I want to touch him everywhere. I lean down and kiss his collarbone, because a girl has to start somewhere.

"Yes, angel," he whispers. "So nice."

The praise lights me up. As I kiss his neck, I let my hands wander over his body.

His hands wander, too, but there's more skill in it. He traces a thick fingertip across the swells of my breasts, just above the cups of my camisole. Then he does the same thing at my panty line. I give a full body shiver as that naughty finger dips so near my pleasure center.

"You like that, don'tcha?" I feel his smile more than I see it.

Everything is going so well that I feel emboldened. I slip a hand down those incredible abs, until I find his belt. I unhook that and then go for his trousers.

Ian is on board with this plan. He helps by kicking off the khakis. Then, while we're at it, he tugs down his black briefs and tosses them overboard, too.

"Wow." I swallow roughly as a generous, rosy erection juts proudly into view. Granted, it's been three years since I've seen one of these in person, but Ian seems longer than what I'm used to and maybe has *twice* the girth.

You're in over your head now, aren't you? my inner critic cackles.

You shut up, I tell her privately.

He takes my hand and laces it right on his shaft.

"Mmm," I breathe as I curl my palm around its rigid heat. He drops urgent, wet kisses onto my neck, and I sink against his body, diving into the warmth, homing in on his mouth with my own.

We meet in another deep kiss, and I tease my thumb over the smooth head of him. He's uncut, which I'm unused to. But he gasps happily when I slowly jerk his shaft with soft fingers.

"Lose the rest of your clothes, baby," he says. "The lace is scratchy, and the top is hiding your pretty tits from me."

"Oh!" I sit up quickly, remembering in a rush that he is sensitive to certain synthetics. There's some redness on his hip where my lace panties must have scraped against him. "God, sorry." I reach down and pull them off before flinging them away, like you might do with a venomous snake.

His smile reappears. "First time I was ever happy about that allergy." His eyes go lazy as he looks down at my body. "You are fucking spectacular, you know that?"

No, I really do not. "The camisole stays on, though. It's not lace." It's a super-soft microfiber. I wear these a lot.

His eyebrows lift in a question, but he doesn't argue. He palms my breast and tugs the camisole's cup downward by an inch or two until my nipple pops into view. "All right. I'll work around it." He leans in and sucks my nipple into his mouth. His tongue is firm as he laves it into an achy point.

I let out an uncharacteristic moan that makes him lift hungry blue eyes to mine. "My contessa likes that?" He switches sides, and when the other nipple hardens, I feel an actual rush of wetness between my legs.

Wow. This man has skills.

"Aw, hell," he says. "That sound you just made."

"What sound?" I gasp. "A good sound?"

"Fanfuckingtastic sound," he murmurs against my breast. One of his clever hands reaches down and pulls my body against his.

And then we're mostly naked and kissing like it's our last day on Earth. His tongue is in my mouth and his hands are sliding over my ass. He rolls on top of me, and I love it. The weight of him is so sexy, and the kisses keep coming.

He reaches down with one bossy hand and parts my legs in a businesslike way. And I clench the muscles of my core in a needy fashion. Like I'm ready for him there. Like I'm empty, and he can fill me up with all the things I'm lacking.

Maybe I'm about to learn all the secrets.

Maybe this time sex won't be a huge disappointment.

"There's a condom in the bedside table," I practically slur.

"Patience, contessa." He moves his hungry mouth to my

neck, and when he sucks gently on my skin, it feels indescribably sexy.

And then he slides his thumb *right over my clit* on the first try, and I practically arch off the bed in glee. *"Ohhh,"* I moan.

"Yes, honey." He slides his fingers through my slickness and groans. "So wet for me."

His fingers are *magic*. He kisses his way across the tops of my breasts, all the while teasing my core with a wicked hand. I clench my thighs and whimper, because it's so good.

I'm so turned on that I almost don't notice what he's doing until it's too late—he's kissing his way down my camisole to my hips and teasing my opening with one thick finger. Then he spreads my legs and drops his mouth to the inside of my thigh.

Uh-oh.

Oh no.

Up till now I'd gotten happily carried away. Everything was glorious. Actually, it still is. He drops teasing kisses all over the juncture of my hip and leg and down my thigh... It's *lovely*.

But I'm still me, and as soon as his lovely mouth drops down a little farther, hitting its mark, I know I'm in trouble. I'd forgotten that this is how it all goes bad. Every time.

I fight the good fight, though. I relax against the bed and try to enjoy myself. He's so good at this, and I'm not completely immune to pleasure.

Yet it doesn't matter. I start to tense up. I grip the sheets with both hands, but not in excitement. It's the white-knuckled grip of anxiety. Because I can't give Ian the feedback that the male ego craves. Unless I fake it. And in a few minutes, he's going to get tired of trying to get all the right responses.

Any second now, probably.

I grit my teeth.

"Baby," he says quietly. As I glance down, he rests his chin on my thigh. "Contessa, if this isn't your favorite thing, you can just tell me. I won't be offended."

"It's... I like it, I swear. But I won't be able to... I can't..."

I'm scrambling to sit up now. This is ridiculous. What was I even thinking?

"*Hey*, it's fine," he says calmly. "So what? We'll do something else. I'm *very* creative." He gives me a dirty wink.

"But it doesn't matter." I try to untangle my legs from the bed so I can leave. "Nothing works. You can say it doesn't matter, but eventually you'll get annoyed. So I'll fake it. But apparently, I'm not a great actor, so…" I free myself and aim my feet for the floor.

"Whoa, whoa, whoa," he says, lunging his body in my direction, wrapping one strapping arm around my waist like a big hook. "Hold on there, baby. Don't run away when I'm trying to talk to you. Is that nice?"

I immediately stop fighting. Because he's right. It isn't very nice.

"That's better." Ian tugs down the covers and then scoops me back onto the sheets. He covers us both up and then rolls to his side, facing me. "All right. Now explain this problem to your tutor."

Oh boy. I really don't want to, but I have nobody to blame for this embarrassing moment but myself. "I just can't…finish. Ever. It's probably one of the reasons I'm bad in bed. I get frustrated with myself. And it's hard to be a fun time when you're frustrated."

"You haven't *ever*?" His expression turns to horror.

"Well, not with anyone else in the room." My face is on fire now. I've reached my embarrassment quota for the year, so I'm done here. I roll toward the edge of the bed, and a much-needed escape.

SIXTEEN

You're Weirdly Good at This

IAN

I EASILY CATCH Vera the second time she tries to give me the slip. With an arm around her waist, I slide her back across the sheets, bringing her to rest against my body. "Damn, girl. Just give me a second to think. Where were you going, anyway? You're naked, and this is your bed."

She flops onto her tummy and buries her face in the pillow. "I don't even know." The words are muffled. "Somewhere. Anywhere. This is why I don't date. I forgot how stressful it is, wishing I could be just like any other girl."

Oh hell. I keep an arm around her so she can't easily bolt again. My gut says that if this ends badly for her, she won't put herself in this vulnerable position with a guy again. Maybe ever.

I don't know why I care. We're not exactly best friends. She doesn't even like me.

Still, this deep-seated anxiety she's carrying around can't be very much fun. I guess we all have our quirks.

She lets out a big sigh and turns her face away from mine. Her disappointment is a little heartbreaking for someone who enjoys sex as much as I do. And when I try to imagine her ex telling her that she's no fun... Yeah, what a dick move. No wonder she's got anxiety.

"Hey, lady," I say, giving her a little poke in the ribs. "Tell me something."

"Hmm?" she asks without turning around.

"How extensive is your research, anyway? You mentioned the ex. Maybe you two just weren't sexually compatible. How long were you with him?"

"Since college," she mumbles. "Until three years ago."

"First serious boyfriend?"

She nods at the wall.

"And after the ex? How far did you expand your horizons?"

Vera is silent.

I wait.

She says nothing. At all.

"Oh *shit*," I say slowly. "Really? I'm the first guy you've... In three *years?*"

She jerks her chin up and down just once. Then she sticks her face in the pillow again, as if from embarrassment.

Mind. Blown.

Okay. Wow. That puts a fresh perspective on things. I guess if somebody's got to break her losing streak, I'm not a bad choice. I don't hear a lot of complaints from the women who have the good fortune to enjoy a few hours of my time. Not that I stick around long enough to hear complaints. But that is beside the point.

"Look, I think I get it now. You didn't give me enough information to go on. But this is still a solvable problem."

"It's not a solvable problem," she argues, turning her face toward mine. "Don't worry about it, Ian. You're off the hook."

"Did I *ask* to be let off the hook? I'm still having fun here."

She sits up, the sheet pulled up over her perky breasts. "You can't be serious. We just established that I'm the least fun lay ever to stumble into your bed."

"Technically, *your* bed," I say with a shrug. "But we're not done here. I have some ideas. We can get you to O-town for sure."

"Hold up." She lifts an angry palm, like a cop who's stopping traffic. "Do *not* take this as some kind of macho challenge. I asked you to show me what men like. I didn't ask you to prove your manhood by rocking my world."

Under the covers, I run a hand up her silky leg. "What you don't understand is that both problems are the same. Your ability to enjoy sex is stressing you out. And a stressed-out lover isn't going to rock your ex's world, contessa."

Her face falls. "I know. And that's why this was a stupid idea. I thought if I could just get better at faking it…" She cringes. "It sounds terrible. But if you lived in my head, you'd understand."

"Uh-huh." My mind is working overtime now. "That is a doomed strategy."

"No kidding!" she yelps. "I just proved it."

I prop myself up on an elbow. "You just need a *better* strategy. I have some thoughts. Good thoughts." *Dirty thoughts.*

"Let's just drop it," she argues. "I'm embarrassed enough."

"But this is important to you. Otherwise, you wouldn't have brought it up in the first place." I squeeze her knee. "And I know a lot about the mind-body connection. Every good athlete does. Don't you even want to hear my ideas?"

There's hesitation on her face. "I don't know. Maybe."

She's been in pain over this for a while, I think.

"You gotta break the big goals down," I say before she changes her mind. "Your issue is that you're so focused on winning the whole tournament you forget to focus on the play. You get all clenched up, right? And any hockey player who turns up at the game anticipating failure will *ensure* failure. It's basic sports psychology."

She rolls her eyes. "Yes. Fine. That does sound familiar. But I have a lot of evidence that my buzzer won't light. So there you go."

"That's when you change your objective. What if you don't try to make any goals? Don't even shoot at the net. Instead, you let me do my thing, and you just try to enjoy a few—" I wink. "—laps around the rink for twenty minutes or so."

I expect her to give me hell for that crude analogy. But she says, "*Twenty* minutes? Isn't that a long time to...?" She gulps.

"Baby, no. Not in regulation play."

There's the eye roll I richly deserve.

"Hell, I could go all night. You think going down on you is a chore? Think again." To illustrate the point, I flip the covers off my cock, which is still standing proudly, pointing right at her. "He doesn't lie."

Her gaze goes a little dreamy when she looks down at me. I cock one of my legs just to up the ante, and I give myself a slow stroke. Vera's cheeks go pink.

The girl wants me. She can't help herself. Not that I'm really surprised.

"Please, baby," I say in a raspy voice. "I just need twenty minutes of your time."

"T-ten," she says, as her nipples visibly harden beneath the sheet.

"Fifteen," I barter.

"Okay." She lies back against the pillow. "But this is the weirdest conversation I've *ever* had. And you can't be mad if it doesn't work."

"Wait, wait. You're breaking the rules already." I lift the sheet and slide on top of her. We're skin to skin, my cock cradled against her body. "New objective, remember? You're not supposed to try to come. In fact—it's better if you don't."

"Well, that's easy, then," she grumbles. But she wiggles her hips at the same time. She likes the feel of me. She can't hide it.

It's mutual, too. I lean down and give her a slow kiss. She tastes like a dream. My cock gives an eager twitch.

But that's not what I'm here for. *Later, buddy. You'll get yours.* I lift my wrist and make a show of setting the timer on my watch for fifteen minutes.

"This is loopy," she whispers.

"Shh. Trust your tutor." I dip my head and kiss her neck, and her breathing hitches. "Your one job is to feel good for a little while. That's all."

"O-okay," she says as I slide down to suck on her nipple. I tug her little top down until her breasts are both displayed for me. I wonder why she won't let me take this thing off her. But women sometimes have weird ideas about their tummies, so I'm not gonna force the issue.

I switch sides. Her breasts are so sensitive. I pinch the other nipple, and she groans.

"That's right. You've got it now. Just do this for fifteen minutes. Just *feel*." I suck on her tits until her hips are shifting hungrily beneath me.

"You're weirdly good at this."

"Every guy needs a hobby."

She lets out half a laugh that ends up as a dreamy sigh. My hands are wandering over her smooth thighs. God, I want to bang her. I've been hard for two days straight just thinking about it. That won't happen tonight. But if I do my job—and I love my work—there's hope for me yet.

SEVENTEEN

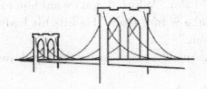

It's Almost Like You're Enjoying Yourself

VERA

IAN KISSES his way down my hips again. He makes a hungry sound as he gently parts my legs. It's a gorgeous, masculine rumble. I love it.

Can I really just lie back and do this for fifteen minutes? Isn't that weird?

Probably.

On the other hand, I love the feel of Ian's broad hands on my thighs. And I love the view of his muscular body stretched out between my legs. When he touched himself for me a couple of minutes ago, it was the sexiest thing I'd *ever* seen.

There are worse ways to spend fifteen minutes.

It's probably fourteen by now, anyway. Then he leans in to slowly kiss me *right there*.

"Oh hel*lo*. Wow."

His chuckle is low and playful. "Relax, baby. All the way."

I sink back against the pillows and remember how to breathe. His tongue is...ahhhh. My heart rate kicks into a higher gear. I grip the sheets again, but in a good way. "That's so..." He flattens his tongue against me, and I whimper. And after a few moments, I realize I've begun to move my hips in time with his caresses.

This is…wow. The man was right. This is fun when you don't care what happens.

"Do you have any lube?"

"W-what?" I slur. "Why?" I don't want him to stop.

"Because lube is fun. Duh." He lifts his body. "I could find some in my room."

"No," I say quickly, reaching for the top drawer of the night table.

He gets the idea, opening the drawer himself. "Oh, look what we have here?" He peers into the drawer, where I realize too late, he can also see my vibrator.

"Take this." I reach into the drawer, grab the lube and throw it at him.

"Impatient, contessa? It's almost as though you're enjoying yourself."

"We need a no-gloating rule."

He snickers. I hear the snick of the bottle, and I close my eyes, waiting to see what he'll do next.

To my surprise, his slicked-up fingertips land on my breast, where he does a naughty circle before giving my nipple a slippery tug. "Oh, fuck," I gasp. And when he switches sides, my back arches off the bed.

"So damn hot," he whispers. "You look like a wet dream right now."

For once in my life, I actually believe him. I *do* feel hot. It's exhilarating. And when he lowers his mouth to my core once again, I moan deeply. His fingers are slick and messy on my breasts, while his tongue is sending licks of heat through my veins.

I clench my thighs together, feeling needy. But his knee puts an end to that, spreading my legs again. Then a thick fingertip runs a teasing circle around my opening.

"Oh, God. I want…" The sentence dies on my tongue, because I realize at the last second that the thing I want is not supposed to be the goal.

What kind of dumb idea was this, anyway?

His chuckle tells me that he knows exactly what I'm thinking. "Not tonight, sweetheart. Not on my watch. Your time isn't up yet."

"Okay," I whimper. Somewhere in the depths of my blissed-out brain I know he's right—the strange rules of Ian's little game are the only reason I'm enjoying myself right now.

"Just enjoy," he says gently, between licks. "Just feel."

Oh, I'm feeling. I'm rocking my hips forward to the beat of my own heart. This is easily the best time I've ever had with a guy's face between my legs. And when I reach down to tug gently on his hair, he moans, too.

Whew! So hot. My time must be almost up, though. I'll probably cry when the timer rings.

But then I hear a low, thumpy rumble instead. "Don't come," Ian warns, before he nudges the blunt cockhead of my vibrator against my body.

"Oh!" I gasp. "That's...cheating." But I can't help myself. I bear down on it.

"Fuck," he curses. "That's...*unnngh.*"

I can barely hear him. My body is a gathering storm as he slowly fucks me with the vibrator. I want it. So badly. I clench my thighs in frustration.

"Vera," he warns. "Relax your body. Just feel."

I try to. I really do, because it's been working for me so far.

All at once he picks up the pace of his torture and leans down to suck my clit between gentle lips.

And I experience a toe-curling, heart-throbbing orgasm like no other. Wave after wave of heady sensation rolls through me, while I moan so loudly that it probably echoes across Lake Como.

It goes on and on, and I'm basically wrung out afterward. The sound of the vibrator halts abruptly. For a moment, all I can hear is my own heavy breathing. I lie there staring up at the ceiling, half in shock, half comatose. And then I hear one more sound.

It's muffled laughter. Ian has pressed his face into the mattress, and his back is shaking.

"What is so funny?" I demand in a wheezy voice.

He laughs for a moment longer and then sits all the way up. "Look." He flops down beside me, holding up his wrist, so I can see his watch.

I look. The timer reads *11:42*, and as I watch, it continues to count down.

"Three minutes," he says with a chuckle that threatens to become more. His voice rises in imitation of mine. "Oh, *Ian*. I can't *possibly* have an o—"

I smack him on the arm. "What did I say about gloating?"

He leans back on the pillow and laughs openly. "Christ, you're fun. Complicated, but fun."

I'm trying not to smile. "Complicated but fun" isn't exactly the comment every girl dreams of, but I'm riding an endorphin high, and there's a hot, naked man lying on the bed next to me. His hair is tousled from my tugging on it. He's got the body of an underwear model, and an erection the size of a New York skyscraper.

Although he's laughing at me.

Welp. I know how to shut him up. I plant a hand on the bed and lean over, taking the head of his cock into my mouth.

Sure enough, the laughter stops immediately. "Wow, baby. That's..."

I give a suck.

"*Nnngh*," he says with a shiver. "Nice. Yeah. Take more." His hand lands on the back of my head. He gathers up my hair in his fist and gives a gentle tug.

Breathing through my nose, I relax and swallow around him. It's been years since I did this. I'm good at it out of necessity. I never really enjoyed it all that much before, but this is different. When I glance up into Ian's face, I find his pupils blown. His lips are parted, and his face is heated. Like he can't stand how turned on he is.

I know it's real. Nobody is faking anything right now. He made me feel like a queen. As I run my hand up and down his shaft and cup his balls, the groan he makes is not for show.

This is what it's supposed to feel like. It's powerful to make a man growl with need. The muscles in his arm flex as he braces himself against the mattress. Like he can't quite find purchase in the wind tunnel of lust.

It's tempting to slow things down and tease him, but I have a point to make here. I dedicate myself to sucking and then licking when I need a break. He's girthy, so this is definitely a challenge. It's a tight fit, and my jaw is already starting to ache.

But who cares? Because Ian is starting to lose his cool in the best possible way. The strong muscles in his neck flex as he groans. He rolls his hips forward in a gentle rhythm, like he just can't stand to hold still.

"Christ, honey," he babbles. "So hot when you look at me like that. Can hardly stand it."

I double down, working him with my mouth, sucking him like I'm in the running for an award.

And maybe I am. I fumble with the bottle of lube and spill some into my palm. When I slide my slicked-up hand across his balls, he grunts loudly. "Look out, baby," he pants. "I can't hold back."

I pop off him and sit up. "Paint me," I demand. "Do it." I jerk him quickly, my knees splayed, my exposed breasts bouncing. It's as free and dirty as I've ever been in my life.

He shudders and groans as he unleashes a hot spurt of semen right across my camisole. "Fuck. Me." His cock jerks again in my hand, before he finally collapses back on the bed, breathing hard. He takes a deep, satisfied breath. "Impressive, contessa. Jesus."

I grab his wrist and hold it up in the air. There's still time on the clock.

He lets out a snort of laughter. Then he sits up and hauls me in for the messiest, most satisfying kiss of my life.

EIGHTEEN

I Just Created a Monster

IAN

FOR THE SECOND time in weeks, I sleep like the dead for eight hours. I wake up dazed, blinking into the sunshine, and wrapped around Vera's mostly naked body, where we'd passed out last night.

My comfort is interrupted, though, by the realization that someone is knocking on the door to my room. I can hear it faintly from here in Vera's room.

Knock knock knock. "Crikey? You coming on this run?"

I slide out of the bed with a curse and trot into my own damn room. "Two minutes!" I call to Castro, who's on the other side of the door. "Right down!"

Castro leaves, and I stumble into my compression shorts and a comfortably worn-out T-shirt. It's quiet in the adjoining room while I pull on my socks and running shoes, and I slip out without waking Vera.

I don't kiss her goodbye or leave a note. Not like I know what I'd say. *Thanks for the surprisingly intense sexual experience. Last night was one of the hotter nights of my adult life, and I couldn't even tell you why.*

Yeah. No. Besides, she knows where to find me later.

When I get downstairs, the guys are waiting for me. "Hung

over?" Drake asks me, handing me a glass of water. "Castro said it was like trying to wake the dead."

"I'm cool. Just sleepy." I pound the water anyway. "Let's go."

We head out into the bright Italian morning with Drake and Castro in the lead. My buddy Anton is telling me stories about what had happened at their poker game after I departed. Castro's wife bluffed her own husband into losing a big pot. "It was awesome," Anton says with a deep chuckle. "The girl had pocket aces and she didn't raise him until the turn."

"Priceless," I say at just the right time. But my head is miles away. I'm still drunk on oxytocin and sexual gratification. One night won't be enough. I wish I could turn around, run back to the villa, and slide back into Vera's bed.

Then again, it's always fun to break a dry spell. That must be why I still feel so keyed up. Even now I'm looking out at some people sunning themselves on the deck of a boat in the lake, and my inner horny boy is wondering what kind of trouble Vera and I could get up to on a boat after dark.

What a great vacation this is shaping up to be.

I love Italy.

WHEN WE GET BACK from our run, the day is heating up, so we all strip off our T-shirts and jump off the dock. The lake is a welcome shock to my system.

We're splashing each other like little boys at summer camp when the women appear, dressed to kill, ready for a day in Milan. Vera is wearing yet another hot little dress, black this time, and heels that make her legs look long enough to wrap around me twice.

I give her a hot look, and she pinks up before tossing her hair and looking away.

"Anyone want to go shopping with us?" Heidi Jo asks.

Cue some loud laughter from the lake.

"Didn't think so," she says with a smile. "Anyone need anything from town?"

"I do!" Drake raises a wet hand. "I need Charli to buy the skimpiest Italian lingerie in Milan and then model it for me later."

"Sure, stud," Charli says. "Just as long as you'll wear a matching set."

We all hoot and laugh and generally act like bozos, until the women take their leave. And then we ravage the sandwich cart and spread out on lounge chairs on the terrace, while Drake streams some tunes through his sweet outdoor speakers.

"This is the life," Anton says. "Can somebody rub sunscreen on my back?"

"All right," Neil agrees. "If you'll do me."

I let out a half-assed cat call, but my heart isn't in it. The Italian sunshine is making me sleepy.

The afternoon passes in a pleasant haze, until I rouse myself to make espressos for my crew. I'm just finishing my own cup when my phone rings. It's O'Doul, and his name on the screen gives me a whiff of anxiety.

What now? More pressure from management?

I answer the call. "Hey, Doulie."

"Hey, man. How's Italy?"

My mind serves up an image of Vera's O-face. "It's everything I needed in this life."

"Glad to hear that." He chuckles. "You staying out of trouble?"

My heart drops. "Of course I am. Why? Is Hugh asking?"

"No, man. I was just teasing you. Everything is fine from where I sit. Did you see your photo on the internet this morning?"

"What?" I set my coffee cup down on the lunch tray. "What photo?"

He laughs. "Is Drake with you? Tell him to check his texts. This is hilarious."

I call over to my teammate, asking him to check his messages. "Is there really a photo of me? From Italy?"

"Yes and no," O'Doul says, amusement in his voice.

A moment later I hear Neil let out a bark of laughter. And then he's crossing the patio to thrust his phone in my face. "Check us out."

The photo is on an Italian site. From the garish font, I assume it's a gossip blog. And there *is* a photo of me. Although, I shouldn't have worried. I'm not holding a drink or anything, I'm merely smiling at Neil. We both look debonaire in our dress shirts. We're stepping off the water taxi onto the dock. And my new short haircut keeps me looking sharp in spite of the wind off the lake.

Vera is at my arm, looking sophisticated in her dress, and I'm holding out a gentlemanly arm to help her off the boat. "Okay. That photo is fine. What's so funny?"

"Read the caption."

"It's in Italian," I argue.

But it doesn't matter. The names listed there are easy enough to make out. *Neil Drake, Jason Castro*, and the name of our team.

"Wait, they got my name wrong?" I yelp.

"They sure did," O'Doul says. "Too bad, because you look very civilized, sir. Way to represent."

I let out a groan of frustration. "So if the PR guy googles my name, he'll still find my mugshot. And not this picture of me helping a lady off a boat."

"Right." O'Doul laughs. "Sorry, Crikey. You have the worst luck."

"Tell me about it." I give Neil his phone back with a sigh.

"I told you I was going to call so we could talk about the captain. Remember?"

"Oh. Yeah." I exit the terrace to put some distance between

me and the boys. "What are your thoughts? Isn't it kind of obvious who it's gonna be?"

"Is it?" he asks. "I don't know if that's true."

"Well, there's really only a couple of obvious choices." I glance back at the terrace, but nobody can hear me now. "Castro's been on the team for more than five years. He's a veteran, but he's got a few good years left. He's a high scorer. He's well-liked, even if he's kind of a grump."

"That's all true," O'Doul agrees. "Great guy, but he doesn't seem interested in the job. And he has a temper, which the refs hate. Besides—he's married to the league commissioner's daughter. Guys might not feel comfortable bringing stuff to him, you know?"

"He and the commissioner aren't close at *all*," I point out.

"You know it. I know it. But a new guy wouldn't. I don't like the optics."

"Fucking optics," I grumble. "But I suppose you've got a point."

"Who's your next pick?"

"Eh..." I look out at the lake, and my mind draws a blank. "The sunshine is making me sleepy, captain. I don't really know."

"Way to pass the buck." He laughs. "But fine. I'll leave you in vacation mode. You need anything? Want me to water your plants while you're gone?"

"If I had plants, you'd be my first call. I'm good, big man. Go out of town. Play golf. Get your wife pregnant. Do whatever it is that retired guys do."

"Sure thing. Just as soon as I figure out what that is. Later, punk."

"Later."

I hang up with him, only to find a haranguing voicemail on my phone. It's from my mother. When I press Play, she gets right to the point. "Ian, did you return that RSVP? It's rude not to answer. People have to plan these things. Let me know when you've done it." *Click.*

Fun times with Mom.

Reluctantly, I leave the sunshine and head upstairs to my quiet room. I fish that damn wedding invitation out of my suitcase and pull it out of the envelope. The paper is so thick you could use it for a drywall job. I put on my glasses and try to read the elaborate script:

> *Mr. and Mrs. Robert Acton Everston*
> *Cordially invite you to the wedding of their daughter*
> *Miss Jaqueline Everston to Her Slick Butthead of a Fiancé*

Okay, maybe it doesn't say that exactly. But I'm severely dyslexic, and sometimes I get things a little wrong.

This damn wedding. My parents need me to go, because my extended family will be there. The groom is my father's cousin's son. And it's not like I want to cause a rift in my family. But do I have to watch the woman who dumped me marry someone else? Seriously?

Once upon a time, we were high school sweethearts who broke up when she went to college. But then we reconnected when I was playing for a minor league team in Hartford. As a young and foolish man at twenty-one, I asked her to move to Connecticut with me.

Seemed like a good idea at the time. And like the nice guy I am, I'd written an email to my second cousin, Carson, asking if there were job opportunities in the statehouse where he worked. After all, Jackie had a degree in history and government. It wasn't a stretch.

Carson put her in touch with some people, and she got a job working as a staffer to a state senator. She loved it right away and began moving up in the ranks. When Carson decided to run for state senate, he asked Jackie to join his campaign.

It's weird, but I knew right away that things were changing.

I could hear it in her voice when she spoke about "the candidate." The breathless admiration. *Carson thinks this*, and *Carson says that*. I think I could tell that her interest in him wasn't just professional, maybe even before she realized it herself.

It was like watching a train wreck in slow motion. She fell for him over late-night meetings and harried press conferences. He was everything I'm not—a scholar, a prep-school boy, a slick-looking guy who's comfortable behind a podium.

One day I got off the bus from a road trip to find that I'd been called up to the big leagues. It was my dream come true. Should have been one of the happiest days of my life.

But when I went home to tell Jackie, I felt dread in the pit of my stomach. I already knew I'd be moving to New York alone. And when she greeted the news with devastation, I laid my heart on the table. "Do you love me enough to move across Long Island Sound?"

The distance was a hundred and twenty miles. Not exactly across the continental divide. And I'd been training for this for years.

When she cried and said, *Ian, I'm so sorry*, I wasn't even surprised. A couple weeks later, the first cozy photo of the two of them kissing showed up on social media.

And now I have to watch them get hitched. Fanfuckingtastic.

I pull an ornate response card from the envelope. My name is already printed on it, and there are two choices: *will attend* and *regrets*.

With gritted teeth, I choose *will attend*. Seeing as my mother already made that choice for me.

Unfortunately, there's one more question on that card—a blank space, with: *seats reserved in your honor*. In other words— am I going alone, or bringing a date?

Huh.

I don't have a date. But I don't want to admit it, so I put "2" in the blank, and seal it up.

Then I find send her a message. *Could you do me a little favor? Can you use your Italian skills to buy a postage stamp? I have to mail a letter back home.* I check the message twice to make sure I spelled everything correctly.

Of course, she replies almost immediately. *If I found you the perfect shirt, do you want it? The seams are cotton. Or maybe they're made of butter. That's how soft they are.*

Sure. Thanks. Get me whatever and I'll pay you back. Go nuts.

She sends back a torrent of clapping hands. *Whee! Off to spend your money.*

I think I just created a monster.

NINETEEN

Crying in the Bathroom

VERA

"MILAN IS TRULY MY SPIRITUAL HOME," I declare as we march down another narrow, curving street with pristine shops on either side. I'm loaded down with shopping bags. "My credit card is going to hate me. But most of this loot is for other people who will eventually pay me back."

"I was done shopping after the second store," Fiona says. "But that lunch was amazing. And the gelato is good." She's on her second cone. "Aly and I are going to peel off and see the cathedral. Anyone want to join us?"

"Me!" Sylvie raises her hand. "I don't need to spend any more money than I already have."

We make a plan to meet up again in an hour, and the three of them depart.

"Quitters," Charli says cheerfully.

"It's just the hardcore shoppers now," Heidi Jo agrees. "Although none of us can out-shop Vera."

"I think I'm going to need a second day in Milan, so I can really dig into the specialty retailers."

"I'm game," Charli says with a shrug. "It's fun watching you work. Where are we headed now?"

"There. Something a little different." I point to a shop that specializes in cashmere and merino knits. "This place intrigues me. It's not all sweaters and socks. They make wool underwear. Wool T-shirts. There's even a sports bra."

"Sounds itchy," Heidi Jo says. But once inside the store, she changes her tune. "Ooh, these tights are luscious," she says, fingering the stockings.

"Aren't they?" Fashion isn't always about a cutting-edge design. A top-quality fabric can turn the ordinary into the extraordinary.

I pause at a table of cashmere sweaters. It's possible to get cashmere for less than a hundred bucks at Macy's or J. Crew. But not all cashmere is *this* cashmere. I run my hand over a brick-toned sweater, and it feels like a cloud.

"That's gorgeous," Charli says.

"Isn't it? The variegation of the yarn is so subtle. My grand-mother would have looked great in this." She's the one I think of whenever I see something gorgeous in shades of red.

Charli squeezes my arm before she moves away, because she knows I really miss my nonna.

But even if she were still alive, I wouldn't have bought the sweater. The only thing Nonna and I ever fought about was my passion for fashion. She raised me alone. We never had any money, and I resented my thrift-store clothes and hand-me-downs from people at church.

"You don't need fancy clothes to look beautiful," she used to say. But I disagreed. And every time there was a big event requiring special clothes, it became a source of tension.

The first high school dance, for example. Nonna wanted to send me in someone's borrowed Easter dress. But at fourteen, I was really small for my age. And the borrowed dress was childish—purple and frilly. A real horror show. I wanted to borrow fifty dollars and buy a cocktail dress in size 0 from Century 21 in lower Manhattan.

She said no. We had a huge fight about it. On the night of the dance, I told my new friends that I had a stomachache, and I stayed home and cried.

When springtime rolled around, there was another semi-formal. This time I wore a dress that one of our church friends had grown out of. It was an A-line with chiffon sleeves and a V-neck, in a dark-green color that made it look very grown-up to me.

I loved it. Spent the three days before the dance trying it on and admiring myself in the mirror. I spent five dollars—all my spending money—on a new pair of pantyhose. My shoes were boring black flats, but I didn't care because the rest of me looked great.

The night of the dance, I did my hair in a French twist and borrowed a pair of earrings from my grandma. There's a snap-shot of me in that dress somewhere. I looked great.

Unfortunately, the girl who had given it to us—Rosalie Carrera—was a classmate. And she made a point to tell absolutely everyone at the dance that the dress used to be hers, and that my Nonna had told *her* mother the story of how I stayed home from the last dance because we were too poor to buy nice clothes.

I overheard her about twenty minutes after the dance began. And then I heard the other girls snickering. So I spent the next hour crying in a bathroom stall.

Nonna never heard that story. And it took her a long time to come around to my choice of career.

I give the red sweater one more pat and then move on to the menswear section.

My thoughts turn automatically to Ian, as they have every five minutes or so all day. Maybe it's ridiculous, but last night he gave me the hottest sexual experience of my life. I'm twenty-seven years old, and I never knew I could be turned on like that.

Honestly, my orgasm wasn't even the most shocking thing about last night. It was Ian's attitude that surprised me the most. So playful. So confident.

So *tender*, too, as he coaxed me to trust him. He could have laughed at me, but he didn't. And afterwards, when he curled up beside me in bed, I lay there fighting sleep, not wanting the night to end.

I'd misjudged him completely.

"Watcha looking at?" Charli asks. "Who's that for?"

I focus my eyes on the merino T-shirt in my hands. It's a beautiful knit in a heathered, charcoal gray. "This is gorgeous. I was thinking about it for Ian." I check the printed tag inside—a hundred percent merino. I run a finger over the interior seams and find that they're knitted together like a sweater. The effect is silky smooth.

This thing costs a hundred euros, my critical inner voice points out. *Plus, if you shower him with attention, you'll look desperate.*

There's that. And if he doesn't tolerate wool, he won't even be able to wear it.

I turn to the clerk behind the counter. *"Mi scusi signore. Qual è la vostra politica di reso?"* What is your return policy?

"Trenta giorni," he replies. Thirty days.

"Grazie." I can work with that.

"Here's another version," Charli says from the other side of the table. She holds up the shirt. "Raglan seams."

"Ooh, that's even better. It fits closer to the body." I circle the table for a better look.

She swings a hip playfully into mine. "Close to the body, huh? How close are we getting these days?"

My gaze snaps up to hers. "Why?"

Charli laughs. "Come on, I'm dying here. That dreamy look on your face tells the whole story. It says—Ian spent the night in my bed."

My eyes bug out. "You're a sorceress."

She laughs so hard that her shopping bag slides to the floor. "Oh, Vera. You should see your face."

"What's so funny?" Heidi Jo asks. She's holding a shopping basket with socks and tights inside.

"Last night Ian left the poker game with *two* glasses of scotch." Charli says with a smile. "This morning I went into Vera's room, and there they were on her windowsill. Untouched, I think."

"Whoa, girl!" Heidi Jo gasps. "You work fast."

I snort, because nothing could be further from the truth. "Do *not* be impressed. I threw myself at him in the most awkward way possible."

She shrugs. "It took me two tries to seduce Jason, and I humiliated myself on the first round. So, well done, sister."

"Really?" Charli's eyes light up. "I've never heard this story."

"Oh, it was brutal." She smiles. "I got drunk and threw up in his bathroom, so he put me to bed like a toddler. I had to sneak out the next morning at dawn."

We all laugh, and I suddenly feel lighter. Heidi Jo seems so competent at everything. It's nice to hear that she can be awkward, too.

"I've never had a vacation fling," Charli says. "But I think it suits you."

"She's right," Heidi Jo agrees. "As my darling husband used to say during his wild days—*nothing ventured, nothing banged.*"

There hasn't been any banging, but I keep that to myself. "Ian told me I could style him. And T-shirts weren't part of the brief, but I think he'd like this."

"Then get it," Charli says. "We have one more shop after this, right? For dresses?"

"Right," I agree. "Let's go."

OUR FINAL STOP is the showroom of the young Italian designer Isabella Fieri. She makes evening dresses, and I've always admired them.

"Is this a client thing or a you thing?" Charli asks, sweeping her hand down a dark-green strapless chiffon dress.

"Me," I admit. "I'm on the hunt for a dress for the gala. A spectacular dress."

"Well, let's see one on you," Charli suggests. "What is it you always tell the clients? The right dress can make magic."

"Good line," Heidi Jo says.

"Thanks." But it's not a line. I really believe that. Fieri's dresses are sumptuous and definitely out of my price range. "Charli, you would look amazing in green silk." And she can probably afford it.

"Fine, but you try this one," Charli says, pointing at a dress the color of an amethyst.

My skin color is deep enough to work with darker tones, and the purple hue will give me a rosy complexion. "All right. Let's see how we look."

Five minutes later Heidi Jo is taking our photo in front of an Instagram wall with the designer's logo all over it. The saleswoman clucks around, hoping to make a sale.

I'm going to have to disappoint her, though, because this dress is way out of my budget.

"Vera, that dress is *you*," Heidi Jo says. "Your ex won't know what hit him."

I stare into the mirror for a moment and try to picture Danforth's reaction. I can't, though. Maybe because we haven't spent any time together in so long.

Or maybe because he was never very enthusiastic about you in the first place, my inner critic suggests.

"Knocking him dead is my goal," I agree. "But not if I have to sell a kidney to do it."

"Fine. Be practical." She shrugs like I'm hopeless.

Back in the dressing room, I carefully remove the nicest dress in Italy.

"So who's better in the sack?" Heidi Jo asks over the door. "Which of your two men?"

The question startles me, and I practically trip on the sandal I'm putting back on. "I don't have two men," I point out. "There's the one who dumped me and the one who is only after a few nights of fun. Hell—he might not even want *that*." It's occurred to me that a one-and-done kind of guy might avoid me for the rest of the trip.

And won't that be awkward.

"Answer the question," Charli says from another stall. "From where we sit, sex with professional athletes is always the way to go."

"Mmm," I say, trying not to sound dreamy. "I won't kiss and tell. They're very different men. And sex isn't everything."

Charli and Heidi Jo both laugh uproariously.

TWENTY

I Made It Weird

IAN

WE'RE DRINKING beer on the terrace when the women come back, loaded down with shopping bags. Vera sets her bags down beside a giant planter full of flowers. When she straightens up, we lock eyes, and she gives me a secretive smile that makes my heart lift in an unfamiliar way.

My grin says, *Hello gorgeous. Did you miss me?*

Her eyes dance, and then she looks away.

"Uh-oh," Castro says. "How much trouble did you ladies get into?"

"Well, shopping with Vera is an experience," Heidi Jo says. "But don't worry—she's a professional. All these purchases were strictly necessary."

"Now hang on," Vera says, adopting a stance of pure sass, one hand on her hip. "I'm not taking the fall for those shoes you bought." Her eyes are bright, and her hair is rolled into some kind of sleek arrangement that makes her look like a runway model.

I just want to grab her, throw her over my shoulder, and haul her upstairs with me. Then I want to pull those clips out of

146

her hair until it makes a tousled curtain across her bare shoulders.

She takes another glance at me, like she can't help herself. And suddenly there are way too many people on this terrace.

"Who needs a drink?" Neil asks, ever the host. He opens a bottle of pinot grigio and starts pouring. But I'm just counting the seconds until I can get Vera away from the crowd without being too obvious about it.

Finally, she carries her wine glass closer to my lounge chair. "Hi, Ian."

"Hi, pretty lady. Did you have fun keeping all the shops of Milan in business?"

She gives me an arch look. "You know I did. Some of my haul was for you, big guy. Can I have a moment of your time to show you my stuff?"

There are so many filthy ways to reply to that request. But Vera prefers well-behaved men, and I'm no fool. "Sure, contessa. Let's go. Show me your stuff." I cross to the massive pile of bags and ask, "Are these all yours?"

"Don't judge," she says.

"I'm not. I'm helping." Not that it's easy. I've got shopping bags hanging from nearly every appendage by the time I've picked them all up.

"Let me carry something," she says.

"No can do. A man doesn't let a lady carry anything as long as he has at least one functioning arm."

"All right, bossypants. Thank you." She strides on long legs up the stairway, and I find myself standing there admiring the view for a moment. The woman knows how to move, that's for sure.

Charli clears her throat. Loudly. And when I look at her, she gives me a sly wink. I don't know what that's all about, but I also don't care. I follow Vera up the stairs and then down the hall to her bedroom.

Inside, one glance at her bed is all it takes to remind my

libido that this is the scene of last night's fun times. If I play my cards right, we can do it again. Except Vera is still treating me a little like a stranger.

"Thank you for carrying those," she says primly. "Just drop them anywhere."

"All right." I do exactly that, dropping the bags from my hands. And even as they hit the floor, I'm crossing the room to where she stands.

She makes a small noise of surprise as I swiftly remove the wineglass from her hand, set it on the mantel, and pull her against me.

And, yup, I've needed to do this all day. She tastes like wine and sunshine as I steal the first kiss. Her mouth is firm beneath mine for at least a half a second. Then she softens, her arms sliding around my body as I back her up against the bathroom door.

I pin her against the wood, plundering her mouth. My desire roars to life like a fire with fresh fuel. The whimper she makes stirs me up even more.

"Contessa," I rasp. "Don't you want to practice your technique?"

She lifts slightly dazed eyes to mine. "Yes?"

"Then where was my kiss hello? And I didn't get a single sexy text from you today. No teasing. No dressing room selfies. No, 'I can't stop thinking about the way I came all over your tongue last night, Ian'."

She groans and then kisses me again, shutting me up.

So naturally I break the kiss and take a step backward. "Gotta leave 'em wanting more, honey. Now was there something you wanted to show me?"

She just blinks at me for a moment before recovering herself. "I bought you a few things. Shirts and a pair of chinos. Everything is returnable."

"Ah, my favorite topic," I tease. "Fashion. Are the shirts all cotton?"

"What? You think I'd *forget?*" She gives me an irritable look. "Let me show you."

Vera crosses to her bounty and pulls out a couple of bags from the pile. She unwraps two button-down shirts—one is blue with a subtle white thread pattern and the other is white with dove-gray checks. "These colors will coordinate well with your coloring. And feel the seams." She passes me a shirt.

I tuck my hand inside the collar and run a finger along the shoulder seam. It's soft to the touch and barely there. "Nice pick, contessa. I'll totally wear these."

Her smile pops back into place. "I'll wash them both if you think they'll work for you. And these are the pants." She thrusts them into my hands. "The fabric is just so lovely, and they're cut in a way that accommodates a hockey butt."

I laugh. "Yeah, baby! This is the first I've heard that you noticed my ass." I turn around slowly and wiggle it a little, just to be, well, an ass.

"Oh, I definitely noticed it. In a professional capacity." She gives me a sly smile.

"See, this is a good lesson. Part of seduction is letting a guy know you've noticed things about him. You told me a minute ago that the shirts will—" I mimic her. "—coordinate with my coloring. But you *could* have turned that into a compliment."

She rolls her eyes. "I think you're just fishing for compliments. It's not like you don't know you're hot."

"Hey now. That's where you're a little mixed up." I cup her face in one hand and stroke her cheek with my thumb. And her expression softens. "Nobody feels desirable all the time, unless he's truly obnoxious. So don't assume that the dude you're trying to seduce won't want to be reminded that he turns you on. Trust me, he wants to hear it. No matter who he is. Besides, if you make the assumption that he's on some higher plane, then you're putting the guy on a pedestal he probably doesn't deserve."

Her big eyes dip. She rubs her cheek into my hand like a

happy cat before lifting her gaze to mine once again. "Well, Mr. Crikey..." She takes a deep breath. "If you must know, I think you're the hottest thing on two legs. It's a miracle I didn't buy all the wrong things in all the wrong sizes today. Because I barely had two brain cells at my disposal. I couldn't stop thinking about you, especially when I was choosing clothes for you. I practically needed a cold shower afterward."

I grin just picturing that. And hell, it *is* flattering. "Now that's a compliment, contessa. Nice work. A-plus grade from your tutor."

"Thank you." She takes a step back. "There's something more I'd like to give you now."

"Is it another blowjob?" I ask hopefully.

"No sir," she says with a smile before turning toward her shopping bags. "How do you feel about wool?"

I make a face, because wool is not half as interesting to me as she is. "It's what suits are made of? It's fine. Why do you ask?"

"These are wildly expensive, but also returnable. Could you try this on?" She pulls out a soft gray tee. "This is merino, which is unusual in a T-shirt. But the people who love wool *really* love it. It wicks like synthetics. And you said that synthetics are a problem for you. This could be a solution. And the salesman swore there was no sizing on the fabric. Wool doesn't need it."

"All right, contessa. I'll try anything once. If I break out in hives, you can give me a soothing sponge bath."

She blushes. "It's a deal. Here."

"Maybe you're just trying to get me naked," I tease, shucking off my shirt. I pull the new one carefully over my head. If she hadn't told me it was wool, I don't think I would have guessed, because the fabric isn't thick or hairy like a sweater. "It's super soft," I point out as the fabric slides into place on my chest. "I'll give this a try."

"It's pricey," she says quietly. "A hundred euros. It's a little outrageous. But I wanted you to see it."

"Money is not one of my issues," I say, looking at the shirt in the mirror over her dressing table. "Can you snip this tag off? I know I gave you a lot of shit for wanting to shop for me. But I think I like it. Can you do the suits, too, when we're back in New York?"

She beams like I've given her a dozen roses. "It would be my *pleasure.*"

"Oh, please. I know better ways to give you pleasure. Is tonight the right time for your next lesson?"

Her mouth opens and then closes again. She swallows. "If it's no trouble."

I bark out a laugh. "Seriously, contessa. Don't get too excited. This guy you're trying to impress—is he going to be bowled over by 'if it's no trouble'?"

"Obviously not," she says, crossing her arms in front of her chest. "But he won't be doing me some kind of weird favor, either." She frowns. "Hopefully."

"Christ." I put my hands on both her shoulders and give them a squeeze. "We've got to work on your self-esteem. Do you think I'm looking forward to tonight because I feel like doing a *weird favor*?"

"I have no idea," she says softly. "I made it weird by making it weird, and I don't know how to make it not weird."

"Weird is not a concern of mine, doll. I don't care if I dress weird. I don't care if I look weird, and I don't care that you propositioned me for sex lessons. I'm not big on doing sexual favors when I'm not in the mood. But I'm big on doing *you*. Have I not made that clear several times?"

She tilts her head and looks up at me with wide brown eyes. Her face is so expressive, she really ought to be an actor. "Yes, I guess you have."

I have the strongest urge to unbutton my shorts and do her

right this second. But someone is yelling "dinnertime!" down
the hallway.

So it will have to wait.

TWENTY-ONE

Seduction is Fun

VERA

DINNER TONIGHT IS A COOKOUT—GRILLED burgers and sausages out on the patio. Afterwards, Neil pours us each a glass of prosecco so we can toast the sunset together.

I'm sitting in a lounge chair, feeling lazy and satisfied as the sky turns orange, pink, and then purple. I'm perfectly content.

But then Charli moves off her chair and goes to share Neil's. He puts an arm around her and kisses her passionately.

And, ouch. It hits me right in the center of the chest. I want what they have. I don't mean the seven-bedroom villa on Lake Como, although I'd take one of those, too. But I want that magic—I want a man who's looking forward to being crowded in his chair just so he can kiss me.

Charli is special, though, my inner voice reminds me. *A top athlete. Bolder than you by half. And stunningly pretty, too.*

"Hey, I'm working on it," I tell that voice.

"Sorry? What did you say?"

I glance up and see Ian standing over me, holding the bottle of wine. "I was, um, talking to myself. Oops."

He gives me a smirk. "More hooch?"

"Sure. Thanks." I hold up my glass, and he squats down

beside me and pours out the rest into my glass. "Wait. Don't you want more?"

"Fuck no. I'm moving on to beer." He pins me with a hot glance. "Am I invited over later?"

"Yes," I say without hesitation. "In fact, I was thinking of heading upstairs soon. Give me a head start?"

His smirk returns. "Sure, contessa. Will do. Can't wait to see what moves you're going to try on me tonight." Then he gets up and saunters off.

SO NOW I'M NERVOUS. Obviously. The perfect sunset is forgotten as I realize that Ian is expecting me to seduce him. I drink my second glass of prosecco in nervous gulps. Because I don't have a plan.

At all.

There's always lingerie, my inner voice reminds me. *If you can't be original, you can still dress well.*

I carry my empty glass into the kitchen and wash it. Then I march upstairs and open up my lingerie drawer.

There are lots of choices, because I believe in dressing well from the inside out. I pull out a sexy red camisole trimmed with lace. But then I remember how Ian is sensitive to synthetics. So that's out. In fact, most of my lingerie involves lace of one kind or another.

Uh-oh. Now I've spent ten minutes rifling through my own underwear drawer. That's not seduction. That's indecision.

Crap.

I pull out my travel candle and a book of matches, and I light the candle, placing it on the dresser. It's not much, but it's something.

Then I hurry into the bathroom, put the plug in the tub, and crank the faucets. I pour in some bubble bath that I'd brought along, because Charli had told me about the clawfoot tubs in every bathroom. I haven't tried mine yet, because I was worried about Ian walking in on me.

But now that's kind of the point. As I watch the bubbles rise, I twist my hair into a topknot and shed my clothes. Back in the bedroom, I douse all the lights but leave the candle glowing on the dresser.

Then I slip into the hot water, sinking down to hide the part of my body that's not very sexy. It feels *great*. I immediately relax, because baths are one of my hobbies. This is my favorite way to chill out at home, too, even though the surroundings aren't nearly as glam.

I've been soaking for only a few minutes when I hear Ian enter his room. A moment later, the bathroom door opens after a polite tap. He peers into the room, spots me in the bath, and smiles. *"Nice work*, contessa. It's a simple setup, but classic."

"Right?" I agree. "I'm all, 'Oh, I'm just here taking a bath, don't mind me.'"

His sexy smirk appears. "Meanwhile you're wearin' nothing but the bubbles. Men are visual creatures. You got all my attention now."

"Excellent." The praise lights me up more than I would like to admit.

Ian sits down on the edge of the tub and strips off the merino T-shirt. He folds it and sets it on the towel bar.

For a moment I just blink up at his chest. It's like a brand-new miracle every time I see it.

"I am invited in, right?" He tests the water temp with his hand.

"Sure. Yup," I prattle, busy watching his arm muscles flex as he unzips his shorts. My tongue is practically hanging out as he pushes them down, revealing strong thighs, the most muscular ass I've ever seen in person, and a thick cock that's already half hard.

I know I saw it all last night, but apparently, I'm not over it. "You see something you like, honey?"

"Uh, yes?" I drag my eyes off his penis and try to meet his gaze. "I'm messing this up already, aren't I?"

"No way." He flexes a muscular thigh and steps into the bath. I bend my knees to make room, and he sinks down opposite me. "B-minus for the conversational skills, but the look in your eye gets top grades from your tutor."

He's grading on a curve, because you're naked and he's horny, my critical voice announces.

"You fluster me," I admit. "You're kind of an impressive specimen. Maybe I'd be less of a wreck with an ordinary guy."

Doubt it, my inner voice cracks.

Ian props one magnificent arm on the side of the tub and places his chin in his hand. "So tell me about this ex that you want to impress. Is he an 'ordinary guy?'" He puts air quotes around that last part.

"Well..." It seems weird to talk about Danforth when I'm sitting in a bathtub with Ian. "I've known him since I was nineteen. He was always a smart kid, and I admired him. We were *both* smart, but he was on a whole other level."

Ian's smile fades. "Okay. So you like brainiacs. What else?"

"He's just finished Harvard Business School. He's ambitious."

"Ambition is often sexy, at least to me," Ian agrees.

"You think so?" I'm surprised. "Ambitious women are often perceived as cold and bitchy."

"Love 'em." His knee knocks against mine for emphasis. "The opposite of ambitious is lazy, and there's nothing sexy about that. Well, not unless it's Sunday morning and she wants to stay in bed all day. But that's not lazy, not the way I do it."

I smile just thinking about it. A whole *day* in bed with Ian. So scandalous. "Yeah, I take your point."

"So, he's ambitious. What else makes him attractive to you?"

"Well..." I have to close my eyes, because it's the only way I can remember Danforth when I'm sitting in a bathtub with Ian. "He takes care of himself. Runs marathons. Looks good in a suit. Kind of a foodie, which can be fun. During college we visited every well-reviewed pizza place in the five boroughs. Including Staten Island."

"Nothing against pizza, but we need something more personal to go on. What has he done or said to *you* that made you feel sexy?"

"Right, okay. He..." My eyes flutter open. It's not an easy question.

He chose you, my inner voice reminds me. *That's the best you ever got from that dude. Validation.*

That can't be all, though. And I'm kind of done talking about Danforth. "Look, maybe it's all the steamy water." I dip my eyes and smile. "And the steamy *view*. But I'm drawing a blank on him right now."

"Girl, you're a natural at this." He reaches over and taps my wrist. "That was some first-class flirting right there."

"Thank you."

"Now come over here and show me some more of your moves."

"Over there?" I'm not even sure how that would work.

But he beckons to me, and when I lean forward, he straightens his legs, so I can climb into his lap.

Now we're face to face at point-blank range, and I can see all the shades of blue in those chilly eyes. "Hey—did the merino T-shirt feel comfortable?"

"It did, countess. I'm going to try it under my hockey pads, too."

"It's washable," I point out. "But you'll have to lay it out flat to dry."

A wrinkle appears in the center of his forehead. "Don't take this the wrong way, honey, but your dirty-talk game is weak."

I laugh suddenly, and the sound bounces off the walls of the bathroom. "You think I don't know that? Dirty talk is totally above my pay grade. I'll never be able to do that."

"*Sure,* you can," he insists. "That's tonight's lesson, then. Right after you figure out that I've been in this bathtub for a few minutes already, but I haven't gotten any kisses." He snaps his fingers. "Let's go, champ. Let the seduction start."

"But now you're making me self-conscious," I complain, even as I flatten my palm against his sexy chest tattoo. "What if I can't work in these conditions?"

"Just try," he says, his voice gravel. "I'll take one for the team and try to enjoy it."

"*Try,*" I scoff. "You liar." I dip my hand in the bubbles and then scoop some onto his chest. I trace his collarbone with wet fingertips. "You don't enjoy this?"

"Do it again. Let me think about it," he says with a smile.

"All right." I lean in, and the soap bubbles tingle and pop as I compress them. Placing a single kiss to the underside of his jaw, I stroke his cheek with my hand.

"That's real nice," he says softly. "You keep touching me, I'll keep enjoying it. But pro tip—you can take it up a notch if you touch yourself instead of me."

Not hardly, my inner voice says. *You'd look ridiculous. Like a cut-rate porn star.*

But I look up and catch the gleam in Ian's eye. It's hungry, not mocking. And suddenly I want to please him more than I care to worry about how it looks.

I lift both hands and cup my breasts. It's not the most outrageous maneuver, but it feels nice, and the bubbles make it fun. I smooth my thumbs in circles around my nipples, which are already peaking.

Ian lifts his eyes to the ceiling and groans. "I think you're a fast learner, countess. Fuck." His greedy eyes return to my chest, and he licks his lips.

I'm enjoying myself now. Dipping my hands in the water, I

rinse the bubbles off my chest. My skin is shimmering and wet, my breasts prominently displayed right under his nose.

That's when I lean forward and kiss him for real. He groans again, pulling me closer. Wet skin slips against wet skin. My knees bump vaguely against the porcelain, but I don't even care. As our tongues clash, I run my palms down his arms, enjoying the feeling of all that muscle.

And then I submerge my hand and wrap it shamelessly around his cock, which is stiff and thick for me already.

God, seduction is fun. I get it now.

"Countess," he says against my mouth. "What do you want to do to me tonight?"

"Mmm." I can't answer the question just yet, because I'm kissing him again. No wonder I spent the day fantasizing about this. He tastes like heat, and he kisses like a sinner.

"Tell me," he whispers a few minutes later. "I want to hear you say it."

"Why?" I gasp. "I'm a shower not a teller."

He chuckles against my tongue. "Action is good. I'm a man of action. But don't be afraid to use your words, lady. You might as well own your choices."

"Fine. Then I think we should get out of this tub," I point out.

"But then what?" He tucks an escaped tendril of my hair behind my ear. "Give me a hint."

The warm look in his eye brings me courage. "The sight of you naked in my bed is something I definitely need to see again."

"Good answer. Hang on." His arms wrap around me, and then I rise suddenly up into the air.

I let out a little shriek of surprise. "Ian! Careful."

"Oh, I'm careful." He laughs. "I'm also eager." He sets me down on the bathmat, where I grab a towel and yank it to my stomach.

I'm still not ready to let him see that skin up close. I don't want to break the mood.

He steps out of the tub, and I hand him another fluffy, peach-colored towel off the bar.

"Lead the way, princess. Tell me more about your plans for me."

Hastily drying myself off, I head towards the bed, wondering what I'm even going to say.

TWENTY-TWO

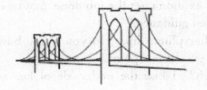

Professional Development

IAN

THIS GIRL HAS HAD me revved up all day, and she doesn't even know it. If I ever meet this dickhead who told her she wasn't sexy, I'm going to punch him in the kisser.

Sure, Vera might be the kind of woman who needs a few extra minutes to get herself into the mood. But so what? She's got it going on, even if she doesn't trust it.

That ex she's trying to impress must be a real dingus not to appreciate her. But his loss is my gain. As Vera pulls back the covers and slides into bed, I feel like the winner here.

Then? She reaches up to unclip her thick, dark hair, which cascades down over her bare shoulders and all over the pillow.

She looks like a goddess, and I let out a shameless little moan as I climb onto the bed. "Nice move, baby. I think you've got this seduction thing down pat. Time to work on your dirty talking."

"Oh, you wish."

She pulls me in for a kiss, but I resist, holding myself above her pretty face. "Now hang on. Dirty talk is useful. How will I know what you want, if you don't tell me?"

"Please." She pats my cheek. "Like you don't already have a lesson plan? What kind of teacher are you?"

I shake my head. "This *is* the lesson plan. Speaking your mind is sexy. Asking for what you want is sexy. Besides, if you want a man to please you, you gotta know where to start. If your dickhead ex didn't get the job done, maybe it's because the poor fool needed guidance."

She bites her plump lip. "Do you know how much I hate admitting that you have a point?"

"How much?" I kiss the underside of her smile. "A lot, I hope."

"It hurts me a great deal," she sniffs.

I drop my voice and whisper into her ear. "Tell me where it hurts, so I can lick it better."

"Ian." She shivers. "I really like the naughty things you say."

"Do you, now? Tell me how much you like it. And tell me how I'm going to make you scream tonight."

She takes my head in two hands and positions her lips right at my ear. And when she finally speaks, her breath tickles, making a shiver run down my back. "I need you to fuck me," she whispers. "Not softly, either. I don't want you to treat me like it's amateur hour. I'm tired of wondering what it's really like to be with you."

Whew. Is it hot in here? "Baby." My voice actually cracks like I'm thirteen again. That's how much I want it, too. "I'm so happy to hear that. And for the record, hearing you whisper *fuck me* into my ear made me hard as an iron spike." Just to prove my point, I drop my hips onto hers, so that my cock is poised between her legs.

Her eyes go into soft focus. "You feel so nice."

"Nice?" I snicker. "Of all the things I feel right now, *nice* is not near the top of the list. More like ravenous." I reach down and demonstrate by nipping the juncture of her neck and shoulder. Then I kiss it better.

I start to kiss my way down her body. Her skin is steamy from the bath. The window is open a crack, and there's a floral-scented breeze off the lake. "Now this is living," I murmur against her skin.

Her hands grasp my face. "Stop right there, please," she whispers. "Not my stomach."

My lips pause at the underside of her breast. "Why?"

"Because," she says. "Just because." She puts both hands on her stomach, like she's guarding it.

"Okay, contessa," I say slowly. I want to know more, but I refuse to ruin the mood.

Instead, I kiss and lick and tease her soft breasts until she moans my name.

"That's right. You make that sound, and say my name? I get even harder."

I think we're past the point of instruction. She shifts her hips with impatience as I kiss the backs of her hands, which are still poised above her stomach. And then I shift purposefully down her body toward her pussy.

A month ago, if you'd asked me if pint-sized, fussy women who work in fashion were my type, I would have told you no. But this one is. She's so damn responsive, moaning as I nudge her knees apart, and whimpering when I brush a teasing hand across her mound. "I am goddamn *seduced*," I growl. "You win."

"What's my prize?" she gasps.

"This." I drop my head down and give her a slow, dirty lick, right where she needs me.

Her hands grip the comforter as she lets out a happy cry.

I spend the next half hour pleasuring her. I bring her right to the edge of bliss, and then back off again. After the first two times, she figures out that I'm teasing her intentionally. And she doesn't take it well.

"God, you're mean," she pants, glassy-eyed. "Last night you convinced me that I could get there. And now you won't let me. Who does that?"

I hide my face against her thigh and laugh. "A greedy man, that's who. You got condoms in that drawer of yours?"

She groans. "No, I don't."

"Don't panic, girly." I heave myself up off the bed and head for the bathroom. "I've got us covered."

After a quick visit to my suitcase, I return to find that she's put on another one of her stretchy little tank tops. But no panties, thank God. And she's propped herself up against the pillows.

"Sexy, contessa," I say, sitting back down onto the bed. "You are the hottest thing I've ever seen."

She gives me a happy smile. "No need to exaggerate. I'm not going to back out now."

"But I'm not lying." I crawl up her body until we're nose to nose. "Don't know how I got so lucky as to be part of your vacation plans. But I'm not going to question it."

Big brown eyes blink back at me. "Is it still dirty talk if I tell you I need your mouth on mine?"

"Absofuckinglutely," I whisper.

I don't know who moves first, but we crash together again. Limbs tangling. Hands grasping. Tongues searching the darkness for more of this perfect heat. Candlelight flickers on the walls, and we can't stop kissing.

Even when I sit up to put on the condom, she's right there, her arms around me, whispering sweetly in my ear. "Hurry, Ian."

But I'm trying not to. I'm the happiest I've felt in months. Vera takes me out of my head. There's no way to worry about the past or the future when I'm trying to bring her pleasure.

It's perfect.

Once I've suited myself up with clumsy hands, I lay her back on the pillows. She stares up at me with wide eyes as I grasp one of her smooth knees and lift it to my hip.

"Hold on, contessa. Rough ride ahead." I tease the blunt end of my cock against her body, and her eyes go a little hazy with yearning.

"Do it," she begs.

I don't wait for a second invitation. I push inside to find a tight, hot heaven. "Fuuuuuck," I growl. And then I sink into her mouth for a kiss.

Warm hands caress my shoulders as I set a selfish, eager pace. I need to slow down, but I don't want to. I crave her too much. And Vera bucks beneath me, her knees tightening around my body. Her eyes heavy-lidded with desire.

This is supposed to be about her, though. Mastering myself, I roll my hips.

She grips my biceps and moans. "You feel so good. Don't stop."

"Don't want to stop," I agree, leaning in for another endless kiss.

I'm drowning in pleasure. After a while, it takes everything I have to hold back. "Come with me," I beg.

"Don't need to. Go on," she murmurs against my lips.

But I don't want to leave her behind. I need her to feel a little of what I'm feeling. I kiss her one more time and then rise up to look her in the eye. "You want me to show you what a guy really likes?"

"What?" she asks breathlessly.

"When you touch yourself." I grab her hand and move it between our bodies. "Sexiest fucking thing in the world."

Her mouth opens with surprise. "No, don't worry about me."

"Oh, I'm not," I lie. But I want her to have a good time. I want it so bad. "Visual creatures," I remind her. "This is for extra credit. Do you trust your tutor?"

Slowly she nods.

"Then blow my mind, honey. The most confident thing a woman can do is to take charge of her own pleasure. And no guy could resist the sight of you touching yourself while I'm inside you. Do it. Now." I push myself up off her body and look down between us.

And, sweet Jesus, it's the most erotic sight I've ever known. Vera's fingertips slowly circling the place where we're joined.

It's so sexy that I lose my rhythm before remembering to keep up my end of the bargain with slow, dragging strokes. Each time I move, my body quivers on the brink. Every thrust feels like it's pushing me closer to the cliff's edge.

"Oh...geez," she gasps, her lips parted. "Oh, *Ian*."

"Baby, *yes*," I babble. "My name on your tongue, your hand on my cock..." God only knows the sounds I'm making right now. Sweat rolls down my back as I try to hold myself in check.

"So...close," she whimpers. Her brown eyes open again, but her gaze is unfocused. "Oh, *please*." She sounds agitated.

"Shh," I whisper. "Who's this show for, anyway? Don't come. It's not your turn yet."

She lets out a whimper of protest.

I pick up the pace, one more time. It's the best kind of torture. My balls are tight, my heart wild. "Touch yourself. Faster."

When I look down, I see her slicked fingers working, our bodies shimmering in the candlelight together. "Fucking beautiful. So hot. I can't hold out any longer. Fuuuuck. You wrecked me."

At that, I drop into another hot kiss, and she gasps against my tongue. And then I feel it, that delicious pulse of her body milking me for all I'm worth.

And I let it all go, climaxing in a bright shower of release. All the while, she moans my name, making me feel like a sex god. Two more thrusts and I'm wrung out, collapsing between her legs, my head on her chest. Her heartbeat flutters wildly beneath my ear.

I hear a great gust of air, and I realize it's me, exhaling like I've just invented it.

Finally, I relax. Sweet fingers rustle my hair, their fingertips running mindlessly across my scalp. For the first time in a long time, I feel hollowed out and peaceful. And surprisingly tender toward this little woman with a big heart.

It's so nice. I never intended to find a surprising sexual chemistry with my neighbor. But I'm grateful just the same.

We lie together for many long minutes, until I finally heave myself up to toss the condom. Then I climb right back into her bed, still drunk on kisses and sexual satisfaction. "Well? Do you feel like a new woman? Did I rock your world?"

"Don't be smug," she murmurs. "You know you did."

"Thought so. I think you got what you came for, baby. You've officially graduated from the Ian Crikey school of seduction."

Vera blinks. "I'm done?"

"Oh, you're very done. I just did you myself." I laugh.

She gives me a poke in the ribs. "You're so smug."

"It's true." I run my fingers down her back, and she shivers. "And look, just because you already know how to seduce a man, doesn't mean we have to waste the rest of the trip. You'll need some maintenance training. What did they call it in school? Oh yeah—professional development sessions."

Vera turns her face into the pillow and laughs.

"Extra seminars. Special topics." I kiss her neck. "Private study sessions with the Dean of Dirty Talking and the Professor of Pussy—"

She puts a playful hand over my mouth. "Enough. Don't be crass."

I lick her palm, and she yanks her hand away. "This is me, baby. Take me or leave me. My vast experience comes with a side of raunchy. If you remain a student in my classroom for the rest of our vacation, you get the full experience. I won't rein it in for anybody."

Her eyes gleam, and a sexy little smile plays at the corners of her mouth. "The rest of our vacation, huh?"

"Well, yeah." I pull her against my chest.

"I'm sure I can put up with this until then," she says.

"Good choice, contessa." I yawn and snuggle in beside her. This is the moment when I'd usually kiss a woman good night and go back to my own room. But somehow, I don't even have the urge.

"Night, Ian," she says.

I stroke her hip in reply, and my finger catches on the little tank top. "Contessa? Why don't you want me to touch your stomach?"

She hesitates for a beat. "I just don't."

That answer is entirely unsatisfying, but I let it go.

And for the second time in ages, I sleep all the way through the night.

TWENTY-THREE

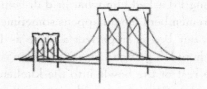

Is There a Secret Handshake?

VERA

I GATHER up the last few gelato bowls and spoons off the patio table. The sun is low in the sky, and in a little while, I'll be treated to yet another Italian sunset.

This trip is a fairy tale. The whole crew has just enjoyed our nightly gelato treat. It's our little ritual—each night a new flavor. And afterwards we gather on the terrace to watch the sunset. Sometimes we sit in the hot tub, and sometimes we sit on the lounge chairs.

The last few evenings, I've joined Ian on his chair. We aren't truly a couple, but we're behaving like one, if only for a little while. Every night we have *all* the sex and fall asleep in my bed. It's dreamy.

Actually, for Ian, the "dream" part of the night isn't always great. I've discovered that he has nightmares. A few times I've awakened to find him struggling against a foe in his sleep—his upper body twitching, his breath labored.

I always put a hand on his bare shoulder and whisper: "Baby, you're dreaming."

Twice he's rolled over and continued to sleep without a peep. But other times he'll sit up like a shot—his back heaving as he catches his breath. "Sorry," he'll mutter. "Just a dream."

He rises to visit the bathroom and get some water. Then he gets back into bed and hugs me around the waist, and we always go right to sleep.

This morning I'd asked him what he'd dreamt about, and he said he didn't remember. "That happens sometimes."

Otherwise, our bed is as perfect a place as I've ever been. And I wonder how I'm going to give it up when the trip is over.

I carry the rest of the bowls into the kitchen, where Ian is wiping the counter. My tummy still gets a little fluttery whenever I walk into a room where he is.

As I start to load the bowls into the dishwasher, I notice something weird. "Hold on. I sorted these spoons and forks. Did you just mix them up? On *purpose*?"

"Of course." Ian looks at me as if I'm speaking Swahili. "If you put all the spoons together, they *nest*. And they won't get clean enough."

"What? I *always* sort the silverware—that makes putting it away easier. And it always gets *perfectly* clean."

"So you say," he argues.

"Like I can't tell the difference?" I yelp. "Just admit that you're making extra work for yourself."

"Nah," he says. "I wouldn't do that. I'm not one of those people who sorts their laundry into colors, either."

"Seriously?" I sputter. "I *always* sort the laundry! What kind of heathen lets their white T-shirts turn pink?"

He holds out his arms and looks down at himself. He's wearing another threadbare T-shirt announcing a charity road race from seven years ago, plus a pair of khaki shorts. "None of my laundry turns pink, countess. I rest my case."

"Please," I scoff. "Like I'd ever take life advice from somebody who puts the toilet paper backwards on the holder."

Ian and I might be perfectly compatible in bed, but otherwise, we bicker. A lot. It's just a thing with us. And I can't seem to stop.

"*Guys!*" Charli calls from the terrace, where all our friends are waiting. "Stop your strange version of foreplay and get your butts back out here. It's almost sunset!"

Ian and I lock gazes, not quite ready to give up the Great Dishwasher Debate. But then his clear eyes soften as he gives me a sexy little grin that says, *busted again*. He opens the refrigerator to grab a six-pack of beer and a chilled bottle of wine.

I pick up a basket of unbreakable wine glasses and hurry toward the terrace door. "Coming!" I yell,

"Yeah, you'll be doing that later," he drawls under his breath as I pass him.

His voice resonates inside my body in several delicious places. But I march onto the terrace as if I haven't heard him.

I'm not sure why we bicker so much. Maybe we're just the kind of people who only get along when the clothes come off.

Outside in the golden evening sunlight, Heidi Jo takes the glasses from me and pulls a corkscrew out of her pocket. Then she takes the wine from Ian, who's right on my heels. "Neil got outvoted on poker," she says as she works on opening the bottle. "So it looks like it's movie night."

"Awesome!" I chirp. "And it's the women's turn to pick."

"No," Ian grouses. "You guys chose that true-crime thing the other night."

"That didn't count!" I argue immediately. "That was a compromise pick."

Heidi Jo smiles at me and then shakes her head. "I don't mean to kink-shame, but you two are at it again. All that bickering."

"Works for us," Ian says mildly, grabbing a beer. "Brewski, anyone?" As he asks the question, he puts a hand on the back of my neck. His thumb slides slowly up and down, raising goosebumps all over my body.

My face heats. Okay, *all* of me heats. Our nightly trysts are public knowledge, and Ian doesn't have an embarrassed bone in his body, so his frequent hot looks and handsy affection are pretty hard to miss.

I don't even care. In a while we'll go up to bed, where he'll slowly (or maybe very quickly) turn me into a quaking, shivering, shuddering puddle. I've never had so much sex in my life. Yesterday we had to take a water taxi into town to buy more condoms, because we'd run through his supply.

It's like I'm a completely different person than I was a week ago. *This* Vera likes sex. A lot. She doesn't get stressed out about where to put her hands or anxious about whether or not it will be any fun.

Because it always is. Every time. If I weren't enjoying myself so much, I might feel a little foolish. I was so hung up about it for so long. I'd created a problem where there wasn't one. And Ian fixed it so effortlessly.

"Come here, contessa," Ian says, beckoning to me from a lounge chair. "It's showtime."

I take my glass of white wine over and set myself on the edge of the chair. Unsatisfied, Ian grabs me around the waist and pulls me back until I'm seated between his legs, my back against his strong chest. "That's better," he says.

Indeed. The sky is turning a bright orange-pink, which is reflected on the lake's surface. Everything is dazzling and colorful, including the tinted fronts of the waterfront villas dotting the shoreline. In the far distance, the mountain range is Easter-egg purple.

It's magical. I loll back against Ian, sip my wine, and feel more joy than I've ever felt before. "We have sunsets in Brooklyn, too. But somehow, I never look at them. I guess I never go over to the promenade at the right time and look toward South Jersey."

He takes a swig of beer and then plays with my hair in his free hand. "I see a lot of sunsets out the window of the team jet. But it isn't the same."

"Mmm." The sensation of his fingers trailing through my hair is almost as remarkable as the sky turning from pink to purple. And I realize that watching the sunset with him is more or less the exact thing Ian taught me to do in bed—stop thinking for fifteen minutes and just feel.

This vacation has been a revelation in so many ways. Every morning I wake up and wonder whose life I've stumbled into.

This morning, for example, I opened my eyes to see Ian Crikey's bare body striding toward the bathroom. I've never had thoughts about a man's backside before, but that ass is worthy of poetry. The front of him is even more mind-blowing.

The whole experience has been a little surreal. And I wouldn't be me if I didn't realize that all this gratuitous pleasure comes with a new set of concerns. Namely, what am I going to do when it ends? In six short days, we'll be back on a flight to New York. I'll be super busy, working a string of twelve-hour days to make up for missed business.

And Ian will be off to training camp. He and the other hockey players are already working out like beasts, running eight or ten miles in the morning, followed by trips to the gym.

Real life is waiting to pounce on all of us the moment we return. My time in Italy—and my all-consuming affair with Ian —will pop like a soap bubble.

We'll be over just as quickly as we began. And I won't be ready.

It's the same story all over again—I hadn't known how to casually start a vacation fling, and now I don't know how to end one. Is there a protocol? What are my lines? When I see him on the street, do I just wave and smile?

Is there a secret handshake for people who briefly had earth-shattering sex on vacation?

Only you would worry about this, my inner critic points out.

And she's right. But I still lack answers.

I take a sip of wine and notice that all around me, couples are kissing. And I do mean *all* around me. Anton is nibbling on Sylvie's ear. Charli and Neil are neck deep in a make-out session. Fiona has her head on Aly's chest, while Aly drops gentle kisses onto her head. And Castro and Heidi Jo are snuggling and laughing together in the hammock down on the lawn.

And then there's us, the not-couple who are not kissing. But maybe sunset kisses are too intimate for a vacation fling?

"Do you smell that?" Ian asks suddenly.

"What? I don't smell anything."

He sniffs the air. Twice. "I smell smoke. Like an engine burning up. Is someone thinking too hard around here? Oh wait, it's you."

"Ian," I growl.

"Come on." He chuckles. "You're the only one on this terrace who's thinkin' so hard."

"Am I?" I shoot back. "You think you're so slick? I say you're thinking too hard about my thinking too hard."

"Touché," he says. "What are you thinking about, anyway? Fashion? Or how many extra suitcases you're gonna need to get all your loot home?"

You. I'm thinking about you.

"Look who's judgy," I complain. "You didn't mind so much yesterday when I bought those see-through panties."

"No, I didn't mind," he agrees in a low, hungry voice. "Filed that away in the spank bank. But still, I only left it on your hot body for about six seconds. It was blockin' my view. So lingerie is pointless."

"Ha. You say that as if I wear lingerie for you. But I don't. I wear it for *me*."

And now we're bickering again. That's probably why this fling will crumble to dust the minute we leave Italy.

"Huh. Funny how that lingerie that you wear for *you* showed up in Bruisers purple, though."

"That was a coincidence," I snap.

Liar. My inner voice snickers.

"You're hot when you argue with me," he says with a wicked grin. "It's a seduction technique all on its own."

"That's ridiculous." I turn my shoulders to get an even better look at him. "Now you're just mocking me."

I expect him to fire back. But he kisses me instead, right here on the world's most romantic terrace. Firm, generous lips on mine. Purple twilight painting his face. I can't resist leaning in, and the glass of wine is removed from my hand and set aside.

I barely notice. I'm too busy enjoying the moment. His kisses are magic. Two hands land on my rump and spin me around until I'm straddling him.

That only makes it easier to wrap my arms around his broad neck, and sink into his deep, drugging kisses. I lean in as he shamelessly parts my mouth with his tongue and tastes me.

Five nights of this have practically turned me into Ian's puppet. He touches me, and I do whatever he wants. Here in the purple twilight, with his hands stroking my back, I can't even remember what life was like before it had so many kisses in it.

I forget myself until Ian pulls back, breathless, some minutes later. "Damn, contessa." He's watching me with wonder in his eyes.

Slowly, I realize how hot and heavy we've become, right out here in the open. How shameless I am in his lap. That's the effect he has on me. He turns me into a wild woman that I hardly recognize.

Face burning, I sit back, too. "Okay. Time out." I pat my hair back into shape. It's hopeless. Tendrils are escaping everywhere. "I'm sure this will go straight to your oversized ego. but I need a little space or I'm going to embarrass myself and everyone else by mauling you."

"That's one way to play it," he says with a smirk, as his eyes move lazily over my body. "But I have a better idea."

"What?"

But that's all I manage to ask before Ian scoops me into his arms and stands.

"Ian!" I hiss. "Put me down."

"Hush, honey. We're going upstairs now." He heads toward the double doors.

"What the... This is highly irregular."

He laughs. "This is *fun*."

I hold onto his neck as he strides purposefully through the kitchen and toward the carpeted staircase. "Did I say I wanted to go upstairs?"

"You said it with your eyes and your tongue."

"My eyes lied," I say grumpily. All our friends are probably snickering right now.

"Don't you want to go upstairs? Fine. We'll stop here." He stops abruptly and sets me down. We're only halfway up the stairs. Still, he gently nudges me to a seated position and then leans over to kiss me again.

I sprawl backward on the stairs and play along. It shouldn't be fun. I'm not even comfortable. But Ian is a wild man who knows every secret my body holds. When he puts his tongue in my mouth and his hand up my skirt, I gasp with both surprise and pleasure.

"You're naughty," I whisper against his lips.

"So are you," he whispers back. "You just didn't know it yet."

TWENTY-FOUR

Best Neighbor on Hudson

IAN

I'M LYING on my back on Vera's bed. Naked. Sweaty. She's lying on top of me, catching her breath. And I don't ever want to move. I mean that literally, which is a problem, because our trip is over in another week.

Vera traces a shape on my chest. "Did you read that thing I sent you from the lawyer? It sounds like he can help you set up your LLC pretty easily."

"Not yet," I admit. It's just one of the many things I don't want to think about. The emails and messages are piling up on my phone. The lawyer. My mother, asking about that damn wedding. Do I have a decent suit? The PR guy, with his list of charities to look over. Even O'Doul wants to talk again about the whole captain thing.

"If you write back to the lawyer," Vera says, "you could have that LLC sorted out right after you get back. Isn't that what he said?"

"Possibly," I hedge. "I actually didn't read his letter. It's a PDF."

"My phone can handle those," she offers.

"Yeah, so can mine." I sweep her hair off her neck and kiss it. Then I surprise myself by actually telling her the problem.

"But I can't, Vera. I'm super dyslexic, and I rely on dark mode, certain fonts, and sometimes a text-to-speech app for certain documents. But PDFs make that hard."

"Well, shoot." She pops up onto her hands, and I inwardly flinch. Vera is a perfectionist. She probably never lets an email linger for longer than thirty minutes without dealing with it. "I'm so sorry," she says. "I didn't know."

"It's no big deal." I pull her back down onto my chest. "Just a hassle. Slows everything down."

"Can I help you? Can I just read it to you and type your reply? It gets one thing off your plate."

I hesitate, although it's a really tempting offer. "You don't want to do that. We were having a nice time."

She rolls onto the mattress and smiles at me. "I'm still having a nice time. And if you go downstairs and get me the glass of wine you didn't let me finish, then I'll still be having a nice time. But also, your email to the lawyer will be written and done."

"Well…" There's really no reason not to take her up on that offer, except for the age-old shame of not wanting to be that guy who can't read his own mail. "Okay, sure. One sec. Let me get our drinks and my phone."

TEN MINUTES LATER, I'm pleased with my decision. Vera, long legs draped over mine, is tapping out a reply to the lawyer. All he needs is a check and a couple other details to form a corporation.

Oh, and a name for it. "All right, what are we calling this LLC? *Hudson Avenue Co?*"

Vera makes a face, her fingers pausing. "No way. That's boring. Besides, that name is too common. Someone else probably used it."

"What's your big idea, then?"

"How about *Hot and Frisky Hockey Player Co?*"

I crack a smile. "Aren't you hilarious? Okay, I've got it. Try this—*Best Neighbor on Hudson LLC.*"

I expect Vera to give me some shit about how I am not, in fact, the best neighbor on the block. But her eyes soften, instead. "That's fun. I'm writing that." She taps madly on my phone screen.

Huh. I'd meant it as a joke. Then again, I don't really care what the title is. I'm just stoked that Vera ran point on connecting me with this lawyer and answering his email for me. "Okay, done?"

"Done," she confirms. "Got anything else that needs doing? I've never seen an inbox before where *every* message was starred for follow-up. Is that because you're on vacation?"

"It's bad, right?" I scrub my forehead. "This is how it always goes with me. I'm always behind on email. You'd think being an athlete would mean that I didn't have a lot of paperwork. But it's not true, and I'm salty about it."

Vera rubs my thigh with a smooth hand. "Anything else I can help you with?"

I hesitate. "Maybe just the one from the PR guy? I'm supposed to choose from a list of charities, and then do some volunteer work. And if I don't answer, he'll think I'm trying to get out of it. You see one from Tommy?"

"Yep," she says, tapping happily on the screen, as if this were actually fun. She takes a sip of wine and then sets it aside before reading. "Okay—here's the list. We've got Boys and Girls Clubs of Brooklyn."

"A solid choice. But a lot of guys do that one. What else is there?"

"There's a dozen more. A Brooklyn women's shelter. A children's hospital. An organization for teaching sports to kids. Oh! And here's Look Good, Feel Better. They're great."

I snort. "There's a charity for looking good? How is that a thing?"

Vera gives me an arch look. "There you go again assuming that someone is shallow before you have all the information. I work with that charity, Ian. It might even be on the list because I mentioned it to Neil."

Uh-oh. Stuck my foot in it again. "All right. Let's hear it. Tell me again how I'm an ass." I wrap an arm around her shoulders, hoping she won't hold it against me. But I *do* shoot my mouth off when I feel defensive. And, yeah, I could stand to stop.

"Let me tell you a story," she says, her voice less frosty already. "I was raised by my Nonna after social services took me away from my mother."

Oh geez. "I didn't know that."

She shrugs. "My nonna loved me. She was great. But she felt a lot like you do about fashion. She wanted me to become an accountant. Or a dental hygienist, like my cousin Maria. She was a very practical lady. But even when I was a very little girl, I was already deep into fashion. Other girls were checking out American Girl books at the library, but I checked out back issues of Vogue."

I laugh, but I can totally picture it—a young Vera flipping pages in a magazine instead of doing her homework. "You know, I was the same way but with hockey. And knowing what you want out of life is handy."

"Sure." She smiles at me. "But Nonna and I fought about it all through high school. My college program was focused on the business of fashion. But Nonna kept trying to persuade me to drop the fashion part and just learn business finance."

"Yeah, it's pretty frustrating when your family disagrees with your choices."

"Well…" Vera drains her wine. "When I was almost done with the program, she was diagnosed with cancer. It was bad, too. She had ignored some symptoms. She had metastatic melanoma."

"Oh God, I'm sorry."

Vera takes a slow breath in through her nose, and her eyes

look a little red. "It was pretty awful. She got a lot of treatment, and for a little while things were looking up. But she died after a long battle."

She looks so sad that I pull her into my lap and kiss her bare shoulder. "I'm so sorry, baby. How long ago was that?"

"More than a year now. It wasn't sudden." She takes another deep breath. "But anyway, she did a lot of surgeries. There were drugs, too, with serious side effects. Eventually they tried chemotherapy as a last resort. She lost a ton of weight, and she lost her hair. She got depressed and didn't go out as much.

"She wasn't playing bridge or seeing her friends. She didn't look or feel like herself. And that's when I called Look Good, Feel Better. They provided her with a very realistic wig. And they taught us some skincare tips for dealing with the side effects of her treatments. That's what that charity does—they help people who are undergoing cancer treatment look good on the *outside*, so that they feel more like themselves on the inside."

"*Oh*," I say, feeling like the world's biggest ass. "I had no idea."

"I know." She gives me a tiny smile. "That's the thing, Ian. She didn't either. And after she got her wig, I made a reservation at the next church supper. And I bought her a dress in her favorite color—red. She said I shouldn't have spent the money. I told her it was on sale, even though it wasn't. We got all dolled up and went out together, just like in the old days. And this nice older man complimented her dress *and* her hairdo, which made us both laugh. He didn't know it was a wig."

Vera stops to press her fingertips against her tear ducts, and I hold her a little closer.

She takes one more deep breath. "Anyway, after we got home, she looked in the mirror and said, 'Vera, I'm sorry I always gave you such a hard time about the things you love. I think I understand you now. And finding a job you love is something to celebrate. I'm sorry if I made you feel like I didn't respect your choices.'" She swallows hard. "I didn't realize how much I'd needed to hear that, but she finally gave that to me. Then she died. A month later."

"Wow, honey. I'm so sorry."

Vera presses her face against my chest, and I can feel tears leaking into my T-shirt. "At the end, when she gave her last wishes to my aunt, she'd chosen that red dress for her burial. The one I gave her."

My heart breaks right in half. "You must miss her terribly."

"I do," she says through a sniffle. "I still have family—aunts and uncles and cousins. But she was really my only parent."

I stroke her hair for another couple minutes until she composes herself. "Thank you for explaining to me what that charity does."

"Don't mention it," she sniffs. "You know how much I enjoy proving you wrong. You and everyone else, I guess."

I take her face in both hands. "Then I'm glad I could provide you with this opportunity."

When she finally smiles, I kiss her.

TWENTY-FIVE

Is This Golf Day? Or Team Shrink Day?

IAN

I SQUINT up the fairway toward the hole, wondering how to handle this next shot. My golf game is not very graceful. I can move the ball—just not always where I want it to go.

"So, is this going anywhere?" Neil asks me.

"Let's hope so. Which club should I use?" Neil knows golf better than I ever will.

"Here." He hands me an iron from my bag of rented clubs. "But I wasn't talking about the twelfth hole. I was talking about Vera."

"Oh." That wasn't the question I expected. "No, man. She has some big date coming up when we go back. An old flame. Long term was never our plan." I square the club's head with the little white ball. I set my shoulders the way you're supposed to, and then I draw back and whack it.

The ball flies through the blue Italian sky before landing a good ten yards past its destination.

"Too much heat," Castro says.

"Yeah, yeah." We pick up our golf bags and head toward the green.

"You two would be good together, though," Neil says. "Long term."

"You're the only one who thinks so." I laugh. "We have exactly nothing in common, except for sexual chemistry."

"That's a good start," he says. "But I bet you're wrong. Having stuff in common is more than golf versus shopping. It's how you look at life. Vera is a really good person. Loyal to the core. Willing to do anything for her friends. You're kind of the same, but with a side of trust issues."

"Is this golf day? Or team shrink day? And I do not have trust issues."

"Uh-huh," says Castro, who's known me even longer than Neil has. "I was there when your ex hopped into bed with her new man about ten minutes after you joined the team. You gave a big speech on the jet about how relationships were for suckers. Women just exist to fuck with you—that's a quote. And how you would never again trust one of them. Then you got that massive tattoo on your chest because your ex hated tattoos. And Massey talked you out of adding 'NEVER AGAIN' in giant letters, too."

"That was *years* ago," I scoff.

"Exactly," Castro says. "And you never dated anyone since." He lines up his shot and chips the damn ball right into the hole.

"Nice shot," I say, trying to change the subject. "What are we doing for lunch later?"

But Neil isn't ready to let it go. "Isn't your ex's wedding coming up?"

I never should have told my guys about that damn wedding. "Sure. So what?"

Neil dusts off his putter. "You should take Vera. You'd have more fun, and she could meet some wealthy social climbers who buy dresses and designer shoes."

"My ex's wedding? That's *not* a woman's dream date. Not to mention that she would have to meet my parents. My mother would assume that Vera and I were dating, and then I'd have to answer questions about that." Worst idea ever.

"It was just a thought," Neil says, lining up a perfect putt.

But now he's got me thinking about it. The truth is, I'm starting to really enjoy Vera's company. Neil is right that matching hobbies isn't everything. Not that I'll admit it to his face.

Besides, having Vera along at the wedding to dance with me and critique everybody's outfit would actually make the whole thing much more entertaining.

It's tempting. But then my mother would get big ideas...

Nope. That idea is as terrible as my golf swing. It takes me two putts to get my ball into the hole, for the worst score of our foursome.

We head for the next hole. And Neil has the gall to ask, "So what's this big date Vera has with her ex?"

My reaction to the question is immediate and angry. "How the fuck should I know? Ask her yourself if you're so curious."

Neil just chuckles, like he's caught me out.

And maybe he has. I like her a little more than I ever anticipated.

That's not a good thing.

A WHILE later we're seated at an outdoor table at the golf club, eating sandwiches, when all our phones start chiming with texts. All within a few seconds of each other.

The four of us exchange worried glances. Because that can't be good.

Castro is the first to reach for his phone. He squints at the screen. "What the hell? *Puck Daddy's* says: *Massive 3-team trade between Brooklyn, Boston and Vegas in the works.*"

My stomach bottoms out. "Fuck a duck. If one of us got traded while we were golfing, I will not be responsible for my actions."

Castro holds his phone out for all of us to see. There's a text from Bess, his agent. *IT'S NOT YOU. CALM DOWN.*

185

"I got that same message from Eric," Anton says. Then he wipes imaginary sweat from his brow.

Neil lifts his sandwich. "I have a no-trade clause."

"You do?" I yelp. "How is that?"

"Took a twenty-five percent pay cut to get it," he says with a shrug.

A beat after he says this, the rest of us each throw a potato chip at him. "Rich fucker," Anton says. "It's a good thing we like you."

Neil just laughs, because he's a great guy who doesn't care how ridiculous it is for a bunch of millionaires to throw shade at him for being a billionaire. Especially while we're staying at his Italian villa.

And I'm still the only person at this table who doesn't have the all-clear on whatever trade is going down.

Pushing my plate away, I get up and carry my phone outside the dining area. I stand beside a wall that's climbing with vines and bright, exotic flowers. The lake shimmers in the distance. But a pit of cold fear gathers in my stomach, nonetheless.

Until this year, I'd been living a charmed life. So few men get five or more years in the NHL. So few get the chances I've gotten.

But I'd always felt I'd *deserved* those opportunities. Hockey was my one thing—my only real skill. My purpose. Even if my family never quite understood me, it didn't matter. I had hockey in my corner, and I thought it would never turn on me.

Suddenly, I'm not so sure. I've had sleepless nights wondering how I hurt that Boston rookie so badly. And now my team thinks I have an image problem. They see me as a liability, not an asset.

If I get traded, it could mean the beginning of the end. Some guys have a downward spiral at the end of their careers. I'm not ready for that to be me.

I'm not ready.

With cold dread washing over me, I pull out my phone

and scan my notifications. Several friends have sent me that same gossipy post about a three-way "multiple player" trade. But there aren't any messages from my agent or from management.

The closest thing I've got is a day-old message from the PR guy, asking about the date of my return from Italy. *So we can get you started on charity work.*

I'm dying here. I tap O'Doul's number and wait for the ring.

"I don't think it's you," is how he answers.

That's not quite the reassurance I need, but I let out a sigh of relief anyway. "Why? You know who it is?"

He hesitates. "I got an inkling. I shouldn't say, though. Management would kill me."

"Doulie, I'm losing my mind, here."

He chuckles. "You know that getting traded wouldn't be the end of your life, right? This is hockey, not a mafia flick."

"Says the man who played his whole career for one team."

"Yeah, fair. Okay, I think Ivo is one of them. I saw his agent walk into the building for a meeting. I didn't see Ivo, though, so the meeting could have been something else. Like a contract negotiation."

"Oh, wow." I let out a great gust of air. "So if it was Ivo getting traded, then—"

"It wouldn't make much sense to trade both of you," he says, which was my first thought, too.

"Too disruptive to have that much turnover," I add. The Finnish kid and I play the same position, and it would be awkward to ship out both of us at once.

"No calls from the GM, right? No calls from your agent?"

"Right. Nothing."

"Then don't let the rumors make you crazy. And for fuck's sake—never read the comments on those gossip pieces. They'll just make you ragey."

"Oh God, I know." Armchair hockey fans will be speculating like crazy right now. They'll have the whole team traded twice over by cocktail hour. "I'm probably at the top of the fans' list for a trade."

"The fans don't matter," O'Doul reminds me. "They haven't skated a mile in your shoes. They don't know you. They can't squat five hundred pounds. They don't get hit in the face for a living. They. Don't. *Matter*."

"Right," I say quietly. This is exactly the pep talk I needed. "What the hell am I going to do without you next season? *Fuck*."

O'Doul chuckles. "I'm flattered, kid. But change is just part of the equation. It won't kill you."

The way I feel nauseated right now? I'm not sure he's right.

"But now that I have you, let's talk about the captaincy again. Who's getting it? What do you think?"

"Uh…" This is literally the last thing on my mind. "I thought Castro, but you said no. So the next obvious choice is Trevi. He's a high scorer. The refs like him. He's got an honest face. Already a leader. Looks good on a brochure."

O'Doul laughs. "I know. He's the whole package. But there's another conflict of interest. He's married to the coach's daughter."

"Nobody thinks Leo is a snitch," I point out. "He's such a stand-up guy. Even *you* like him now."

O'Doul laughs, because he remembers their rocky start, too. The captain was not a big fan of Trevi's when he was a rookie.

That feels like a million years ago, though.

"I know, man. Leo is a great guy, and he's a natural leader. But we need somebody who doesn't have a link to management. A solid guy who doesn't have a temper. A hard worker with seniority in the organization."

"We got plenty of those," I say, weary of this conversation. "You'll figure it out."

He sighs. "Okay, if you don't want to help."

I snicker. "No guilt, man. If you haven't decided by the time I get back, I'll put names in a hat, and you can pick one."

"It's a deal. Now go have fun and don't worry about this

trade. It's probably not going to happen to you. And if it does, you'll deal."

"Thanks," I say gruffly. We hang up, and I feel better.

A little.

For the first time since I can remember, my excitement for the upcoming season is tempered with nerves. That's not like me. But I can't seem to shake it.

TWENTY-SIX

I'm Actually Tired of Shopping

VERA

"IT'S hard for me to admit this, but I'm actually tired of shopping." I make this dramatic announcement as Charli, Heidi Jo, and I drop into cafe chairs on one of the cute streets of Lugano.

Charli had asked me if I was interested in driving to this Swiss town for the day, and I'd jumped at the chance to double the number of foreign countries on my first international trip. But now I'm bushed.

"My feet hurt," Heidi Jo admits. "But I thought we saved the best store for last?"

"We did," Charli says. "And we have to go in, because Vera and I still don't have dresses for the gala."

"Maybe I'm not meant to go," I mumble. "It's a sign from the fashion gods to stay home."

"Who *are* you? And what have you done with Vera?" Charli demands. "And if I have to go to this thing, you have to go. That's a rule."

A waiter appears and begins unloading cups of espresso onto the table.

"Grazie mille," I say in thanks.

"You definitely need caffeine," Charli says, pushing a cup

into my hands. "Drink this. And then we're going to find your dress."

"Maybe," I concede. We've been to Milan twice now, though, and I also shopped Bellagio from end to end. But the only dresses I've liked have been way out of my price range.

Maybe it *is* a sign. The right dress is magic. And the absence of magic is notable, in this case.

And—here's a rebellious thought—I can't picture my ex tromping all over two different countries looking for just the right suit to impress *me*.

Funny how this never occurred to me before now.

After coffee, we head for *La Boutique Rosa*, where several sparkly dresses adorn the window. And I promise myself I won't try on anything I can't afford. Danforth isn't worth the stress of a credit card bill I can't pay, right?

Right, my inner critic agrees. *Unless this is your last chance to make him love you again. Just saying.*

"You shut up," I whisper under my breath as my girls and I fan out in the shop.

Heidi Jo holds up a salmon ball gown. "I need to go to more fancy parties," Heidi Jo complains. "So that I'll have somewhere to wear this."

"You'd look beautiful in that," I agree. But a glance at the price tag confirms that I'm in over my head here.

The shop is lovely, though. I enjoy my time pulling dresses off the rack, admiring the Italian and French designers' style and thinking about all the trends I'm seeing. Fringe is back, and feathers are also in. Asymmetrical necklines are everywhere. I take an Instagram pic of a whole row of dresses in begonia pink, a color that's having a moment.

"Vera!" Charli whistles for me. "Come here a second."

I look around, but don't spot her. And then I see a hand waving to me from the very back of the shop. There's a rack marked *prezzo ridotto*. Reduced price. And Charli is holding up a floor-length ballgown in a simple style with a high waist and a sweeping skirt. There's a sweetheart neckline and slender shoulder straps.

And the whole thing is done in a rich shade of dark red that would look spectacular against my Italy tan.

"Okay," I say slowly. "That's gorgeous."

"I love the hem," she says. "There's a soft wire inside it that makes the shape of the skirt more interesting."

She's right. The hem detail makes the dress. "That is really cute. Do you mean this for me or you? That color could go either way."

"It's for you, dingus. But that hem couldn't easily be shortened. Maybe that's why it didn't sell? It has to be exactly the right length, or it won't work. This one is a petite length, though. Try it on?"

"Wow, all right. Good eye, girly."

She gives me a happy shrug. "You never know. Could be the one."

I find a saleswoman who helps me into a fitting room. I remove my sundress and carefully step into the ballgown. The fabric is a low-luster silk blend. And the price tag? Reduced to just two hundred euros. It's a lot of money—but not for an Italian designer ball gown.

"Can I zip you?" Charli asks from the other side of the door.

"Yes, please." I come out, and Charli's smile widens. "Oh heck! The length is going to work, isn't it? Turn around." She zips me into the dress, and I step past her to find the three-way mirror.

And *wow*. It fits me like it was made for me. The bodice is sleek against my chest, the straps don't dig or roll, and the hem hits the floor.

"Stand on your tiptoes," Charli demands. "Let's see what a low heel would do."

I raise myself up an inch and then turn in a slow circle, while the skirts swish neatly at the floor.

"Holy cannoli," Heidi Jo says. "You look like an Oscar nominee."

"The bust even fits," I murmur. "That never happens."

"That's the *one*," Charli whispers. "That's your dress. Tell me I'm not crazy."

"Not about this," I agree. "Thank you for finding it for me."

Charli laughs. "You do the same for me all the time. I'm just trying to return the favor."

WITH MY NEW dress packed carefully in tissue paper, we ride back to the villa in the limousine, making only one quick stop for a couple of pints of gelato for our evening ritual. The other two women send me into the gelato shop alone, because they know I like to practice my Italian.

"I hope nobody minds my choice," I say when I emerge. "It's a little weird but the guy gave me a sample, and I thought it was amazing."

"How weird could it be?" Charli demands. "My favorite so far was the guava you chose."

"Well, brace yourselves. This one is olive oil and rosemary."

Heidi Jo shrugs. "That sounds different, but if they made it fattening, I'll probably love it." She pats her tummy affectionately. "I'm up at least five pounds on this trip."

The driver zips us back to the villa before the ice cream melts, and I remind myself that I'm going to have to travel like a normal person again—on the subway—in a few short days. I'd better enjoy myself as much as I can before I turn into a pumpkin again.

After putting the gelato in the freezer, I head upstairs and put my dress away. The bathroom I share with Ian is unoccupied, so I go in to splash some water on my face. The door to his room is open, and I spot him perched on the end of the bed, shirtless, elbows on his knees, phone in hand.

My heart does a belly flop. It's not just because he's physically attractive, although he is. But now I know how it feels to sleep against that body. And the surprising tenderness of those strong hands.

He is beautiful, but also familiar. He looks like... Wow, this is bad. But he looks like *mine*.

What the hell are you smoking? my inner meanie demands. *He's not yours. And if you said that out loud, he'd laugh in your face.*

Ian looks up, catching me watching him. And that's when I notice the worry lines on his forehead.

"Hey, what's the matter?" I ask immediately. "What's wrong?"

He tries for a smile, although it looks startled. "Hi, contessa. How was shopping trip number eighty-nine?"

I cross to the bed and sit down beside him. "You can poke fun at my hobbies if you want to, tough guy. But why do you look like someone just ate the last donut?"

He rubs his handsome jaw, as if trying to work out a puzzle. "There's nothing wrong, exactly. But there's some kind of big trade brewing in Brooklyn, and it's got me on edge. I'm not in a good place with my team, and I'm worried they'll ship me to Vegas or somewhere if they think I'm a lot of trouble."

"B-because of your arrest?" I babble as my heart quietly detonates.

"Yeah, partly," he says. He sets his phone aside and then lies back on the bed, his feet dangling over the edge, his arms over his face. "The reputation thing is certainly a factor. There's a lot of changes happening on our team. It would be easy for management to push me off the table. Make me someone else's problem."

Wait. What? "They *can't* trade you away." My head spins. He can't just leave Brooklyn. "You just bought a building!"

"I know, right?" His laugh sounds a little hysterical. "Do you have any interest in becoming the superintendent of a small apartment building? I might have to hire someone, starting a couple weeks from now."

I taste acid. I might even be sick. "They can *do* that?"

"They can," he says miserably. "It's one of the wild things about my job. The pay is good, and you don't have to sit at a desk. But they can ship your ass anywhere they want with no notice."

Shocked, I lie back on the bed beside him. I stare up at the ceiling with unseeing eyes. If Ian gets traded, I'd be the one to blame. He *can't* get traded. "How will you find out?"

His hand closes over mine. It feels so good, but I don't deserve it. "The GM will call me with my agent on the line. O'Doul doesn't think I'll be traded. He's got a theory that they're trading someone else. I won't relax until they announce the deal, though. I know I must be on their list of consideration."

"I'm sorry," I say.

"It's okay," he says. "Might not happen. And it's not your fault."

Except maybe it is.

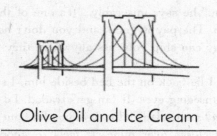

TWENTY-SEVEN

Olive Oil and Ice Cream

IAN

VERA and I take a spontaneous nap on my bed.

That ought to be nice, except I have a fucking bad dream in the middle of it. After I punch him, the rookie from Boston looks up at me and says, "Now you're going to be traded."

I wake up sweaty and miserable.

At least I don't wake up Vera. She's curled on her side, looking sweet and peaceful. I get up and tiptoe to the shower to try to feel human again.

THAT NIGHT AFTER DINNER, I start a ridiculous argument with Vera. I argue against olive oil as an ice cream flavor. (But can you blame me?) I argue about fashion.

I think I do this to convince myself we're not really a couple. If we're arguing, I won't miss her after I get traded to Vegas or where-the-fuck-ever.

The argument is so unimportant that I actually lose my train of thought in the middle of it. We're standing in the living room, just the two of us. And my stressed-out mind can't take even another minute of pretense. Instead of finishing my thought, I pull Vera to me and kiss her hungrily.

She doesn't even seem surprised. Her eager fingers thread through my hair, and she kisses me back with passion and focus.

I need her. Badly. And I can't even be bothered to be subtle about it. After a couple of minutes of hardcore making out, I pick her up and carry her up the stairs.

She doesn't argue this time. Not even when I drop her on the bed and announce, "Take off your dress. I want to tie your wrists to the bedpost and then lick you all over."

"Why? Is that a thing I need to learn?" she asks, pulling her dress over her head.

"Fuck no." My voice is gruff. "It's just a thing I want to do."

"Oh," she murmurs. For a second, I think she'll argue with me. We're so good at arguing. Just like we're good at making each other moan.

But she doesn't. She lies back on the bed in a silky camisole and tiny panties. My mouth is watering, and I already know I'm going to make this a night to remember. You have to use the skills God gives you, even if they're not the ones the rest of the world wants.

I need something to tie her hands, and I don't have a lot of options. "Did you buy me any new ties on your shopping spree?" I ask.

She lifts her head off the pillow. "Ian Joseph Crikey! If you make knots in that new Valentino tie I bought, before you even wear it, I will not be responsible for my actions. Look in the top drawer of my dresser. There are some cotton scarves."

It only takes me a second to find them, thank God. A moment later I'm straddling her body, tying her wrists loosely together, and then tying the ends of the scarf to the bedpost.

Vera looks up at me with wide eyes. But her gaze isn't nervous at all. She's focused on my chest, where the tattoo flexes as I work. "What do the wings mean, anyway?"

"Freedom," I say, without offering any further explanation. "Not in the mood to talk, contessa." To prove it, I move down her body. Then I lean over and catch the strap of her tiny panties between my teeth.

Her breath catches as I drag them down her body. "Oh geez. Oh boy," she gasps.

"Yeah, I'm in a mood." I toss the panties onto the floor. Then I pick up the second scarf and roll it. "Close your eyes."

She slams them shut with gratifying speed. I lay the scarf carefully across her eyes, and she lifts her head to allow me to tie it.

"You tell me if you don't like anything I do," I say gruffly.

The little vixen smiles. "Yes, sir."

Christ. "You're a quick learner." As if this had anything to do with lessons anymore. We're way past that. My hands are quick and needy as I reach down to tug down her tank until it reveals her breasts, and she arches into my touch.

This woman has given me a hell of a lot more than I've ever given her. Right now, she's giving me her trust, which feels like a beautiful gift. I lie down on the bed beside her. Leaning over one perfect tit, I gently blow on her nipple.

She shivers deliciously and lifts her body toward me. But I'm not in the mood to be all that predictable. I lick the other nipple, instead, and she whimpers.

Rising onto my hands and knees, I commence my unpredictable seduction. A kiss to her neck. A kiss to her breast. A brush of my lips across her thigh. A hungry series of kisses across the top of her mound.

"Ian," she gasps, her hips twitching with anticipation.

"I like you like this. Naked, spread out like a feast. Don't ever let anyone tell you that you aren't as sexy as the day is long. That man is a liar."

I drop my mouth to her hip bone for another wet kiss, and she squeezes her thighs together in a needy way. "More," she demands.

"You'll get more. Spread your legs for me."

She parts them.

"Wider," I demand. "All the way. I want to look at you."

After the briefest hesitation, she complies.

Now she's spread out like a feast. And I get busy pleasuring her with my tongue and my hands. This is exactly what I need.

She's exactly what I need. Even if I get traded tomorrow, I'll never forget this night.

After many minutes of fun, I've got her begging and whimpering. I sit up and grab a condom. As I slide it on, I notice that her tank top is ruched up to reveal her belly. Much of it is smooth, but there's a broad section of skin that's a slightly different color. And the texture looks different.

"Contessa," I say gently. "Do you have a birthmark on your stomach?"

Her body stiffens. Then she tugs one of her hands out of the scarf, freeing herself and quickly yanking her tank back down.

Well, shit. With gentle hands, I lift the scarf off her eyes and look down at her. "I'm sorry. Did I ruin the mood?"

With a sigh, she wiggles her other hand, and I reach up to help her free it. And then we're just staring at each other while I wait to hear whether or not she'll tell me what's wrong.

"It's a burn," she says quietly. "When I was a kid, I got burned a little. And even though I've had some laser treatments, it's ugly."

"A burn...?" How does a kid get a burn on her tummy?

She doesn't elaborate.

"That's why you leave your top on?"

"I've been told it's unattractive."

I don't ask who said that. I guess it's none of my business. But it makes me angry anyway. "Scars are part of life. I got a few." I point to a scar on my shoulder where I got cut by a skate blade while playing pond hockey as a teenager.

"Men are supposed to be battle-worthy," she points out. "Women are supposed to be smooth and lovely."

I open my mouth to argue, but then I stop myself. Because I bet it's true. There are lots of people who'd tell her so, anyway. And they never say that shit to me, so I don't really get to dispute the point. "Nobody is smooth and lovely all the time," I say instead. "And if they are, we don't like them very much."

Vera suddenly cracks a smile. "Agreed."

"If I shut up now, can I make love to you?"

She laughs softly. "Anytime you're ready."

I take her hands in mine, and I move them onto my chest. And then—without further discussion—I slide home.

"Oh," she says, her mouth falling open as I enter her. Then she moans as her body surrenders to mine.

This time I make myself go slowly. We're running out of time together. I can make this last.

So I draw it out as long as I can. But I'm not used to so much raw connection—all that eye contact and deep, deep kisses.

I'm supposed to be the teacher here—the one who knows what he's doing. But when she whispers my name, I'm lost.

And I don't even think I care.

SOMETIME LATER WE both collapse in her bed. Sleeping together is something I've gotten used to in a hurry. My eyes always fall closed with remarkable speed.

But not so quickly that I don't have time to grab my phone one more time and look for news of the trade.

Nothing yet. Just a text from O'Doul. *Stay cool*, he says.

As if.

TWENTY-EIGHT

I Don't Groove on Pageantry

VERA

AFTER OUR EPIC SEX FEST, I lie awake for a while, my mind too busy to sleep.

Ian is passed out next to me, breathing deeply. His handsome face is serene against the pillow. One of his legs lies against mine, as if trying to hold onto the powerful connection we found earlier.

Or maybe I just wish that were true.

On our first day in Italy, I'd told the other women that I wasn't a vacation-fling kind of person. And—in spite of the naked evidence at hand—that's still true. Flings confuse me. I'm confused right now.

I'd told Ian that I didn't really understand sex, and he'd quickly proven me wrong. At least I understand it better now than I ever have before. But now that I know how good it can be, I don't quite know what to do with that information. I don't know how you go from staring into someone's eyes and moaning his name to waving hello as you pass on the sidewalk.

The way Ian makes me feel is like a miracle. And it seems wrong to throw miracles away.

Except he's wrong for me in so many other ways. We don't care about the same things in life. We argue constantly. And—

most crucially—he doesn't date. Staying with him was never an option.

And then there's Danforth. I never got over him. I never made peace with the way we ended. We had plans together. I still remember all the things we said we'd do together.

I still want all those things—the coop apartment we were going to save up for. The dog we agreed we'd adopt when we both had good jobs. The restaurants on our endless list that we never got to try.

The apology he never gave me. *I'm sorry, Vera. What was I thinking? You're the perfect woman for me.*

Eyes closed, I try to picture Danforth saying it. It's difficult, but not impossible. And then I try to picture Danforth removing my panties with his teeth and ravishing me. That's even harder to imagine than the apology.

I've always believed in manifestation—that creating a vision for what you want will help you get it. But what if you no longer know what you want?

What then?

I WAKE up bleary and way too early. It's only six thirty when I roll out of bed and quietly put on shorts and a T-shirt.

Leaving Ian sleeping peacefully, I go in search of coffee.

Charli is sitting at the kitchen table, already sipping a cappuccino. "Good morning!" She gives me a radiant smile before hopping out of her chair. "Want a coffee? I was hoping someone would wake up and talk to me."

"My goodness, you're chipper."

She presses a button on the gleaming automatic espresso machine and shoves a cup into place. "I had a little trouble sleeping."

"Been there," I murmur.

"I was too happy. Too excited. Look." She holds out her hand, and there's a giant, gleaming diamond on it.

"Holy cow! That's so *beautiful*. Is that... Did Neil give it to you last night?" I'd noticed that neither she nor Neil wore a wedding ring. I'd chalked it up to hockey players having no interest in bling. But I didn't ask.

"He did," she says, gazing at it. "Neil and I did *not* have a typical wedding, Vera."

"You eloped in Vegas. I know." She'd told me that the two of them got drunk and tied the knot, shocking Neil's family. There was some drama, but I don't know the details, and I haven't wanted to pry.

"It wasn't just that we eloped." She moves the cup under the steamed-milk attachment and presses another button. "We never planned to get married. And for a long time, I assumed we'd end up getting divorced."

I take a gasping breath, because I hate that idea. "But you guys are so perfect together."

She laughs. "You say that, and I believe you now. But I didn't always understand. And I was afraid to trust him, even when he looked me in the eyes and said, 'I want this, I love you.'"

I've forgotten to breathe. It's been a long time since anyone said that to me, and when Danforth *un*said it, it broke my heart.

But I still want that. It's still worth it.

And I don't want to settle for someone who isn't crazy for me.

"Neil never gave up on me." She sets the coffee in front of me and sits back down. "He waited until I was ready. I finally got there. This was his grandmother's ring." She holds out her hand and admires it again. "And when he put it on my finger last night, I finally realized that it belongs there."

I look down at the ring and smile. My eyes get hot, and my voice cracks a little when I speak. "It's beautiful, and I'm so happy for you. Couldn't have happened to a better girl."

Then I reach over and give her the big hug she deserves.

Hearing her story galvanizes me. I don't need a giant diamond. Charli would be the first to agree that bling doesn't matter. As Nonna used to say, it's the thought that counts.

But I do need a man who will give me his whole heart and not ask me to settle for scraps. That means holding out for a man who can love me as much as Neil loves Charli.

Even if it hurts.

SEVERAL HOURS LATER, I hurry downstairs and out the villa's front door, where there's a plush little motorcoach and driver waiting to drive us to the Italian city of Verona.

Glancing around, I realize I'm the last to appear. "Sorry," I say. "The time got away from me."

"But you look incredible," Ian says, taking in the purple satin dress I'd brought just for this occasion. "I take back every nasty thing I said about fashion."

"Really? Then why do you keep tugging on that tie?" I nudge his hand away from the knot in the silk. It's a blue tie with tiny yellow flowers on it. I chose it myself. "Leave this alone. It's perfect."

"Wearing a tie is never perfect," he argues. "I got no trouble with women's fashion. But I'd wear joggers to this opera if you let me."

"But we didn't," Charli says cheerfully. "Now everybody in the coach."

We sit in four rows of three, Ian and I next to each other, his hand resting lovingly on my knee.

Everyone looks elegant tonight. "Hockey players clean up well, don't they?" Heidi Jo says.

"Yes, we do," Charli agrees, the diamond glinting on her finger. She's wearing a slit-leg crepe dress in a sleek shade of midnight blue. Not only does it make her skin look luminous, but when I brought it over to their apartment for her to try on, she declared it "surprisingly comfortable," which is high praise from Charli.

As I watch, Neil takes her hand and gives her a happy smile.

That smile is something I feel in the pit of my stomach. That smile is *goals*. I take a calming breath. But then I also take an unconscious glance at Ian, who... is looking at his phone. Not at me.

And that's fine. It is what it is.

"Hey Ian, you're going to break that thing," Castro says as we roll down another pristine Italian road.

"What?" Ian grunts, his attention still on his phone.

"They won't announce the trade any faster just because you keep refreshing your email."

Ian raises his middle finger without even looking at Castro. "It's not your ass swinging in the wind, is it?"

"I wonder what Vegas is like this time of year?" Anton asks. "Let's check the weather. Oh, look at that. 107 degrees?"

"You dick," Ian grumbles.

"Hey, I'm just teasing." Anton reaches up from the row behind us and squeezes Ian's shoulder. "We just don't know why you're so fixated on *this* trade. The possibility is always there. And yet here we still are together."

Ian looks out the window, not answering the question. He isn't an unfeeling man. I don't believe that anymore. But he tries to pretend he is, and I think I know why he's so distracted. This trade comes at a difficult moment for him.

That's your fault, my critical voice reminds me. *Nice job*.

My own phone lights up with a text. It's from Danforth.

Hi V! Are you back from your trip? Any chance you could find me a new tux shirt before the gala? Mine's old now, and you're so good at stuff like this. He adds a winking emoji.

Somehow, I feel more irritated than flattered. Did he invite me to the gala simply to ask this favor?

No, that's ridiculous. Presumably he's been sourcing all his own clothes for the past three years. I decide to give him the benefit of the doubt, at least for now. I'm still keeping my options open. Maybe I'll date him. Maybe I'll even seduce him.

Hi D! I write back. *I'm not back yet but if you email me your measurements, I'll find one in time for the gala.*

I sneak another glance at Ian, thinking of all the advice he'd given me on the topic of seduction. And I force myself to admit that it's advice that Ian genuinely intends for me to use on other men. Like Danforth.

It's a sobering thought. If Ian had feelings for me, he'd say so. That's the kind of man he is.

Seduction is all about anticipation, he'd said. With that in mind, I add one more text for Danforth. *I found a stunning dress for this event. I'd show you a photo, but that would be cheating…*

That's it. That's all I'm giving him. I tuck the phone away, so I won't be tempted to see if he replied.

WHEN WE ARRIVE at the Arena di Verona, Ian helps me out of the coach with gentle hands. I'll miss those hands after this trip. But now is not the moment to dwell on that, because he's leading me through a stone archway into an ancient colosseum.

"Wow," I gasp. "This looks like the set of *Ben Hur*."

"Crazy, right?" Ian agrees, squeezing my hand.

I've never seen anything like it. A portion of the oval structure is taken up by the stage, which is a modern addition. But the rest of the space—the floor and the stonework sides—are given over to row upon row of red velvet seats. It must seat ten thousand people.

Neil leads us straight up the center aisle, all the way up to the third row from the stage.

"Isn't this fancy," Ian mutters. "When I fall asleep, the whole cast will notice."

"You wouldn't dare," I growl.

His answering smile is cheeky. "I don't groove on pageantry, contessa. But I'll try to keep an open mind."

"That's okay," I tell him. "I'm excited enough for both of us. *La Traviata* is a classic."

He gives me an indulgent smile. A short time later, the conductor walks out in a white tie and tailcoat. Ten thousand people applaud. And then a hush falls over the crowd as he raises his baton in a gloved hand. When he brings it down again, several dozen violins send their music up into the nighttime sky.

Soon the stage is crowded with cast members dressed in finery. They're singing so mightily that the hair stands up on my arms. As I watch, Violetta — a courtesan — meets and falls in love with the high-born Alfredo.

I'm transfixed. "It's so beautiful," I whisper between scenes.

Ian moves his mouth to my ear. "Yeah, it is, contessa, but I can't understand a word they're saying."

Never missing an opportunity to argue, I lean in and answer, "You don't need the words. I've been to one of your hockey games, and I didn't understand a thing. But I still knew who won and who lost."

Ian chuckles as the lights come up again. Then he turns his attention back to the stage.

And he does not fall asleep.

THE TRAGIC ENDING WRECKS ME. I'd known what was going to happen, but I still wasn't prepared to watch Violetta die. When it's over, I shoot out of my seat for a standing ovation.

Ian is slower to applaud and claps with a grumpy look on his face. "That's it? Really? He comes back to her, but she just *dies*?"

"Yep," I say with a yawn. "If his father had been less of an ass, they could have had more time together."

"Nobody told me opera was so depressing. I wore a suit for this."

"And you look very handsome," I say as we head for the coach.

Ian helps me up into the vehicle, and I take a seat near the window. It's probably less than ten minutes into the ride when I fall asleep with my head on his shoulder.

I wake up groggy and confused sometime later, with Ian patting my hand. "Come on, contessa. We're home."

We're not, though. This place isn't home, even if I sometimes wish it were. Sleepily, I get off the coach.

Tomorrow, we go home for real. This is my last night in Italy.

I'm not ready.

MOST OF MY packing is already done in preparation for tomorrow's departure. The open suitcases on the floor ruin the illusion that this room is my pretty space and my pretty life.

Back to Kansas, Dorothy, my inner voice reminds me.

I feel subdued as I get ready for bed. I pull my bathrobe around my body to the sound of Ian brushing his teeth in our bathroom. After the water shuts off, I tap on the door and then try the knob. It opens, so I slip inside to brush my teeth, too.

"Contessa."

I look up to see Ian leaning on the doorframe to his room. His tie is draped lazily around his neck, and his shirt is unbuttoned, revealing the tattoo I might never see again after tonight. He looks like an ad in a high-end magazine—the poster boy for money, sex, and sin. If this is my one and only vacation fling, I chose well.

Still, I have to spit out the toothpaste before I can answer him.

Sexy, my inner critic snorts.

"Yes?" I finally say, grabbing a towel.

"Um…" He hesitates, which isn't like him. "I have to go to a wedding in Connecticut after we get back. You should feel no obligation, but I was wondering if you might consider going with me?"

Wait, what? My mind reels as I dab water off my face. "A wedding? Your ex's?" Then I wince because there's no way I'd know that short of googling him.

"Yeah," he says easily. "It's August seventh."

August seventh. My sluggish mind rolls that date around for a moment before realizing why it sounds familiar. "Oh! That's the night of the gala," I blurt out.

Ian's expression shutters. "Oh right. Your gala. Should'a figured you'd have plans." He starts to turn away.

That wakes me up fast, but I'm still playing catch up. "Okay, but…" Did Ian really just ask me to his ex's wedding? "What if…"

When he turns, he's already shaking his head. His cool eyes grow cooler. "Nah, go to your party. Haven't you been planning for that for weeks? Wasn't that the whole point of this…" He waves a hand between us. "To set you up for that night?"

"Well, it *was*, but… But I…" The sentence dies on my tongue. Because it's no longer true. What began as a ridiculous plot to learn to seduce Danforth became so much more the very first moment Ian kissed me.

But he doesn't want to hear that, does he? What would he even say if I told him I feel *gutted* at the thought of not waking up next to him again?

He'd laugh, my inner critic says. *He'd back away real fast.*

"Look," he says, leaning against the doorframe. "Forget I mentioned it. Don't blow this chance with your guy. Not for a crappy night in a wedding hall. He's supposed to be your forever guy. Not me."

Well, ouch.

"Right," I say numbly. "Of course."

Ian's eyes dip. He clears his throat. "You don't need me anymore. You know that, right?"

Not true! I want to shriek. But I don't scream it. I don't even whisper it.

Because I know a dismissal when I hear one.

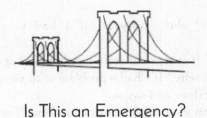

TWENTY-NINE

Is This an Emergency?

IAN

I WATCH VERA'S REACTION. She looks conflicted. Maybe a little hurt. I have to fight my own reaction, which is to step farther into the room, lift her up onto that bathroom counter, and kiss her senseless.

But I can't do that anymore, can I? I can't pretend to offer her more than we've already had.

Why would she blow off her ex for a wreck like me? I've got a trade hanging over my head. And if that doesn't blow up in my face, I'm still diving back into another brutal season, hitting the road for a hundred nights this year, and working twice as hard to prove myself again.

And yet I seem to be stuck here in the doorway. My feet won't move to go into my own room, where I haven't slept since the first or second night of this trip.

"Listen, there's something I need to tell you," Vera says. She folds a towel with nervous fingers and sets it down. Then she lifts vulnerable eyes to mine, and my heart stutters.

Come to bed with me. I don't want to end things yet. I think I might love you. These are all the things I'm both hoping and terrified to hear.

But when she opens her mouth, she breaks my heart

instead. "I called the police when your party got loud. It was me."

"What?" It's so unexpected that I'm not sure I heard correctly.

"I'm sorry," she whispers. "If I had to do it again, I wouldn't."

"But *why?*" It comes out sounding harsh. Anger flares inside me. "Seriously, why? If I had a problem with your party, I'd just knock on your door and say so."

"I know you would." She looks stricken. "I'm sorry. I never meant for it to cause you all kinds of trouble."

"Fine. I see." There's a heavy feeling behind my ribs where my heart used to beat. "Just had to get that off your chest?"

"I'm *sorry*," she repeats. "I really am."

I nod like a wooden marionette. "Yeah, okay. Good night."

She flinches. "Don't *go*," she says. "Let's talk about this."

"Let's not," I say stiffly. "Talking isn't what you asked of me anyway, right?"

"*Ian*," Vera gasps.

"Forget it. Don't worry about it. Good night." That's when I finally leave the bathroom, closing the door behind me with an abrupt click. The untouched bed is waiting for me, so I turn down the covers and climb in, punching the pillow and flopping onto my back.

The plaster ceiling looks back at me. I lie beneath it, feeling mad at the world. My anger is like a warm cloak around me, keeping me warm. Vera shouldn't have called the police. That's a bullshit thing to do.

And how could Vera—the person who's made me feel more alive than I have in a long time—be the one who caused me so much distress?

She didn't, barks a voice in my head. *You did it to yourself, asswipe. Should'na had such a loud party. Shouldn't expect a hundred and ten pound female to feel comfortable asking a bunch of rowdy athletes to shut up.*

He makes a few good points.

Oh, and you shouldn't've hit that rookie from Boston so hard. That's your real problem. And if you don't man up and go see that kid, you're the biggest pussy who ever lived. Wait—no. You're a coward. Pussy is too good a' word for you.

My conscience has a potty mouth. But I know it's all true.

I roll over in bed a few times, trying to fall asleep, but it's no use. I grab my phone and note the time. It's one in the morning here, but back in New York it's only dinner hour. I dial the damn PR guy.

"Hey, Mr. Crikey. Is this an emergency?" Tommy asks when he answers.

"Not at all. You need me to call back?"

"No, no. Just making sure I didn't need to find you some bail money."

He chuckles, but I don't find it the least bit funny. "I'm calling because I want to take you up on that idea of visiting the guy with the, uh, badly broken collarbone."

"*Oh.*" There's a pregnant pause. "Wonderful. I'll reach out, and we'll set that up."

Except now I wonder if he knows something I don't. Right this minute he could be drafting a press release about trading me to Vegas. "And I picked two charities," I add. "If you want to know what they are."

"Great! Yeah. Just grabbing a pen. Okay, shoot."

"I'd like to teach one of those soccer clinics that O'Doul did last year. Maybe I can even get his retired ass to help me."

"Nice," he says. "Good call. What's the other one? You might not have time for both."

"It will be fine, because I only want to make a financial donation to the other one. It's the, uh, Look Good Feel Nice one. Whatever that thing is called. My friend is involved—she says they do good work. They helped her grandmother."

"Got it. That's a nice way to honor her grandmother. I'll get you the information."

"Thanks," I grunt. "You take care."

We hang up, and I listen to the silence for a moment. The villa is so quiet at night. And when I close my eyes, I picture Vera in her dress at the opera, smiling as the stage lights reflect on her pretty face.

I can also feel the weight of her sleepy head on my shoulder in the van on the way back. And remember the scent of her cologne.

This trip was everything. I needed to get out of Brooklyn and get out of my head. Spending time with her turned into something so special that I can barely stand to give it up.

Except I know in my gut that I don't deserve that girl right now. And maybe I never will. Tomorrow I'm going back to New York, where I'm going to have to face every problem I've created for myself. It won't be easy.

I lift my phone again and hit O'Doul's number this time.

"Hey," he says after only one ring. "Still no news."

"I know," I say with a sigh. "Just wanted to tell you that I'm gonna visit that rookie in Boston. I'm going to tell him how sorry I am that he got hurt."

There's a beat of silence on the line. "That's real brave, man. But I think it will help you."

"Yeah." I clear my throat. "I also think maybe I might be depressed."

Patrick whistles. "You think maybe?"

"Well, uh…" I clear my throat again. "I am. It's not, uh, super bad. But it's not great, either. I'm still having those dreams sometimes."

"Are you finally gonna tell Doc Mulvey about 'em?"

"Yeah, sure," I say, feeling sheepish. "Not sure why that matters."

"Just try it," O'Doul presses. "It's like… you tell him, and you just feel different afterwards. Instead of cramming it all inside you. Shit looks different when you say it out loud."

"All right. Fine," I say, capitulating.

"You come home tomorrow afternoon?"

"Yeah."

"I'll text him. I'll make you an appointment."

"Okay, sure." He's probably thinking I'll blow it off if I have the chance.

He might be right.

We hang up, and the last person I text is my mom. I tell her I RSVP'd to the wedding and that I'll see here there.

That wedding is just another hurdle to jump. I'll show up and clap at all the right times and smile when I'm expected to.

But I don't have to like it.

That done, I finally close my eyes. And when I do, I see Vera's bright smile on the backs of my eyelids.

THE NEXT DAY we're all a bit quiet as we prepare to leave the villa behind.

"The end of a vacation is hard," Charli says as I carry my suitcase downstairs.

"It is," I agree. I'm peeved to see that Vera has already carried her extensive luggage downstairs without my help. She's chatting with Fiona and Aly while we wait for the limos.

And she's ignoring me, which I probably deserve.

She ducks me on the jet, too, passing right by me to sit at the table in back with Anton and Sylvie.

I wonder if she's taken her anxiety medication.

I wonder if she's scared.

But it's not my turn to help her anymore. I don't get to hold her. I gave that up last night by acting like a prick. So I take a seat alone.

Drake's fancy jet has wifi. I spend the flight alternately watching old *Mission Impossible* movies and checking my phone for news of the trade.

When we land, my whole body is stiff. I open Uber to get a

car, then swivel around to look for Vera. "Hey, want to share a cab?"

"I'm going with Sylvie and Anton," she chirps without making eye contact. "But thanks."

My friends all give me the side-eye like I'm radioactive. "What happened there?" Drake asks under his breath.

"I was a dick," I grumble. "But we weren't a serious thing, anyway."

"Hmm," he says. "If you apologize, maybe you *could* be a serious thing."

"Doubt it." I plan to apologize when I get the chance. But not before I make a few necessary changes.

I get into my Uber alone. We're crossing the George Washington Bridge when my phone starts pinging with texts. My stomach drops as I pull it out to look. *Three-way Trade Changes the Face of Bruisers Hockey*, reads the first headline I see.

With my heart in my mouth, I click on it.

I read the article three times through before I remember to breathe. There are two of my teammates' names in that article. But mine isn't there.

My exhale is full of relief. A huge bullet dodged.

So why do I not feel happy?

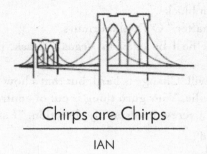

THIRTY

Chirps are Chirps

IAN

"A LITTLE TO THE LEFT," I say, squinting into the space between the wall and the back of the TV we're hanging. "There," I say when O'Doul and I have it lined up just right. "That's it."

We both ease our hands off the TV and step back to admire our work. "Nice," he says. "This place looks great with the furniture in it."

"Thanks for your help, man. Want a sandwich? The jetlag had me up at four in the morning, so I ordered groceries."

"Nah, I'm good. Let's hook up your speakers now. It'll be awesome when it's done."

I pick up the box of cables and set them on my coffee table. "I appreciate the help, but there's probably somewhere else you're supposed to be."

O'Doul plucks a coil of speaker wire from the table and shrugs. "Not really."

"Look, I'm all right," I tell him, suspecting that his help today has more to do with me telling him I'm depressed than with my home-movie setup. "You don't have to do this."

"I know you're okay," he says, poking at one of my speakers. "But this is what we do. I'm pretty sure you and I installed Ivo's

TV when he rented my place. And now we're gonna uninstall it for him when he moves out next week."

He's not wrong. "Kid was a long way from home, though. I only moved ten blocks."

"Doesn't matter," O'Doul murmurs.

"You think he'll be okay in Vegas?" I ask, picking up the other speaker.

"Yeah, he will. Change is hard, but that's how we grow."

"Fuck, Doulie. Your guru thing is out of control."

He points a screwdriver in my direction. "I said that just to make you cringe."

"It worked."

He grins. "Any final thoughts on the captain appointment?"

"Not now, man. I don't want to choose. I already have survivor's guilt over this trade."

O'Doul laughs. "Fair enough. I think I know who I want in that seat anyway."

"Don't tell me, so I don't have to try to act surprised when I hear it."

"I wasn't going to."

The doorbell buzzes, and the effect it has on me is strange. I immediately think *Vera*, and then feel a lift inside my chest. It's been a constant struggle not to think about her. And as I nearly trip myself sprinting for the buzzer box, I realize I'm failing.

But who else would arrive at my door?

I press the button. "Hello?"

"Hey Ian, it's Doc Mulvey."

My head swivels to O'Doul, who already looks sheepish. "Oh, did I forget to mention that your appointment is today?"

I press the button that unlocks the door, but I also glare at my teammate. "That's a dick move, Doulie."

"Is it?" He gives me a smirk. "Easier than hounding you to lock in an appointment. Later." He heads for the door, greeting the shrink in the hallway on his way out.

That's how I find myself standing in the middle of my living room, trying to hide my scowl as Doc Mulvey strolls in wearing khakis and a polo shirt. He's the least intimidating man in the world. He's a nice enough guy, but I still don't really want to talk to him.

"Didn't know you made house calls," I say grumpily, closing the door behind him.

"It's nice to get out of the office sometimes. This is a great apartment. Did I hear you're working on it yourself?"

"I did the dumb-guy work—sanding and painting. I can hold a paintbrush as well as anyone. But I hired contractors for the electric and the plumbing. Want a soda?"

"Sure. Thanks."

I get two drinks from the kitchen, but then the conversation stalls. After sitting down, I take a sip of my drink and fidget while he makes himself comfortable.

"Mr. Crikey, you and I talk several times a year. This is no different."

"Isn't it? Usually, we're talking about sports psychology. Maintaining my focus and all that. But nobody wants to hear a professional athlete whine about his nightmares."

"We're here to talk about your focus and well-being, same as always. It's just that you happen to be struggling a little bit right now. And Ian, everybody struggles. It's how you face it that makes you who you are. I can tell you for sure that ignoring your problems is a crappy strategy."

"All right," I grunt.

"So tell me how long you've felt unsteady. Patrick says you're having trouble sleeping. Has this happened all season?"

"No way." I shake my head. "It started in the spring. After that, uh, incident."

"Define *incident*."

"You know the one." This is what I don't like about shrinks. They don't let you get away with anything. "I sent a player to the hospital. He's had—what—three surgeries already? And he's not coming back."

"You feel responsible."

"Of course I do."

"Let me ask you this—have you ever gotten hurt by another player in a game?"

"Yeah, but that's different. I've been punched. I've even broken a bone. But I've never been hurt so bad as I hurt that kid."

"Why do you think it happened like that?"

I take a deep drink of my soda to stall for time. The man has only been in my apartment for five minutes, and he's found the thing that I least want to talk about. "I don't really know what happened. I have relived that moment so many times."

"Try," he says quietly. "What do you remember about that night?"

"Well, the kid skates up to me…"

"No, before that. What kind of a night were you having? Was this a home game?"

"Yeah. It wasn't really a special day. I went to morning skate. Came home. Went through the mail…" I stall out.

"The mail," he prompts. "And?"

I sigh, because I know he's gonna make a big thing of this. "There was a wedding invitation. My ex is marrying my second cousin. I don't really want to go to the wedding. But we broke up a few years ago. It's not exactly a big deal."

"And why did the two of you break up?"

"Um…" I let out a strained chuckle. "She grew out of me. Thought the whole tough-guy thing was attractive in high school, I guess. But then she decided she wanted a slick guy. The kind of guy who looks good in a suit, standing at a podium or working the room. And in the end, she chose my second cousin." I shrug.

"Did that make you mad?"

"Well, sure. But like I said, this all went down years ago. Having to go to the wedding is just sort of, as they say, insult to injury."

He nods. "And later that night—after you opened this invitation—you gave somebody a real injury."

"You know I did."

"Tell me about the fight. Did you know you were going to fight this guy? Did you prep for it?"

"No way." I snort. "I watched some video of that team's veteran enforcer. But I'd never seen this rookie before. No idea why he took the fight. I've been asking myself that ever since."

"He just comes up to you out of the blue and throws down his gloves?"

I try to think. "We'd just drawn a penalty against their guy. So it wasn't completely unmotivated."

"Who drew the penalty?" the doctor asks.

"Um…" I search my memory and come up blank. "I forget. Sorry. It wasn't a big deal. Just a Thursday night in hockey, you know?"

He nods. "Go on."

"Yeah, so…" I feel a tightness in my chest, and the words don't come as easily as they should. "He comes up to me at the end of the second period. He says something kind of obnoxious to me. I ask if he's challenging me to a fight. He throws down his gloves. And the crowd starts doing their thing. Yelling. Whistling."

"What does that feel like?" the doc asks. "When the crowd starts up?"

My face feels hot all of a sudden. It's like I'm there hearing the fans snarl. "They sound angry. Always. It's a rush, knowing I have everybody's attention. I always feel really… alive. Even though I'm also kind of nervous I might lose. But not because I'm afraid of the pain."

"No? The pain would matter a great deal to *me*."

I shake my head, my throat dry. I still feel hot and strange. "It's the dread. The moment when you realize you're the one who's gonna end up on the ground. That span of time is short, but it's the worst feeling in the world."

"You didn't end up on the ground this time, did you?"

Another shake of my head. "No. We danced around for a minute. I had trouble getting a grip on that kid. He was fast, but his reach wasn't as long as mine. I was getting frustrated. And he kept up with the chirps..."

Ugh.

"What were the chirps? Do you remember?"

I swallow. "Yeah, but it shouldn't make a difference. Chirps are chirps. That kid didn't know me from Adam."

"What, though?" the shrink presses. "Did he say, 'I heard your ex is marrying your cousin'?"

I laugh, because it's so ridiculous. "He said, 'You're old and fucking slow. No wonder the women don't want you.'" My heart starts to pound as I raise my eyes to the doc's. Because that lame-ass chirp practically made me lose my mind. "I mean, a fourth-grader could do better."

"But this isn't a playground, right?"

"No." I shake my head. "He was trying to bait me. It worked, and I hit him hard. Twice. Got lucky to land the left lead to his jaw. His head snapped back, so the right cross landed here." I stop and press a hand against my own collarbone, as if testing its strength. "And I felt it go. It just...*popped*." Reliving that awful moment makes me visibly shudder. "He went down so hard. Like instantly. His head bounced off the ice, his helmet flew off..." I stop and breathe, tasting bile at the back of my throat.

Doc nudges my soda toward me on the coffee table. "Then what happened?"

I gulp my drink for a moment and pull myself together. "They took him off on a stretcher, and he was vomiting blood in the locker room before the ambulance came. Someone said maybe a bone fragment caused internal bleeding. He might have died."

The shrink sits back in his chair. "Ian, that is a really bad day at the office, don't get me wrong. But this guy skated up to you, insulted you, and asked you to fight him. And that same thing happens at every rink on the continent."

"Yeah, but how often does it end like *that?* I must have lost my mind out there, Doc. Or else I have fucking terrible luck. How do I figure out which it is?"

And what if it happens again? That's the scariest question of all.

Doc studies me with kind eyes. "The fact that his injury bothers you says important things about you. You're allowed to feel however you feel. But you're never getting a note from God, Ian. Perfect clarity is too lofty a goal."

"Yeah, yeah."

"That doesn't mean you can't find some peace, though. It happened, and we can't change that. But you're sitting here, doing the work, asking the hard questions. You're struggling with yourself. None of this is easy. But the next time you come up against a fight, this work you're doing will make you better able to handle it."

"Hope so," I grit out.

"How often do you have these dreams about the fight?"

"I had a lot of 'em during the playoffs. Had one last night, too. But Italy was better."

"Interesting." He folds his hands over his knee. "What was different in Italy?"

One word: Vera. "Well, I wasn't alone. Lots of friends around. But also…" My chuckle is awkward. "I hung out with a great woman. But then I screwed that up, too."

His face fills with empathy. "Did you tell her about the dreams?"

"No way." I shake my head. "Nobody wants to hear about that."

"Hmm." It's the sound of someone who's about to tell you something you don't want to hear. "In my experience, no relationship can survive without the truth. You know what Ari tells you guys in yoga class—no mud, no lotus."

"People love that expression," I grumble.

223

"Maybe because it's true," he says.

BY THE TIME the doctor leaves, my eyes are drooping. Who knew the truth was so exhausting? I stretch out on my sofa to take a nap, but after just a minute or so, somebody rings the doorbell.

Just like before, I leap up, excited by the possibility that Vera has come to see me. I buzz the visitor in, sight unseen.

But it's not Vera. It's a stranger bearing a garment bag. "Sign here, please."

"What is this?" I ask as he hands me the pen.

"Delivery from Peter Tailor's Menswear."

I take the bag and unzip it the moment he leaves. Inside is a beautiful gray suit in a lightweight wool, a crisply ironed white shirt, and a tie finely striped in blue and a peach color.

There's also a note:

DEAR IAN,

I promised you suits.

Perhaps you'd rather not work with me on fashion anymore, but I know you have a wedding to attend this weekend, so I'm sending you this ensemble in your size.

Once again, I'm sorry for having called the police. It seemed reasonable at the time.

And I just want you to know how much I enjoyed spending time with you in Italy. Maybe we don't have much in common (and the way you load a dishwasher is still all kinds of wrong), but you made me smile so many times, and I will always be grateful.

V.

I GRAB my phone off the coffee table and pull up her number. In the first place, I need to make my own apology, because she deserves one. Second, I need to thank her for the suit, which was a kindness I don't deserve.

But as my thumb hovers above the Call button, I stop myself. If I call her right now, there's a decent chance I'll ask her to reconsider going to that gala with her ex.

And that's not fair. She deserves to attend that thing with an open heart.

Truly, I'm dreading this Saturday night. Not only will I be at my ex's wedding, but it's going to kill me to know she's out there in some killer dress spending the evening on another man's arm.

And who gave her pointers on how to seduce him afterwards? Me. I did that.

Fuck my life. What the hell was I thinking?

So instead of calling her—which would probably lead to me begging her not to go anywhere with that asshole—I go into my bedroom and dictate a note on my computer.

Then I spell-check it. I'm just about ready to print it out when I realize I could add a photo.

I'm too lazy to put on the whole suit, so I make do with the shirt and the tie. When it comes time to pose, I get a little creative.

She might still choose the banker over me. But I'm not going down without a fight.

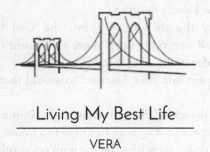

THIRTY-ONE

Living My Best Life

VERA

August

ON FRIDAY I check the mail. In addition to the usual bills, I find that someone has slipped a folded letter into my box. When I notice that it's from Ian, my heart beats a little bit faster.

Hey V—

The suit is great. Thank you so much.

If I never told you this before, you're a generous and helpful person. I don't deserve this favor, but I am going to wear it anyway. You do amazing work. And if anyone asks me where I got it, I'm giving him your number.

Be well. Have fun this weekend. I miss you already.

I.

There's a photo printed below the note—and it's a thirst trap! Sure, the shirt and tie are in the photo. Barely. Ian is leaning against his bed with the shirt unbuttoned. The tie is strung around his shoulders, as if he's too sexy to actually put it on. And his eyes look out at me, full of sexy heat.

Damn that man. Damn his hurtful attitude on our last night in Italy.

Damn his sweet thank-you note.

I fold the letter again so I don't have to look at it and shove it to the bottom of my stack of mail.

I can't let him get into my head. Tomorrow night is the gala, and in a short while, I'm meeting Danforth in Manhattan to deliver his new tuxedo shirt. Not that it's convenient. But Danforth asked nicely. He also told me to bring him a short stack of business cards, so that he'd have them at his office in case anyone might need a stylist.

It's promising enough to get me on the subway even at the end of a busy week. After putting on a very carefully selected outfit, I hustle onto the train for a two o'clock coffee meeting at Danforth's Park Avenue office tower.

When I reach the marble lobby, I hand over my ID. They give me a visitor's pass and direct me to the 14th floor.

In the elevator, I check my makeup in the shiny steel doors. My daytime smoky eye is in full force. I'm wearing a plain black Burberry dress that I bought with my employee discount right before I quit the department store. And a pair of bright red patent-leather heels that my grandmother would have loved. My lipstick matches my shoes, and my hair is swept up into an elegant twist.

I'm strangely nervous, though. As if I were marching off to an important audition.

When the elevator doors part, I step out. My heart leaps to find Danforth waiting there beside the reception desk. Then it leaps again when he gives me a big smile.

I used to do anything for that smile.

Please, my inner voice chirps. *Like you wouldn't now?*

"V! You look beautiful today." He kisses my cheek hello, like the debonaire man that he is.

"Thank you." I return his smile. "It's been a busy day running around, trying to make all my clients happy." I hand over the garment bag I've brought.

"Oh, I bet. Thank you for this." He crosses the reception

area to a coat closet and deposits the shirt inside. "Now let's get some coffee. There's a cafeteria down on the tenth floor."

Well, it's not exactly the cozy sit-down I'd envisioned. But he's probably very busy.

In the cafeteria, Danforth uses his corporate ID to pay for two cups of coffee before leading me to a table by the window.

We sit down on opposite sides of the table. When he lifts his coffee cup, I marvel at how familiar his hands are to me, with their long, elegant fingers. We used to hold hands on all our many dates across the city.

Danforth is objectively handsome. His skin is a warm, coppery brown, and he has thick black hair and a model's bright smile. He's a lovely blend of his Pakistani mother and his Italian father.

"How's your nonna?" I ask. He has one of those, too.

"Good, good," he says. "How's yours?"

I blink. "She *died*, Danny. A year after you left. You sent me a card."

"Oh God!" His eyes widen. "Of course she did. I'm sorry, V." He sounds genuinely horrified to have forgotten.

But yikes. I guess he didn't spend nearly as much time thinking about me as I did him after he left.

And you're surprised about this?

Well, no.

"How's business?" he asks now. "Do you like making your own hours?"

"I do, except I think I'm working twice as hard. Oh! The cards." I pull my stack of business cards from my bag and set them in front of him.

He lifts the top one and smiles at the line drawing of a necktie. "This is really cute. Nice look."

"I did it myself. See?" I reach over and flip the card, so he can see there's a drawing of a dress on the opposite side. "Something for everyone."

"Good branding," he says cheerfully. "Can we talk about the gala? My department took a table for ten — five couples."

"Of course. Tell me who's important."

He pulls out a card where he's written down everyone's name. "Arnold Kretcher is the head of my department."

"So if I spill my drink, make sure it's not on him?"

Danforth looks startled. "God, no."

While maintaining eye contact, I reach across the table and squeeze his forearm. "That's a joke, Dan. Relax." Then I give him a sexy smile.

My ex blinks. Then, slowly, he smiles. And it lights up his face. "I've missed you, Vera. I forgot how funny you are."

I feel like doing cartwheels.

WE SIT THERE and talk longer than either of us expected. Until Danforth's phone chirps. He checks it, then makes a sad face. "Aw, crap. I have a meeting in ten minutes. I'm sorry."

"Hey, it's all good." I push my chair back and pick up our empty cups. "I have a million things to do, anyway."

He walks me slowly in the direction of the elevator bank. "Hell, Vera. It's been fun catching up with you. I'm glad we get to do this again tomorrow."

Okay, here goes nothing. My heart starts to hammer, but Operation Seduction has to start now.

I step closer to Danforth, putting a brave hand in the middle of his chest, right over his Ferragamo tie. "I'm off now. But I expect a slow dance tomorrow night."

Then I lick my lips.

The whole performance is ridiculously suggestive. For a panicky moment, I wonder if he'll laugh at me.

But he doesn't. Instead, I watch with fascination as his eyes land on my mouth. Then he licks his lips, too. "Yeah, about that dance. I can't wait."

And I'm stunned at my own power. I can do this. It's not even that hard.

But then I remember Ian's first lesson. *Seduction is about anticipation.* I take a step backward, leaving Danforth wanting more. "Just wait until you see my new dress," I say with a slow smile. "It's *perfect.*"

His eyes go a little darker, and his chuckle is low and gravelly. "I can't wait for that, too."

I close the distance to the elevator bank and press the button. "Text me where I should meet up with you."

"Of course." He gives me a big, hot smile—the *exact* smile I'd been hoping to get from him when he walked back into my life.

Wow. This is it. It's *working.*

"Later, Dan." I swing my hips with a little extra mojo as I step into the elevator. I manage to give him a cheeky wave before the doors slide closed.

There we go. I've dropped the bait in the water, and tomorrow night I'll reel in my catch.

And then you should throw it back into the lake, my inner voice whispers.

I shush her and make my way home.

SATURDAY IS DEVOTED TO PRIMPING.

First, I sleep in for the first time since we got back from Italy. Then I go to a yoga class, which I follow up with a leisurely bubble bath.

Both the yoga *and* the bath remind me of Ian. It's hard to avoid thoughts of him today. He's probably on his way to Connecticut for that wedding. Maybe he's even dressed in the suit I chose for him.

Thoughts of him are a bit like a bruise that's slow to heal. It hurts, but there's no use crying over it. I have to move on.

Whether it's with Danforth or someone else, my needs are the same—I need a man who's ready to love me. And Ian isn't that man.

After my bath, I meet Charli at a salon where we treat ourselves to blowouts in adjacent chairs. "I even sat still for a manicure last night," she says. "Be proud of me."

"Oh, I am," I assure her.

As soon as our hair looks glamorous, we head to my place. Charli does my makeup before she leaves to do her own. "See you at six? We'll pick you up."

"Can't wait," I assure her. "I got a bottle of prosecco for the ride. Do I need to bring glasses?"

"Nope. They have them in the limo." She rolls her eyes. "That car is ridiculous."

"Surprised you noticed the glasses," I tease her, because Charli once confided in me that she and Neil got carried away in the back of that limo one night.

"You shut up."

I cackle as she leaves. But then it's time to get as beautiful as I can possibly be. Sexy strapless bra? Check. Matching panties? Check. Not to mention that I'm waxed and shaved and plucked and perfumed. My nails are polished—fingers and toes.

It's go time. With nervous fingers, I unzip the red dress and remove it from its satin hanger. When I'd tried it on in Switzerland, I'd thought it was perfect. Magical, even. The kind of dress that could transform me into the woman I need to be for this event.

Carefully, I step into the dress and ease it up my body. The fabric has a pleasantly dry hand, and luckily the zipper isn't too hard to reach. A partner's assistance would come in handy right about now. I wiggle the zipper up to the middle of my back, then switch to an overhead grip to pull it the last few inches.

I adjust the straps on my shoulders, hold my breath, and then step in front of my three-way mirror.

And *wow*. My memory hadn't even done this dress justice.

It's *perfect*—the cut is flattering, and the fit is divine. The color brings out the warmth in my Italian skin tone.

This is the magic of finding the perfect style—I've achieved for myself what I'm always trying to do for my clients.

Naturally, I take a few selfies for Instagram. It would be a shame to waste this hairdo and this moment. Even if I'm not living my best life, I'm living my most photogenic one.

Then I take one more pic, this time for Danforth. It shows a cropped view of my face and one shoulder strap's worth of the dress. It teases. You can see that my lipstick is a perfect match for my dress, but you can't see the whole effect.

"Seduction requires anticipation," I whisper, hitting Send.

I swear to God the phone rings three seconds later. It's Danforth, of course. "Hey, V. That picture is *fire*."

"Isn't it?" I agree lightly. "Are you ready? New tux shirt okay?"

"Terrific work, as always."

"Thanks. I'll see you outside just before seven, unless there's a traffic catastrophe."

"Perfect," he says. "Oh, and V? I need one little favor."

"Hmm?"

"At the gala tonight, I need you to introduce me to Neil Drake."

"Neil Drake," I repeat slowly, as a strange prickly feeling finds the back of my neck. "Why?"

"He's on the board of the solar initiative," Danforth explains. "I expect he'll be at the gala. It would be a real coup if I could get a meeting with him. He invests in several different energy technologies."

I think back to the conversation I'd had with Danforth in this very apartment. I'd talked about my trip to Italy. I'd probably dropped Neil's name when I mentioned the villa.

And a few minutes after that, Danforth had invited me to this gala.

"Oh," I say.

Ohhhhhhhhhh, my inner voice says. *Well, of course. You really should have seen that coming.*

I hadn't, though.

Wow. I really am an idiot.

"You *do* know him, right?" Danforth asks. "Didn't you just go to Italy with the guy?"

"Of course, I did." I swallow hard. "He's picking me up in half an hour."

"Score, babe. Well done. Great networking."

"But..." My heart trembles. "Did you ask me to the gala just so you could meet him?"

There's a telling pause. "Don't be like that," he says after a beat. "I definitely want to meet the billionaire. He could change the whole path of my career. But that's how we roll, V. We're ambitious. I took a stack of your business cards because you want to expand your clientele. And I want to expand mine. You're the one who used to say we were going to become a power couple. This is how it's done."

"Right," I say, although my throat feels tight.

He's right. I used to say that very thing. It's just that I cared more about the *couple* part of that phrase than the *power.* And I still do.

"See you soon," he says. "Can't wait to see more of that dress."

"Yes," I say woodenly. "See you soon."

I hang up the phone and tuck it away in my clutch bag. I step in front of my mirror again and study the full effect.

The dress is still magic. I can live my best life tonight. I can draw eyes from across the room.

It's just that I think I picked the wrong room.

THIRTY-TWO

Pink Stuff on a Cracker

IAN

DISCREETLY HIDING my phone behind my beer, I tap out a text. *My cheeks hurt from smiling. They literally hurt. That's how pleasant I've been today.*

Drake must be bored at his gala, because he replies almost immediately. *Maybe you just don't use those muscles enough. We can work on that in the gym.*

He adds a biceps emoji, and I snort.

My mother gives me an elbow to the ribs. "Put away your phone. That's rude."

"Ma, I've been on my best behavior going on twelve hours now." Actually, it's only been three hours. But it feels like twelve when you're at your ex's wedding, and the girl you really want is on a dream date with someone else. "You know, they shouldn't be able to call it a cocktail 'hour' if it goes on forever. Are you sure they're planning to serve actual food at some point?"

"Here, try one of these." She passes me a tiny plate, and I eye the hors d'oeuvre with suspicion.

Pink stuff on a cracker. "What is this, anyway?"

"Salmon pâté en croûte."

I shove one of them into my mouth. "It's tasty, but I prefer when my food doesn't look pre-chewed."

My father laughs so suddenly that he chokes on his white wine, and now it's his turn to get my mother's evil eye. I check my messages again.

Drake: Aren't you going to ask how my night is going?

Crikey: You're the one who had to put on a tux, so I already know how that's going.

At least I'm comfortable. As usual, the clothes that Vera picked out for me are tasteful and suited to my fabric issues.

I hope she found my thank-you note.

And I hope she spent a long time looking at the photo.

Drake: I thought you'd be asking me how Vera's date is going.

Crikey: I don't want to know. But after I send that, I get worried. *Why? Did something happen to her?*

Drake: She's fine. And I met the guy. He introduced himself to me.

Crikey: All right, I'll bite. Is he an okay guy?

Drake: He's smart. Polished. Firm handshake. Your basic nightmare.

When I laugh loudly, my mother sighs. "I have the best friends, Mom."

"I'm so glad," she grumbles. "But put away your phone."

But I don't, because it rings. *Drake calling*. I answer the call while walking hastily to the edge of the ocean-view terrace and hiding behind a potted topiary. "What's up, man?"

"Just checking up on you, my friend. I know you're hung up on Vera even if you won't say so."

"What's there to say?" I argue. "She wants another chance with her ex. I was just the stand-in. And not a very good one, if I'm honest."

"I guess I don't understand why the two of you aren't together tonight."

"I tried, man. I invited her to this wedding, but she declined."

"That is a tough break." Drake sighs.

"You bored or something? I thought you were supposed to be dancing with your lovely wife right now."

"Oh, I will be after they serve dinner. I'm starving."

"Same."

"At least you can get drunk," Neil says. "To that end, I'm sending you a little something to help you on your way. It's a very fine bottle of scotch."

"What? Dude, I'm not even home."

"I know that. It's coming to you at the wedding. Aren't you at the Belle Haven Boat Club? I'll text you when my driver pulls up. You just have to run outside and get it."

"That's a little excessive, man." Christ, I must've been acting more depressed than I thought this summer. "I'll take it, though. But I'm okay. I mean that."

"Oh, I know you are. But it's weird attending your ex's wedding."

"Eh, I guess." I peek around the topiary and look for the bride. It's easy enough to find a woman wearing a giant white dress. "She looks good and everything. But I've been over her for a long time. Swear to God. I hope she's happy."

"That's great, man. Look for my text in twenty minutes, okay? Charli's giving me the stink eye to get off the phone."

"I bet. Later, dude. Thanks for everything."

"Glad you're still on my team, Crikey. Call me tomorrow."

"Will do."

AT LONG LAST, they call us inside for dinner, and the crowd begins to slowly funnel through a set of double doors and into a vast dining room overlooking the water.

"How do we find table number sixteen?" my father grumbles. "I'm too weak from hunger to look."

"Follow me," my mother says calmly "I'll save you."

Table sixteen is against the windows overlooking the

marina. I pull out my mother's chair.

"Now isn't this nice?" my mom says, taking her seat.

"So nice," I deadpan. "But is it just me, or is there no food on this table?"

"Patience," my mother says. "They need to announce the bride and groom first."

"Announce them? Didn't we all just watch them get married?" God, I hate pageantry.

My mother just shakes her head.

We're joined by a couple of my cousins and their spouses, and my father strikes up a conversation about Connecticut politics.

I've always been the odd duck at family gatherings. I don't care about politics or business. And besides my father, none of the other Crikeys ever cared for hockey.

"Oh dear, there's an extra place setting," my mother says under her breath. "You really should have told them your date wasn't coming. I'll have them take it away." She raises her hand.

"No," my father and I both say at once, our eyes meeting in silent understanding. What sane man would send extra food away from this table?

"Caterers charge by the head," my mother says quietly. "Saving face is costing the bride and groom money."

I glance toward my ex's father at the head table and realize I don't care that much.

My pocket buzzes, and I pull out my phone to see a text from Drake. *The driver is pulling up now. Enjoy.*

"Excuse me for a quick second," I say to the table as I slide out of my chair and head for the exit. I hurry through a lobby that's decorated with ropes and other boating paraphernalia.

Outside, I see a stretch limo pulling slowly into the curved drive. Hell, it's tempting to flag down Drake's chauffeur and beg the man for a ride back to New York. I've done my duty here. I'd watched my ex pledge her undying love to a man who could not be less like me.

It hadn't even been that difficult, if I'm honest. Closure is real. The wedding was more boring than painful.

The only awkward part was the receiving line, where my ex and I had a brief moment of discomfort while we both tried to decide what was an appropriate greeting for one another. I went for the quick cheek kiss, and she went for the stiff pat on my shoulder.

Whatever. The whole experience makes me feel like one of those barnacle-covered boats in the marina. Sturdier than I imagined and more seaworthy than I knew.

The limo driver gets out and hurries around the front of the vehicle. I lift my hand in a wave, so he'll know I'm the guy he's looking for.

But he doesn't approach me. Instead, he opens the rear door and reaches inside to offer a hand to…

The most beautiful woman I've ever seen. Vera steps out of the limo and straightens up, wearing a stunning red dress and a slightly sheepish smile.

The sight of her lifts a weight off my chest that I didn't even know I was carrying. My reaction is to bend over and brace my hands on my thighs, laughing like a kid at his own surprise party. "Holy hell, contessa. I've never been so excited to see anyone in my life."

"Really?" The uncertainty leaves her smile. "I'm sorry. This…" She waves toward the car. "Was all a little crazy. I was halfway here when I made Neil text you to make sure you hadn't brought another date."

As if there was anyone else I'd want by my side. There isn't, and I'll be sure to tell her that later. First, I cross to her and put my hands on her smooth shoulders. Touching her again is sweet relief. "Wait, contessa. Are you trying to tell me Neil didn't send me a flask of single malt?"

She frowns. "No, that was a ruse…"

I laugh and then don't let her finish that sentence by

planting a very firm kiss on her mouth. "Sorry to tease you. I'm just so fucking happy you're here."

"Is the wedding really that bad?" she asks.

"Fuck no. I just miss you. You look stunning, by the way. Fuck. Do we *have* to go inside?" I'm babbling, and I don't even care.

She stands on her toes and kisses me quickly. "We do, because I put on this dress and came all the way here to be your date for an awkward wedding."

"Fine, fine." I take her hand in mine and lead her back toward the boathouse. "I can at least get you fed before I steal a car and drive you home."

"Steal a car?" She yelps. "Haven't I gotten you arrested enough times this summer already?"

"Aw, honey, that wasn't your fault. I'm sorry I was a dick about it. I've been going through some stuff." We're in the lobby now, but I stop once more to take both of her hands. "You are the only good thing that happened to me this summer. And I screwed it all up, because I wasn't ready to meet you."

She tilts her head and considers me. "Are you ready now? Because you're the best thing that happened to me this summer, too. Even if it took me kind of a long time to admit it."

"Baby, you say the nicest things." I lean down and kiss the juncture of her neck and shoulder. "And let me repeat my praise for this dress. If this is what shopping is for, I get it now."

She laughs, her hand warm against my shirt, her breath at my ear.

"But, baby—" I make myself take a step backwards, because I still don't understand how I got so lucky. "I'd been planning to go see you next week to explain myself. I waited because I thought you needed to go through with that gala with what's-his-fuck. How'd you end up here?"

She winces. "Danforth is not very happy with me right now."

I just bet.

THIRTY-THREE

I'm Good at My Job, What Can I Say?

VERA

"WAS IT BAD?" he asks me. "Are you okay?"

When I look up into Ian's clear eyes, my heart exhales. It was a crazy decision I made to ditch Danforth and show up here. I'm not usually so impulsive. I didn't even know for sure that I'd be welcome.

But Ian and I aren't finished with each other. Not even close.

"I'm okay," I tell him. "In the limousine—on the way into Manhattan—I had a little bit of a freak-out, though." My plan to make Danforth want me back had suddenly felt ridiculous. "It was a shock to realize that Danforth was *never* the right guy for me. It's hard to admit that those three years I spent hoping he would come back were a big waste of time."

"We've all been there," Ian says, his hand a soothing presence on my elbow. The man looks terrific in the suit I picked out for him. That tie makes his eyes look even bluer.

I'm good at my job. What can I say?

"My timing still sucked," I continue. "I realized too late that I was in the car on the way to the wrong event. Charli and Neil calmed me down and told me to take the car to Connecticut. Neil looked up the address and set the whole thing in motion.

When we got to the Met, I had to tell Danforth that I wasn't staying..."

I swallow hard, because that had been an ugly three minutes. Danforth hadn't been gracious at all. I hadn't expected him to be happy, but the things he said were nasty. He'd been red in the face and called me a *vengeful bitch*.

I'm not telling Ian that part, because he'll just get angry. Neil and Charli hadn't heard about it either.

"He said it was a waste of a thousand dollars, and that I was making him look bad. The first thing is silly, because it's for charity. But the second thing is probably true. He said he was embarrassed to go in there and sit down next to an empty plate with my name on it."

Ian laughs suddenly. "I don't see how that's embarrassing at all. He's thinking about this all wrong. Now let's go eat some wedding food, so I can dance with you and then take you home."

"Okay." I grab his hand and give it another squeeze. "Lead the way."

He doesn't, though. His gaze grows hot and lazy, and he leans down to give me a soft kiss.

At least, I think that's what he meant it to be. But Ian's touch flips a switch inside me that only he has ever found. I'm compelled to rise up on my tiptoes and kiss him back. I wrap my arms around his neck and show him how much I missed him.

He makes a happy, sexy noise and pushes me up against a door. I lean back, tilting my chin up so he can kiss me even more deeply.

We spend the next several minutes reminding ourselves how good it always was between us. And why we should stay together. It turns out that having a spark with someone is a big deal, and I'd been a fool to ignore that idea. Kissing Ian is like coming home.

Until someone clears her throat. "Excuse us for a moment? You two are blocking the door."

We break apart. My knees feel a little weak, and I'm trying to catch my breath as I notice the elegant woman in the big white dress who's interrupted us. And the handsome man in the tuxedo beside her.

Oh God. It's the bride and groom. "Sorry!" I gasp. "And congratulations?"

Ian still hasn't snapped out of it. He's looking at me with lusty eyes that swing ever so slowly towards the other couple. "Oops. Sorry, Jackie. This is Vera. Vera, meet Jackie and my cousin Carson. We were just..." His eyes come back to me again, making an appreciative sweep of my body.

"Glad to see you haven't changed much, Ian," the bride says. But her voice isn't mean—it's completely amused. "Still as inappropriate as always. But I really need to get through that door. They can't serve the meal until we show up. You're starving my guests right now, basically."

Ian and I look at each other, and then we both turn at the same time to look at the door. The one we were blocking while we made out like teenagers.

Oh my God.

"Welp, all right," Ian says. His lips twitch as he wraps an arm around my waist and sweeps me aside. "Sorry for the inconvenience."

The groom buries a smile, too. He reaches past his wife and pulls the door open. "Tell you what—why don't you two take a seat? Just let the wedding planner know we're ready."

"Sure!" I say brightly. "Will do!" With my hand clasped around Ian's, I pull him towards the open door. "Nice to meet you both!"

"Likewise," the bride says with a smile. "And that's a *great* dress."

"Thanks!" I say, my smile pasted on. "Yours too! Love the portrait neckline. And that beading is top notch."

Ian propels my chattering self through the door. A wedding planner waits inside with her clipboard, looking aggravated. "What's the holdup?" she asks.

"Not a thing. They're ready for you," Ian says. He leads me past her and across a large room full of guests seated at circular tables.

Every single one of them is staring at us, but Ian seems not to notice. He actually whistles as he leads me to a table against the windows. There are two empty seats, and Ian pulls out a chair for me with a flourish. "My lady."

I sit down, and Ian takes the seat beside me. Not two seconds later, a man with a microphone steps onto a little bandstand in the corner. "May I present Jaqueline and Carson Crikey McNeely!"

The room erupts into applause, and we all stand to clap for the bride and groom. Ian's ex and her new husband stride into the room hand in hand as the band plays a jazzy tune.

Everyone takes their seats again as waiters appear from the kitchen with trays of salad. All the wedding guests start talking at once.

Except at our table, where everyone is staring at me, wondering where I came from.

Two of the people gaping at us can only be Ian's parents. His mother recovers first. "My goodness. Ian, did your date make it after all? Or did you coerce a volunteer you found wandering the property?"

"Mom," Ian snorts. "Be nice. It's not Vera's fault that I'm a hot mess. Vera, these are my parents, Evan and Jillian. They're a little uptight today, but they're mostly cool."

"Hello," I say with a quick smile.

"Hello, dear. And I'm *not* uptight," his mother says. Then she winces. "Much."

Ian roars. He leans back in his seat and wraps an arm around me. "I love you anyway, Mom."

A salad lands in front of me, and another one lands in front of Ian. He plucks a bread basket off a passing tray and hands it to me first. "Good timing on your arrival. Right before the food. That's usually my trick."

"What a lovely dress," Ian's mother says. "Wherever did you find it?"

"Vera is a stylist," Ian says, buttering a roll. "She shopped her way across Italy. Professionally, of course."

"And Switzerland," I admit. "That's where I found this dress."

"A stylist!" Mrs. Crikey's eyes light up. "That sounds fascinating."

"Honestly, there are flaps that go down over my ears when she talks about fabric." Ian shrugs and then takes a big bite of bread. He chews. "And somehow she's still perfect for me."

He smiles at me, and it's *exactly* the kind of smile that Neil gives Charli when he's happy to see her. The real kind.

And I know for sure I made the right choice.

THIRTY-FOUR

Category Five Kisses

IAN

I'M DANCING at my ex's wedding. And I think I like it. I have Vera in my arms as the band plays an Ed Sheeran cover, so nothing else matters.

"Your parents are sweet," she says, smiling up at me. "They obviously love you."

"Oh yeah. In their own, irritating way." I kiss her on the temple. "You got the whole meet-the-parents thing over with in a splashy way, didn't you?"

"Crashing a wedding is a pretty hardcore way to do it."

"You were invited, badass. You just didn't RSVP. Mom is big on RSVPing, so I guess that'll be points off your score."

Vera's eyes widen, and I have to laugh. "Kidding, contessa. My mother could not be happier to meet you. She'll go home tomorrow and start bragging to her friends—'Ian is dating someone who knows designers.'"

She smiles. "We are, right? Dating?"

"If I have anything to say about it." I pull her a little closer.

"But you told me you don't date." Her big brown eyes are full of questions.

"I was too grumpy to date. But then I met this chick who doesn't put up with my bullshit. She doesn't seem to care if I hate shopping or if I can't read my emails very fast. She wants to solve problems instead of telling me I don't fit the mold. And I really dig her."

Vera turns her face away suddenly, and I wonder if I fucked up.

"Hey, honey. Look at me. What's wrong?" She turns, and her eyes look wet. "Oh shit, what did I say?"

"Nothing. Gosh. I'm sorry. I'm being silly. But you're right about some things that took me too long to figure out. I think you might be the genius in this relationship."

"What?" I laugh. "Nobody ever accused me of being smart."

"No, you are." She puts her head on my shoulder. "When my ex broke up with me, he did me a favor. But I was so mad, I spent three years wanting him to admit he was wrong about us. But he wasn't. He thought we weren't a good fit, and he was right."

"He didn't have to be mean about it, though," I point out. "He didn't have to take your self-esteem with him when he moved away."

"True, but I amplified it. I was so fixated on that one failure, I couldn't move forward. And you came along and reminded me what it meant to have fun."

"Baby, we will have *all* the fun—although not all the time. My season starts tomorrow, and my schedule is a drag. It's one of the reasons I gave up on dating. Hockey complicates things."

"Don't worry about that," she says softly. "We can make it work. I'm not as high maintenance as my makeup kit makes me look."

"Wow, good thing." The pace of the music picks up, and I turn her around to the beat. "Look, I want to take you home soon, but I drove up here with one of my cousins. We might have to bribe an Uber driver to take us all the way back to the city."

She gives me a slightly confused look. "We don't need Uber. Neil left the limousine with me."

I stop dancing. "You're kidding me right now. It's just out there, waiting for us? Then what are we doing here?"

"We're *dancing*." With a smile, she takes my hand and starts to boogie.

"Oh, you're cute, but I think you're looking at this all wrong." I dance, too, but I dance us toward the door.

"Ian!" She laughs. "We can't just dance out of here."

"Like hell, we can't. Your tutor is still trying to teach you his ways, contessa. We can do whatever we want."

She gives my chest a little shove. "You aren't allowed to leave here without your suit jacket! I spent a lot of time and attention picking out just the right shade of dove-gray to complement your eyes."

"Oh, well, if it complements my eyes. Why didn't you say so?"

I lead her back toward the table, where my folks are having coffee. "Don't you two look nice together," my mother says. "Would you like coffee? I want to hear more about Vera's job."

"Later," I say, grabbing my jacket off the chair. "We're going back to the city. I have a team meeting tomorrow morning."

"Ian, it's rude to leave before—"

"No, it's not," I argue. "Jackie and Carson couldn't be happier. It's a beautiful wedding, and I did my bit. But I haven't seen my girl in a few days, and my life is about to get very busy. So, if you'll excuse us..."

My father stands up and offers Vera his hand. "Lovely to meet you. Perhaps Jillian and I can come into the city sometime soon for a game. We'll have lunch beforehand. I can't wait to see this house that Ian has bought."

"Now that's a plan," I say, clapping my dad on the shoulder. "You'll love the house. And it was Vera who found that lawyer to fix up the whatzit corporation, by the way. Be grateful."

"Oh I am," Dad says, winking at Vera. "I hope you took her out to a nice meal to show your gratitude."

"Something like that." I give Vera a hot look, and she blushes. "Later, folks."

She says goodbye to my parents, and then I walk my girl outside.

"THIS IS A SWEET RIDE," I remark as we snuggle up together on a leather seat at the very back of Neil's slick car. "Although, I wouldn't have guessed Neil had a stretch limo. He likes to fly under the radar."

"This is his mother's. They only borrow it for big parties. And, well..." Vera's eyes sparkle. "It has sentimental value, apparently. Some shenanigans happened in this car."

"Did they, now?" I hug her a little closer. And then I kiss her neck. Several times. Neck kisses are Vera's kryptonite. She can't keep her hands off me when I'm smoochin' her throat.

"Ian," she breathes.

"Yes?" I shift her into my lap, running a finger across the bustline of her killer dress.

"I need something," she whispers, kissing my jaw.

"Do you, now?" I chuckle.

"Yes. I need you to tell me why you've been so upset this summer."

"Oh baby, no. Make out first, talk later." I kiss her shoulder and squeeze her tit.

She slides off my lap and crosses her arms. "Not so fast, big guy. I actually worry about you, whether you want me to or not."

"Aw." I steal a quick kiss. "I've been getting that from a lot of people. But you don't have to worry anymore, because I'm dealin' with it. I hurt a guy last season, and it messed with me."

"Was it in a fight?" Her eyes are worried. "I worry about that, too."

"You shouldn't." I wrap an arm around her again, because I

can't not touch her. "I'm probably going to fight less often going forward. Learned the hard way that it can screw with your head. This fight was different, though. It was like a perfect storm—all my issues making me crazy, and his collarbone in the wrong spot at the wrong time. I've been carrying a lot of guilt, and that was confusing."

"Maybe there's someone you could talk to," she says softly. "Would you ever consider it?"

"I'm a step ahead of you, contessa. The team's head shrinker and I spent some time together—with a few more dates to come in our very near future. Sports doctors are pretty great. They know how to talk to a hard head like me."

Her body relaxes suddenly. "You have no idea how happy I am to hear that. I had some therapy in college, and it was really helpful. I'm so glad your team cares enough about you to provide that."

"They do care. And I'm going to stick with it. I'm also going to visit the kid who I hurt. I want to know how he's doing."

She squeezes my hand. "That sounds hard. Maybe harder than going to your ex's wedding."

"Well, the wedding turned out to be a piece of cake. I've avoided visiting the kid for a long time, but I'm ready now. I want to apologize. He might be really angry still, but I can take it. Ignoring the whole thing isn't working for me."

Vera puts her head against my chest. "I admire you. I don't think I ever said that before, but it's true. I admire your fearlessness."

"Nobody is fearless all the time, contessa." I stroke her hair. "I admire you, too, if you haven't already figured that out."

"I know it. Getting to know you has been educational for me. And not just sexually." She lifts her eyes and smiles at me. "I thought we didn't have anything in common. But I was counting the wrong things. It doesn't matter if you hate shopping, and I hate beer. We both care a lot about our passions, even when the rest of the world tells us we're wasting our time. That's our shared value—resilience."

"You are a smart girl." I pull her into my lap once again. "And I'm feeling extra resilient tonight, if you take my meaning." I shift my hand down her sleek body, my fingertips dragging slowly against the red fabric. "When we get home, I'm gonna help us both get past the *long* week we just had. And the *hard* times. I'm not good at waiting."

"I noticed. Can you believe us back there? Against the door? When the bride and groom couldn't get past us?" She lifts laughing eyes to mine.

"She called me inappropriate." My lips twitch. "But it was just a kiss."

"*Just* a kiss," Vera repeats. "Only because she stopped us. That kiss was gathering steam and heading for hurricane category four."

I raise an eyebrow. "Is that the highest category?"

"I think so," she says. "Maybe there's category five. But they're rare."

"Hold on. You think I'm not capable of a five?"

"Did I say that?" she yelps. "It's not an insult to your manhood."

"My feathers are ruffled," I insist. "You'd better kiss me to make it better." I tilt her chin upwards, bringing her rosebud mouth to mine.

And the kiss I give her is a category six. At least.

THIRTY-FIVE

Was That So Hard?

VERA

IT ONLY TAKES another half an hour to get back to New York. We spend the whole time making out. And if the ride were any longer, we might've rechristened the backseat of this limo.

I'm practically on fire by the time the car turns down our street. "Whose place are we going to?" I ask between kisses.

"Mine," he says firmly. "I want you in my bed."

It's hard to argue with that sentiment. Besides, the walk of shame to my house would only be a few steps away. It's a point in Ian's favor that I should have considered before now.

When the car stops, he's all action—his jacket in one hand, me in the other. He opens the door and helps me onto the sidewalk before the driver can get there.

"Thank you, sir," Ian says without a glance at the guy. "You have a nice day."

As we trot toward Ian's front steps, I notice his friend Patrick sitting on the stoop, as if waiting for Ian.

Oh no. Doesn't that man have better things to do than bother us right now?

Ian doesn't even slow down. With my hand in his, he walks us right past his friend. "Sorry. Can't chat now. Important business."

251

If my face weren't already flushed from all those kisses, it would be now.

"Yeah well. Our meeting is tomorrow. Eight a.m. And I need to talk to you beforehand," O'Doul says to our backs.

"Text me," Ian grunts. Then he's unlocking the door and pulling me inside.

"Isn't that rude?" I ask. "Don't you need to talk to him?"

"No, he gets it. Shh," Ian says. "I'm going to kiss you up against this door now, and nobody better dare interrupt me."

And then he does.

IAN'S PLACE has furniture now, and I approve—particularly of a giant bed I can see from where I'm standing in his living room.

We've only made it about twenty feet into the apartment in fits and starts. Somewhere along the way, we've shed his tie and his jacket, my purse, and all of my hair pins. And now I'm working on the buttons of his new shirt.

"As much as I enjoy this dress, I'd like to remove it now," he says, his hands curved around my hips.

"Okay," I slur. "There's a zipper."

He grins. "I'm good at those. But I'm probably going to see your tummy, and I know how you hate that."

"Oh," I say. But suddenly I just don't care. "I guess you're going to have to see it at some point."

His eyes are full of tenderness as he looks down at me. "Swear to God, contessa. There are benefits to showing me your tummy."

"Like what?" I have to ask.

"Shower sex is the first thing that leaps to mind," he says. "That's a whole genre we haven't once explored."

"You *are* full of fun ideas."

"See? You gotta trust me. Now let's have this zipper."

I turn around. Clever fingers find and unfurl the zipper. Ian holds the straps of my dress as I carefully step out of it.

Then, holding my breath, I turn around to face him in nothing but a strapless bra and lace panties.

His eyes slide down my body, but there's no disgust there. And then a smile lights his whole face. "Contessa! The only surprise here is that your panties don't match that bra. What would the other stylists say?"

"Ian!"

He lays the dress carefully onto the sofa and then scoops me up off my feet. I wrap my arms around him as he carries me into his bedroom. "You are as beautiful as the day is long," he says. "Was that so hard?"

"No," I admit. Not now. Not when I trust him.

He lays me down on the bed, and I forget all about that dumb scar.

AN HOUR later we're draped together, completely naked and spent. The light has long since faded outside, and it's dark in Ian's bedroom. Nobody can see that scar anymore.

But it's still on my mind. "I would like to explain why I was so reluctant to let you see me."

"Yeah, I still can't get over it. A black bra and red panties?"

I poke him in the hip, and he laughs.

"That dress required a backless bra. I had limited options."

He kisses my hair. "Thank you for trusting me with that."

"You're hilarious."

"I know."

I trace a slow circle on his magnificent chest. "When I was seven, I lived in California with my mother. She was an addict. And possibly mentally ill. She had a boyfriend, and they used to do a lot of drugs together."

"Oh honey," he says. "That sounds rough."

"It was, but it was a really long time ago. And my mother lost custody of me after her awful boyfriend dropped his lit cigarette on me. We were sitting on the couch, and I'd fallen asleep."

"Shit," he whispers. "God." His arms tighten around me, as if he could go back twenty years in time and prevent anyone from harming me.

I snuggle into his tight grip and finish the story. "The top I was wearing had some kind of flammable design on the front. That's what burned me so badly. But the asshole woke up fast and basically ripped it off me when he realized I was on fire. He dislocated my shoulder, but the burn was confined to my stomach. It could have been so much worse."

"*Still,*" he hisses. "Did he go to jail?"

"I don't think so," I admit. "But my mother put me on a plane to Nonna. That was the only other flight I'd taken before Italy. On that first flight, I was recovering from a hospital stay, and I'd figured out I might never see my mother again. I cried for the whole flight."

He pets my hair with soft hands. "I'm really sorry that happened to you, sweetheart. And I'm sorry if anyone ever made you think that scar was ugly. But I don't think it is. Because it's part of you."

I squeeze him tightly. "You say the nicest things."

"Nah, that's just how I feel. And I'd like to punch the guy who told you different."

"He didn't, actually," I say slowly. "I think I told myself. When your mother can't even be bothered to stick around and keep you safe, you internalize a lot of things. Like always trying to look pretty and be perfect."

"Huh." He strokes my skin with loving hands. "I'm here to show you how the other half lives, if you'll let me. The messy, loud, imperfect half."

"I'm a big fan already," I tell him.

THIRTY-SIX

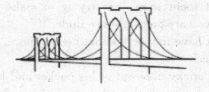

Big Fat Box of Popcorn

IAN

IN THE MORNING—IN spite of the crazy, eventful night I just had, and the lack of sleep—I walk to the Bruisers' headquarters feeling clearheaded for the first time in months.

O'Doul's text had asked me to meet him in the players' lounge before the meeting. *Be early. Bring coffee,* it had ordered. I duck into a deli and buy us two large cups, black. Neither of us cares much for the fancy stuff.

God, I'm going to miss that guy. This early morning huddle is probably just his way of making sure I'm okay. I ought to resent it, but I just can't find it in me.

When I reach the lounge, he's seated alone on the sofa, his feet kicked up onto a coffee table, his arms propped back behind his head in a posture of thoughtful repose.

"Are you gonna miss this place?" I ask as I take a seat beside him.

"You know I am. But this life has been good to me. I get to decide when I'm leaving. I get to go out on a high note." He sits up and cracks open the drinking spout on his cup of coffee. He takes a gulp before he turns to me. "But enough about me. I made my decision about the captain's nomination."

"Good deal, man. You know I'm here for it. This team has

been good to me, too. You can count on my support no matter what happens."

He gives me a funny smile. "See, I know that about you already. I just spent some time trying to make you see it for yourself. But you are one stubborn dude."

"You don't have to worry about me anymore, I promise. I'm in a good place."

He pulls a sticky note out of his pocket and hands it to me. "This is when you're meeting the rookie from Boston. Do you want me to come?"

Oh. I look down at his scrawl. "Does that say October third? Kind of a long time from now."

"But you're a busy guy who's playing a preseason game against Boston on the third. He'll watch the game, and you can meet him at the stadium."

"All right." I clear my throat. "Love to have you there, if you're so inclined."

He grins.

"Am I better at asking for help now? Do I win a prize?"

"Yup." He reaches into a shopping bag at his feet, grabs a jersey, and tosses it to me.

"What's this?" It's a regulation jersey—the kind we always wear—in our color which is officially called eggplant, but it's just purple. CRIKEY is on the back in white block letters, same as always.

But then I spot the C on the arm patch.

C for captain.

"What the…" I look up at Patrick in shock. "Are you kidding me right now?"

"No, man." My friend shakes his head. "Do you want it, though? With you, it's damn hard to tell. Gave you like ten chances to tell me. But you didn't say a peep."

I look down at that patch on the arm, and I'll be damned, but it looks exactly right. "I *do* want it," I say before I even have time to think. "Yeah. I can do this."

"Of course, you can. I never had any doubt. But it sure wasn't easy getting you to say it. So I brought a visual."

I laugh awkwardly. "Dude, I didn't know it was the kind of job you could apply for. I wasn't going to put myself first."

"Right," he says, sounding exasperated. "That's why it's your job. You've always been a rock in the river, Crikey. Sure, last year threw you for a loop. But that just gives you more perspective. You have a lot of history with this team. The guys trust you. You've seen it all. And if you're willing to put in the work and make those tough decisions sometimes, it should be you. I choose you."

Well, fuck. My eyes are weirdly hot, and my face is getting red. I grab my coffee and take a big slug. Then I realize I have an important question. "Wait, is management on board with this?"

"Totally," he says. "Why do you think they crawled up your ass all summer to burnish your reputation? Because they knew this was coming, and they hoped you'd look the part."

"Oh," I say stupidly. "That makes so much more sense now."

O'Doul laughs. Then he takes the jersey from my hands and drops it into the bag, and I realize it's because we have company.

"Hey, guys," Leo Trevi says. "How was the summer?"

"Enlightening," I say as we both stand up to slap him on the back.

"Crikey got a new girlfriend," O'Doul says. "And I think she's a keeper, so now you can all tease him about having to go home at a reasonable hour or needing to call the little woman from the road."

"Oh, Mr. Perpetually Single finally admitted he has a girlfriend?" Castro asks. "What a huge shock, seeing as he spent the whole summer following her around like a puppy."

"Another one bites the dust," says Silas, our goalie, who's claiming a seat against the wall.

The room fills quickly with hockey players. It's not even

eight o'clock, but there's so much energy in here. So much promise.

I feel it like a buzz inside my veins—that preseason excitement. It's a welcome sensation. I've been worried. I thought the optimism and excitement I've always had for the start of hockey season might have deserted me.

But no. It grows with every guy who pushes into the room, until they're taking up all the chairs, covering the window seats, and leaning against the walls.

When the room is full to bursting, the team owner arrives. Rebecca Rowley Kattenberger strolls in, her one year old daughter, Anna, on her hip. "Greetings, boys! Hope you had a great summer, and you're ready to work your hindquarters off."

She gives me a secretive smile and perches on a chair that one of my teammates hastens to free up for her.

O'Doul claps his hands, bringing the meeting to order. "Morning, team. I guess this is my last time addressing you as your captain. But you can still kiss my—" He glances toward the toddler and checks his language. "—Hindquarters, if you feel like it, since I'm not leaving the neighborhood."

The room echoes with laughter and applause and more than one whistle.

"Management is going to officially kick things off in a few minutes. I'm told you're leaving for training camp in twenty-three hours. Tomorrow I'll be eating pancakes in my jammies while you're running ten miles on the beach in Southampton."

A chuckle rolls through the room.

"So get some sleep tonight, fellas. But before I turn you over to the rigors of the season, I gotta announce your new captain. It's been my absolute pleasure to support this team for my entire career. And now I get to pass the torch to someone who has had the same good fortune. Please give a round of applause for your new man: Ian Crikey."

Applause swells as he pulls the jersey out of the bag again and holds it up high. And there's my name for the whole damn world to see. He tosses it to me, and I catch it, red-faced and smiling.

"Crikey! Crikey!" chant a couple of my friends.

Then O'Doul pulls out two jerseys with an A for alternate captain on them and tosses them to Trevi and Castro. There's more good-natured hooting and heckling.

But when all three of us have pulled our new jerseys down over our T-shirts, the room quiets down again. We all turn to O'Doul to hear his very last words of wisdom.

"Boys, this is the beginning of a new era in Brooklyn. Your team has everything it needs to succeed this year. You've got experience with the franchise. You've got great stats and a great lineup. You've got a strong will, and an even stronger work ethic. Be well, men. Make us all proud. I know you can do it. And I'll be in row C, watching with a big fat box of popcorn. And a beer."

That's it. That's the whole speech. We all stand up and cheer, clapping as O'Doul makes his way slowly to the doorway. He turns around once, giving us an overhead wave, and a wide smile.

Then he's gone.

I'm a little sad, but in a good way. And my next thought is— *I can't wait to tell all this to Vera.*

THIRTY-SEVEN

Two Months Later

VERA

October

"BABY, IT'S TIME TO GO!" Ian calls from my living room.

"I know! I'm coming." I put one last pin into my updo and check my look in the mirror. I'm wearing a merino dress in Bruisers purple with a low-slung black belt and ankle boots. My jewelry is silver, including oversized hoops in my ears.

Tonight is going to be big. But I'm ready.

The bedroom door opens, and I hear a whistle behind me.

When I spin around, I spot Ian in the doorway looking hot in another suit I've chosen for him. This one is charcoal, and he wears it with a deep-blue shirt. "What do you think?" I ask him.

"You're just as hot in that dress as you were at our photo shoot last week, contessa. Now move your very stylish ass out of the apartment, because we're going to be late."

"You're nervous," I say, grabbing my bag and following him into the living room.

"A little."

The admission surprises me. "He wouldn't ask to meet you, if he wasn't going to be nice."

"I don't need him to be nice," Ian says, holding my door

open for me. After I pass him to reach the hallway, he locks up with his own key.

Exchanging all kinds of keys is a recent thing. "You're having a whirlwind romance," Charli said a few days ago when I was issued a digital swipe card that allows me access to certain secure areas of the stadium where the Bruisers play their games. "That security pass means this is serious."

And she's not wrong. Every night that Ian is not on the road is a night we've spent together. Sometimes that means a date at a fancy restaurant. But, just as often, it means curling up together to watch a movie. Sometimes I wake up in the wee hours to find that Ian has slid into bed with me after a late flight back from a game.

Maybe I should feel shocked at the speed with which we're moving. But I'm surprisingly calm and centered about the whole thing. Being with Ian just feels right to me. I don't need to measure it or define it.

One big change, though, has been my interest in hockey. The preseason began barely a week ago, and tonight I'm going to my third game.

But first we're on our way to meet Davis Deutsch, the young man who was injured in the fight against Ian last year.

Ian has a cab waiting for us outside. We climb in for the short ride, and Ian begins tapping his fingers on his knee. After a couple of minutes, I place my hand on top of his to silence the drumming.

"Sorry."

"It's okay," I say gently. Ian is in a good place. He doesn't have those bad dreams very often anymore. He seems happier, and the team is doing well.

"I want this. It's important." He sighs. "That doesn't make it easy."

"Right," I agree, curling my hand around his.

Ian wraps his arms around me and kisses my hair, and I hold him for the rest of the ride.

ONCE WE ARRIVE, Ian escorts me through a series of secure doors and checkpoints and then up an elevator I've never seen before.

Patrick O'Doul is waiting for us outside a conference room on the VIP level. He's wearing a suit and a purple tie. "They're here. They're waiting for you."

He hugs Ian, who accepts it with a grim smile. "Let's do this."

Ian lifts his chin and opens the door with his head held high. He smiles as he steps aside for me to pass through first.

There are several people in this room, including PR people from both teams. But I have no trouble picking out the young player seated in a chair beside a woman who must be his girlfriend. They are holding hands. And he looks... not healthy. His face is pale beneath his baseball cap as Ian and Patrick greet him.

When Davis stands up to shake hands, he moves slowly, bracing one hand on the table.

All the joy runs out of me.

"Nice to meet you," I say with a smile when it's my turn to be introduced. His grip is strong, and it calms me.

"I'm Ian Crikey," my boyfriend says when it's his turn to shake.

"Oh, I remember," the kid says with a grin.

The Brooklyn publicist offers beverages all around, and I take a seat off to the side, because this isn't my meeting.

When everyone is settled, Ian regards the other man with a serious expression. "I know it doesn't help, but you have been in my thoughts every day since our fight."

"Not an exaggeration," O'Doul murmurs. "We had a lot of soul searching here in Brooklyn."

"I just want you to know how sorry I am that you got hurt," Ian says. "If I could, I'd do things differently."

Davis shakes his head, a thin smile playing at his lips. "Not sure you should feel that way. That's why we needed to meet. I've gotta tell you a wild story." He clears his throat. "After the punch, my bone shattered. The fragments caused me some immediate soft tissue damage and a lot of bleeding. I don't remember much of the following week. And then came the surgeries."

My stomach clenches, but Ian doesn't flinch or blink. He just listens.

"The doctors had to stabilize me before they could deal with a weird thing they discovered. I have bone cancer. It's pretty rare. Usually hits kids between sixteen and twenty years old. Usually gets you in a limb. Getting it at age twenty-four in my clavicle made for a really unusual case."

"You have... *cancer*," Ian says slowly.

"That's right. That's why the punch shattered the bone in the first place. It wasn't you. It was me."

"*Jesus*," Ian whispers. "I'm so sorry."

The guy shrugs. "Not your fault. I mean—I wish this was your fault, so I'd have somebody to blame. And I actually *did* blame you for a little while. I couldn't wrap my head around it, and I just wanted to go back in time to those hours before the fight, when everything in my life was fine. But it doesn't work that way. And the crazy thing is that if I hadn't challenged you, it might have been a while until I got my diagnosis." He takes a sip of his soda. "Might've mattered to my treatment plan. If anything, I'm supposed to thank you."

Ian leans back in his chair and contemplates the ceiling for a moment. "No need to go that far."

Several people chuckle, but I can't. My eyes are hot.

"Is there anything at all we can do for you?" O'Doul asks.

Davis shakes his head. "I'm getting aggressive care at Dana Farber in Boston. My team has been great. I'd rather be playing hockey, but it is what it is."

"If you think of anything..." Ian says.

Davis grins suddenly. "I s'pose you could foul half the team tonight and spend a lot of time in the penalty box. If you're feeling generous."

Ian finally laughs. "Sure, man. I'll get right on that."

They talk for a few more minutes. Ian asks some questions about his treatment. There's another round of hand shaking and well-wishing, and then Davis leaves the room with his girlfriend and his PR guy.

The door closes, and we all just sit still for a moment in silence.

"Jesus fuck," Doulie says. "That shitshow wasn't even your fault. After all that."

Ian gets up and crosses the room. "Shit. Who even cares? That kid has *cancer*."

I'm still trying to follow along when Ian moves his body with sudden violence. A plastic wastebasket goes flying, hitting the opposite wall with a deafening bang.

"Whoa, now," O'Doul says, already on his feet. He wraps Ian into a bear hug. "Keep it together, man."

Ian flexes, making fists, like he's going to shake Patrick off. But then his shoulders droop, and I hear him take a shaky breath. "I don't feel better."

"I noticed." O'Doul chuckles. "Take a minute." He lets go of Ian and heads for the door.

The publicist sets the wastebasket upright and follows him out, too.

That leaves me and Ian alone. He looks as tense as I've ever seen him, but I don't hesitate to cross to him, leaning in as he folds me into his embrace. "I'm sorry," I say.

"Me too." He takes a deep breath.

"He might be okay."

"He'd better be." His arms tighten around me. "That's not what I was expecting."

"Life never is," I point out. "Not lately."

He kisses my jaw. "Hell, I have to get downstairs. I'm

supposed to play a game now. After that?" His chuckle is dry. "Hey—you ready for tonight?"

"So ready. It kind of makes tonight's special event even more special, doesn't it?"

"Yup." He cups my jaw and kisses me on the mouth. "You make it special, too."

I get one more kiss before we have to get ready for the game.

TWO HOURS LATER, I'm seated in Row A just to the side of the penalty box. These are the captain's comp seats—the best in the house.

"This crowd is crazy," Charli says, looking around. "For a preseason scrimmage. Hell. Good seats to my games are a little easier to come by." She offers me the popcorn.

"You're wrong—front row seats to your first game weren't even available," I tell her. The women's season starts a few weeks from now. "I had to buy in row F."

"Okay, here we go!" she says suddenly. "Warmups are over."

I glance at the ice to see the Bruisers headed back into their tunnel, and my pulse rate moves into a higher gear.

A few minutes ago, the team skated their warmup in plain white jerseys. That's not how it's usually done, but tonight is a special occasion. The players will be skating in breast cancer awareness jerseys that will be auctioned off after the game.

This is a preseason event every year, apparently. But this is the first time the jerseys were designed by *me*. And I still can't believe it.

Right after I began dating Ian, the team owner—Rebecca Rowley Kattenberger—had invited me to take a look at the lineup of Bruisers' spirit wear to see if I wanted to propose any new, more stylish gear. I'd told her I'd be thrilled to do it.

Then, two days later, she'd called me back to explain that they needed twenty special jerseys for this particular October fundraiser. And did I want to source them at my usual fee?

Yes, I certainly did. But because it's a charity gig, I did it for free. And when I hadn't liked the logo options available to me, I'd drawn a new one to show to Rebecca.

"Heck yes!" had been her response. "Do that. It's perfect."

Which is how I came to be sitting here in the front row as the lights go down and music swirls around the crowded stadium. "Ladies and gentlemen," the announcer booms. "Get ready for a preseason matchup between rivals Brooklyn and Boston! Allow me to introduce tonight's starting lineup. Wearing breast cancer awareness jersey number thirty-three, team captain, Ian Crikey!"

I stand up and scream as Ian skates out to loud applause. There's my handiwork right on his broad chest. Then, one by one, he's joined by his teammates, each one wearing the same purple jersey with a muscular bear on the front, clutching a pink ribbon in its paw.

"God, those jerseys are so cute!" Charli laughs. "I want one."

"Get in line," I tell her. "We're going to bid on Ian's. I have a feeling after tonight that he's going to bid high. The money is going to four different cancer research foundations."

"Don't bid on Neil's," she says. "Hands off."

"It's a deal."

After the starting lineup is introduced, the announcer tells the crowd how to bid on the jerseys. "Brooklyn Hockey dot com, slash awareness, folks! You can start now. Bidding ends tomorrow night at ten p.m.! The Brooklyn Hockey Organization would like to thank designer and stylist Vera Vestini for donating her time and design to this fundraising event."

I let out a little gasp, because I hadn't expected to hear my name read aloud.

And then the jumbotron camera zooms in on…me. There I am, smiling and shellshocked, seated beside Charli.

She lets out a cackle and elbows me as she lifts a hand to wave at the camera.

Luckily, I snap to and start to wave. The camera is probably only on me for a few seconds, but time slows down for a few beats of my heart as I have my moment in the spotlight.

The video cuts to Ian, down on the ice. He shows off his jersey with a smile then raises his hands to make a heart shape —like the member of a K-pop band might do.

And then he stuns me by mouthing *I love you, Vera* at the camera.

I let out another little shriek of surprise. Did that really just happen?

"Awwww!" Charli says with a laugh. "Look who's turned into Mr. Romance. He clearly said your name just there."

"He did, didn't he?" My heart flutters, and I'm smiling so hard that I might never stop. "Wow."

"Is that a first?" Charli asks.

"Well, yeah. It's new."

"New, but big," Charli insists. "I guessed it when you gave him that haircut. And when you bought him that shirt. Then I declared victory that first night in Italy when he started putting the moves on you during *Roman Holiday*."

"What? Nobody was supposed to notice that."

"You guys weren't as subtle as you think." She gives me a sly smile. "Now that I think about it, you're like Audrey Hepburn. Cute and stylish. Except *she* left the guy behind after the fun trip to Italy. You don't have to."

I look at Ian again and hope that she's right. Because I'm falling for him. I can't help myself.

THIRTY-EIGHT

This One is Special

IAN

THE GAME IS A GOOD ONE. Both teams have something to prove this year.

Don't we always. But this one is special for me. My boys and I saw a lot of change this summer. We need to come together as a new team and trust each other enough to get it right.

I think we can get there. I really do.

The first two periods are fast and frantic, and we push the score up to 2-2.

"Maybe I should've run a few more miles this summer," Drake complains, toweling off his face.

"You ran all the miles," I remind him. "Blood sugar?"

He checks his phone. "Little low. Huh."

I hand him the glucose drink in the specially marked water bottle as the buzzer rings for the period's end.

My special jersey is drenched with sweat by the middle of the third period. I hope they wash these things before anyone pays twenty grand to buy one. The crowd is a blur as I narrow my focus on the Boston forward I'm guarding.

It's a fast, brutal period, but the score stands. Silas Kelly is guarding the goal with his life, which doesn't hurt our chances.

We give it all we've got as the period wears on. "We can do this, guys. One more before the buzzer."

"Yeah, yeah," Castro says. "I'll find it."

Spoiler: we don't find it. And I manage to foul one of their guys with three minutes on the clock.

"Two minutes for tripping," the announcer says as they open the penalty box for me.

As I skate toward the sin bin, I catch sight of Vera. She's *smiling*, in spite of my fuckup. That's something you don't see every day.

I sit down and take my punishment, gritting my teeth the whole time. My guys work hard to kill the penalty. And they look good doing it. I stand up early so I'm ready when the door opens.

But with six seconds left of my confinement, a Boston player fires the puck through Silas's legs and into the net.

"Fuck."

The lamp lights. Boston celebrates.

I sit my ass back down with a sigh.

Thump. Someone pounds on the plexi.

I don't look, because it's probably just an angry fan.

Thump thump. "Crikey."

When I swivel my head, I see Davis Deutsch smirking at me. "Thanks," he mouths, then gives me the thumbs up. He looks joyous.

I roll my eyes and have to laugh.

"THAT'S what the preseason is for," Castro says, tying his tie an hour later.

"I know it," I agree. "We'll get 'em next time."

It's done, it's over. They won. We shook hands. I gave a few quotes filled with platitudes to the journalists trying to get a story out of a preseason game that doesn't actually count.

Everything is fine. We live to fight another day.

"Hit the Tavern?" Leo Trevi asks.

"Maybe," I hedge. "Gotta find my girl."

"Aw, do you hear that?" Someone makes the familiar sound of a whip.

I know that sound, because I've made it myself a few times when a teammate chose his girlfriend over his buddies.

And I get it now. I just need to see Vera, though, and thank her for hanging with me through the ups and downs. I head for the door, a man on a mission. When I fling it open, there she is in the hall, waiting for me in that purple dress and a big smile.

"Contessa. Come here." I pull her in for a kiss. "Nice job on the jerseys. I heard the bidding got heated even before the game ended."

"Thank you," she says, rubbing the tip of her nose against mine. "That was very exciting."

"You know what else is exciting? Taking you home. I got big plans for you."

"I do enjoy your plans," she whispers. "But do these plans include the Tavern? We've been invited out for a drink."

"I suppose," I hedge. "But we'll have to leave early. I need some alone time with you."

"Yeah?" Her eyes go a little soft-focused. "Whatever for?"

"To tell you again that I love you."

"Oh, sweetheart," she says. "I—"

"You don't have to say it back," I insist.

She puts a hand over my lips. "Don't interrupt a woman who's speaking to you, Ian Crikey. As it happens, I love you, too."

I shake off her hand. "Now we're definitely leaving that bar early. My big plans just got even bigger."

The End

Also by Sarina Bowen